GW00391461

SCATTERED REMAINS

A Nathan Hawk Mystery

COPYRIGHT

© Douglas Watkinson 2021

The moral right of the author has been asserted

All rights reserved. No part of this publication may be reproduced, stored in a retrieval system, or transmitted in any form or by any means, without the prior permission in writing of the publisher.

www.douglaswatkinson.com

Before I became involved…

When Patrick Scott surfaced he didn't know if he was dead or alive, but the fact that he was able to have an internal debate about it suggested the latter. However, the pitch darkness probably meant that he was blind and just as he was about to slip into a panic about that he made out a slit of light in the top left hand corner of his perspective. He took a step towards it only to be whiplashed back, the effect of his hands being fastened behind him to something round and tall. He banged his head backwards and whatever it was rang out hollow and dull. Where was he, though? His imagination ran riot over the possibilities: a tomb, a charnel house, a crypt, a sepulchre, a disused mine, a cave in some remote mountain, a sealed wreck twenty thousand leagues under the sea…

He took a couple of deep breaths and applied some logic, helped by the sound of a cistern flushing way above his head, followed by water rushing down inside whatever he was anchored to. He was in some kind of cellar, then, chained to a downpipe and with any luck the slit of light was the edge of a trap door through which he had entered. And by which he intended to leave. Meantime, this was 'a situation', his father would have said, and to deal with it would require the best of all those qualities the old man so valued: courage, determination, common-sense and many more besides. Right now they seemed far easier to list than to live by.

He tried to give his predicament a context. For the past few days he'd been camping on Bindy's boat, moored in Paddington Basin while she was off on a buying trip. This particular evening had started well enough with a stroll down the canal to The Malvern Café for something to eat and to soak up its inherent calmth as the owner called it. It was half a mile from the boat and he'd managed it for over a week now without the aid of the walking stick. When he'd first used it, in the days immediately following the accident, people had stared at him. One elderly woman in the café had even asked him what he'd done to his leg. Nothing, he replied. He'd done something to his foot which was a totally different matter. She didn't enquire further…

At The Malvern he had taken his drink to a seat at the window which looked out over the canal and when the waitress brought him his Shepherd's Pie she'd said, "The usual for Patrick."

He'd looked up at her. Usual. Usual. If you repeat a word often enough it loses meaning, although right then the tactic didn't seem to be working. Usual. Usual. Christ, he'd become a regular here! He was falling prey to habit. Same place, same time, same dinner. That was how they tracked you down, by latching onto your schedule then striking when you were off guard.

As he'd glanced around the café he'd realised that at least four other people had been present every evening for nearly a week. Two women who were clearly business partners of some kind, were discussing the week's work. The more dominant of the pair was an animated creature with a host of hand gestures and darting eyes, head nodding forward like a bird hollowing out a tree as she made her case. Her friend would turn every so often and catch Patrick's eye, possibly for sympathy, maybe because she liked the look of him but he couldn't rule out a more sinister reason. The other two regulars were men who clearly knew each other but spoke little. The elder of the two was large and frightening, besuited and reading the Evening Standard while he drank tea and snapped at a sandwich. Occasionally he would peer over the top of the paper, glance at Patrick and look quickly away again. His companion younger by ten years, wore jeans and an ill-fitting, bright blue ski jacket which drew attention to his peculiar shape.

"I have to go," said Patrick, rising from the table.

The waitress looked down at the Shepherd's Pie she was carrying, prompting him to take a ten pound note from his back pocket, drop it onto the table, then leave as calmly as possible.

He walked towards the newly paved marina, cobblestones now instead of trustworthy London slabs, and certainly not good for his foot, although the pain helped him to calm down a little. Safely aboard the narrowboat, with the cabin door bolted behind him, he slumped down on the sofa and thought about what he'd just done. He'd panicked, for no reason whatsoever, and as a result he was still hungry. He went through to the galley and poured himself a bowl of cornflakes. His mother would have been appalled. 'Cornflakes for breakfast, lunch and dinner,' she would chide. 'You'll end up looking like one.' Better a cornflake than a flaked almond, he thought, because that's what she was turning into, poor old girl. She was going nuts. In the months leading up to her diagnosis Patrick would have sworn that his father, not his mother, was the one losing the plot. But they were both handling it well, with as much dignity as approaching madness allowed. They'd decided to visit some of the places they had always talked about but never journeyed to, starting with the Great Wall of China early last year, moving to San Francisco in the Spring. Right now they were in Cuba, of all places…

His thoughts were interrupted by someone tapping on the cabin roof. He glanced at his watch and sighed, then called out, irritably, "Please, I've had one hell of a day."

"Patrick, could we have a quick word," said a voice he didn't recognise, a tinny almost girlie voice.

He went to the cabin door and opened it. On the other side stood the two men from the café, the ones he'd identified as regulars, Evening Standard and blue ski-ing jacket. The panic had returned, an increase in heart rate first, followed by prickly heat around his neck and sweat breaking out across his forehead.

"What do you…?" he began, but to no purpose. His two visitors had barged into the cabin, pushing him backwards to give themselves room. The younger one, shorter than his companion by at least six inches, smiled at him.

"Sorry to be so deliberate. We'd like you to come along with us."

"Where to?" Patrick asked.

"It's quite simple. Our business partner would like to talk to you and… well, that's it really."

"Talk about what?"

"Henrietta, of course."

"I've nothing to say."

The man tutted and moved aside to give his companion space in which to operate. The elder man stepped forward and drew a small telescopic cosh from his waistband, slipped his hand through the loop and gripped the handle. With his free hand he grabbed Patrick, turned him 45 degrees and struck him over the side of his neck. Pain first, followed by darkness, then oblivion. A strange paradox, Patrick thought, that he could remember losing consciousness. He'd regained it for about ten seconds, coming to in the back of a car, presumably *en route* to this place. He was jammed up against the man who had half killed him. The shorter man was driving.

"Still alive, then," he said.

His companion took slight umbrage, as if his skill with the cosh had been brought into question. "Course. But is he really worth what they reckon? He don't look it to me."

He'd been kidnapped, then. People usually did that for money. His parents didn't have any. Nor did he. All he had was Henrietta. He hoped to God they hadn't taken her. That was when he must have passed out again and had remained so until now.

Up in the top left corner, the slit of light suddenly widened and what Patrick had rightly assumed to be a trap door yawned open on rusty hinges. Light fell into the cellar and shone on the overflow of family life, an abundance of old furniture, mainly chairs and chests of drawers, carpets rolled up and stored upright, pictures, hundreds of pictures long since denied places on living room walls.

A figure stepped into the square of light and descended the stone steps. He paused seven or eight down, turned and flicked a switch. Patrick screwed up his face against the sudden glare and recognised the man as the younger of his assailants. He was turning keys on a ring, presumably trying to find the one to the padlock which held Patrick to the downpipe.

"We wondered if you were feeling peckish yet," the man said. "The consensus was for Chinese so we've ordered a takeaway…"

"Where's this person who wants to talk to me, your business partner?"

"They'll be joining us."

"Suppose I don't like what they say?"

"Hear them out first, surely."

"And agree to what they propose or that's it for me? Curtains?"

The man found his use of the word curtains mildly amusing and gave a short, giggly laugh.

"Kill you? Don't be so daft, you're far too valuable to kill. No, the plan is to sell you… auction you off to the highest bidder."

I was in Long Field with Martin Falconer, the night we found the metal plate, and like a fool I promised him that I would 'look into it'. I was being polite, of course, hoping that by morning he would have forgotten all about it. No such luck.

God knows why I'd ever wanted to go combine harvesting in the dark, but it had developed into a minor obsession which needed dealing with. I used to lie awake on still nights, listening to the hum of these mechanical monsters in nearby fields and occasionally a beam from their powerful headlights would sweep across the bedroom ceiling as they turned and made their way down yet another strip of rape seed, or whatever they were bringing in. The machines were driven by men I'd come to know during the seven years I'd lived in Winchendon and the tricky part was always going to be asking one of them if I could spend the night with him, up in his cab, just the two of us. Martin Falconer would be the least critical, I thought, but even so I still remember the way he looked at me before saying,

"Of course, Nathan. We're, er… doing a field over in, er… Dorton, er, just past the railway crossing…"

There were too many ers, too many pauses in the invitation for me to feel totally welcome, but I accepted and he told me to join him whenever I felt like it. He would be there most of the night.

I arrived at Long Field just after midnight, later than I'd intended. The Land Rover had shown a reluctance to start, but at that age I guess you're entitled to the odd show of bloody-mindedness. I parked by the gate and watched the John Deere heading towards me, rolling blades out front cutting down all before it, stripping, threshing, winnowing, leaving a cloud of dust to hang in the moonlight. I heard my father's voice, "This bloody machine, driven by one man, is doing the work of a dozen, to say nothing of the team of horses they used for power." It was one of those obvious truths best acknowledged and then forgotten.

With the freshly cut stalks jabbing at my ankles I went over to the combine, scissoring both arms in front of me until the headlights picked me out. Martin brought the machine to a halt and leaned out from the cab door.

"Come on up!" he yelled over the noise of the engine and, at the same pitch, advised caution as I climbed the fire escape of a ladder up into the cab.

It wasn't so much a cab as a flight deck. Computerised and air-conditioned, with Classic FM droning away in the background, Martin told me that this machine was so clever it could be programmed to do the work itself. Having paid close on two hundred thousand pounds for it he hadn't tested that claim, but so much for my father's contention, I thought: this bloody machine didn't need even one man to work it, never mind the dozen or so of his childhood memories.

It took about half an hour for the limited appeal of going up one line and down another to work its lack of magic on me and as I began to think of ways to say this to my friend without offending him, he glanced over his shoulder through a glass partition to the hopper which held the winnowed seed.

"Jesus, didn't see how full it was getting! That's yakking to you." He reached for his mobile as he brought the combine to a halt. "Jan, where are you?"

Jan, pronounced with a Y, wasn't from England, according to his voice on speakerphone.

"Boss, on the road, between farm and you. Trouble with trailer. Nothing to worry. Fix it."

"Quick as you can." Martin finished the call and turned to me. "Jan Zawadski, the new farm manager I told you about."

"Where's the accent from?"

"Same place he is. Poland."

"Plumbers, electricians, now farm managers?"

He nodded out into the night where, half a mile away, we could see tractor headlights dipping and swerving as Jan obeyed his employers's instructions to get here quickly. Minutes later he drove into the field towing a high-sided trailer which he parked alongside the combine. He jumped down from the tractor cab and signalled up to Martin who referred to the computer, fiddled with a mouse-like accessory until a bendable chimney reached out from the harvester and hung over the empty trailer. At the press of a button out spewed the winnowed seed and I saw Jan back away from the dust. I made out in the darkness a tall, fair haired man, early thirties, dressed in the eternal check shirt and baggy cords of farm work. And just as I was wondering, along with my father no doubt, where all the English farm managers had gone something on the ground must have caught Jan's eye. He walked over to it, crouched down and picked it up.

"What's he bloody found?" Martin mumbled as he opened the door and began the climb down to ground level. I did the same my side.

"What is it, Jan?"

"I see it glint in the headlight, Boss. Glint, huh? Is a word?"

"It's a word."

"I see it glint."

He gave it to Martin who handled it as if it were treasure trove, examined it for a few moments and then passed it on to me. I held it towards the light. It was a shiny metallic plate, four centimetres long, one centimetre wide, with four countersunk screw holes in it, precisely engineered. It was made of titanium, I thought, the kind of thing used in orthopaedic surgery. Then I made the mistake of voicing that opinion. I saw the glint in Martin's eye.

"You mean human bone?" he said.

"I suppose I do."

"So where's the skeleton?"

I looked at him, trying to think of ways to unsay what I'd just blurted out, but I held off. It seemed such a cruel thing to do, to a man in search of something to brighten his day. When you spend so much of it grinding up and down fields of rape seed, pausing only to ask yourself why it was given such an unsavoury name, is it any wonder that you long for a little excitement? Classic FM doesn't really provide it.

"Leave it with me, I'll look into it," I said.

Against my better judgement, to say nothing of my urge to chuck it in the nearest hedge, I knew that the plate was… significant. That isn't a bad case of hindsight, of big finishes traceable back to small beginnings, but insight based on 30 years experience as a police officer. Even though I couldn't fill in any details there and then, I knew the object we'd found in Long Field that night would have a disturbing story to tell.

Martin Falconer was dead keen to hear that story and about three weeks later, with the harvest safely in, he started badgering me to keep my word and investigate the whys and wherefores of our discovery. The more he pestered me, the more I resisted. The more he telephoned the less I was in. If he dropped round I would be just about to take a shower. If our paths crossed at the pub, I would have an urgent appointment elsewhere which I was already late for. I must have seemed like the busiest, cleanest man he knew.

I knew it couldn't last and with the inevitability of sunrise itself, early one bright September morning he caught me off guard in my own kitchen. A knock on the back door was greeted by Dogge with a series of barks expelled on a single breath and, like every man I've ever known, I asked quietly, "Who's that?" My friend Doctor Laura Peterson glanced up from *The Observer* and said that she'd no idea but since it was my house surely I should be the one to go and find out.

Every time I see Martin, be it in a cloud of rape seed dust or pure daylight, it occurs to me what a good looking man he is, especially for his age and for a farmer. Both take their toll. He owned up to being fifty-three the last time I enquired and in thirty odd years of adulthood has packed in enough emotional thrills and spills for any man, his latest adventure being an affair with Kate Whitely, a dangerously beautiful neighbour twenty years his junior. It ended badly, of course, and unwilling to go back to his wife he had moved into an empty house adjoining his land and was carrying on his business from there. So far as I knew he wasn't seeing anyone but the youthful looks, the intelligence, the charm, the physique without an ounce of fat on it, the piercing blue eyes, would soon put that right. Christ, I sound as if I've got a crush on the man but I'm actually quoting Laura who, like most women in the village, blames his dalliance with Kate squarely on Kate.

"Martin, this really isn't a good time," I said, as we shook hands at the back door.

"Nonsense!" said Laura. "Jaikie isn't due till one o'clock, and I've just made coffee."

Martin thanked her but dithered until I beckoned him all the way in and sat him at the kitchen table in front of Laura's paper, open where she'd ringed a piece about '*All Good Men and True*'. The film was opening in London at the end of the following week, having already premiered in Los Angeles and New York. It had drawn excellent reviews and the name of my actor son, Jacob Hawk, was now always seen in tandem with that of Josh Hartnett. Martin skim read the article.

"I must tell our Jodie," he said, when he'd finished. "She always had a thing for Jaikie. Who's this Josh Hartnett, though?"

I told him that I knew the name, but the face hadn't stuck.

"Moody, intense and very beautiful," said Laura.

"That narrows it right down," I said, putting a mug of coffee down in front of Martin. He took out his wallet. "It's alright, mate, the coffee's free."

"I should hope so, though I'd expect a bill for any work you did on this, Nathan."

He took a small polythene envelope containing the metal plate from behind one of his credit cards, placed it on the table and explained to Laura that I'd said it was the kind of thing used in orthopaedic surgery. I muttered the correction 'possibly' but it fell on deaf ears. The romantic in Martin had been fired up and he'd assumed that whatever bone the plate had once been attached to was human, part of a skeleton which itself had once been a full blown corpse. Ever since the harvest he had searched for human remains in the field and been undeterred by not finding any. He believed, he wanted to believe, that a body had been buried on his land. He even had an explanation for why the plate might have risen to the surface while the skeleton had not. It was all to do with the properties of titanium and he was about to tell us exactly what they were but Laura stepped in.

"Why don't I try and give it some provenance, as they say in the antiques world. If I can find out who made it, we'll be well on our way."

"Our way to what?" I asked, as flatly as I could.

"I don't know but information is never wasted, you always say."

She was right, I always do. I made a mental note to keep my mouth shut in future. One good thing about Laura's pro-active interest in the plate, however, was that I no longer needed to avoid its current keeper. With any luck the maker would point us towards a reasonable explanation as to why it had turned up in Martin's field and I could go back to answering his phone calls, showering less and having fewer urgent appointments. We could return to enjoying a Friday night beer together, putting the world to rights and alternately moaning and boasting about our children. I'd missed the friendship.

I'd been picturing all kinds of cars from stretch limos to boxy people carriers but when it finally drew up, the other side of the five bar gate, it was a blacked out Mini Cooper. I watched from the window as Jaikie and the driver took two big bags and a school satchel from the back seat and set them down on the verge. The two men exchanged a few words, the driver made a three point turn and departed. Jaikie stood gazing round at the garden, presumably checking that everything was just as he remembered it.

As I went out to greet him it struck me that, even with my children, I'm never sure what to say in those first few moments. He must have felt the same way if his own silence was anything to go by. When we reached the big beech tree, he dropped the bags and we embraced and I felt his strength, which always surprises me. I expect boyish weakness, but then my fixed image of him is as a kid of sixteen. I held him at arms' length and looked him over. He appeared to be much the same as he'd been back in the summer in L.A. His hair was still its natural colour, cut short and parted down the left side for the sake of the movie in which he played a young British gunner from World War Two. His face was still tapered, skin taut, bones visible, not buried beneath the effect of too much good living.

Laura came out of the house, letting Dogge slip past her. She came tear-arsing towards us with Laura yelling in vain for her to stop.

"I'm clean! I'm clean!" Jaikie said as Dogge tried to coral him against his luggage. "Hi, Laura, wonderful to see you again."

He gave her his smile and they kissed in a way I still haven't got the hang of, air kisses left to right. She asked how his flight had been. It was perfect, he said, just three hours late but now, thank God, he was here. He put an arm round her shoulder and drew her towards him, did the same to me with his other arm.

"This really is such a beautiful place, Dad. And it's great to see you, both of you."

He was by nature theatrical, melodramatic if circumstances allowed, but this was him being real. He was genuinely pleased to be home.

A while later Jaikie joined us in the kitchen, having taken a tour of the cottage and told me that he liked what I'd done to the place. I was surprised that he'd noticed I'd done anything and as I drew breath to give him details Laura asked what we were doing about supper.

"I thought we'd go up to *The Crown*," I said.

Jaikie pulled a face and went over to his satchel. From the front pocket he pulled out a stapled document, covered in war-like images, with the words *All Good Men and True* scattered over it.

"My skedule," he said. "You didn't know schedule was spelled with a 'k' did you? I have to be on the road, seven o'clock tomorrow, whole raft of interviews. Then on Tuesday, breakfast telly, have to be out of here five o'clock."

"Supper here then," said Laura. "I made your father a tub of *chilli con carne* the other week. I'll defrost a few portions and do some rice."

She went over to the freezer and found what she needed.

"Is Sophie flying over?" I asked.

I was referring to his long-term girlfriend, Sophie Kent, an English actress who had gone to the States just before he had.

"Blimey, Dad, for a moment I thought I was back in L.A., facing down some gossip hack. No, she isn't."

"Dare I ask?"

"You *are* a gossip hack." He paused. "Sophie and I, we've called it a day."

"I'm sorry."

"Don't be. She had a problem with my success, found it difficult going out with someone who was being talked about all the time." I'd been wondering when the Jaikie I knew and loved would stick his ego above the parapet. "I went out there to get work and struck lucky. Soph couldn't even get a part as an English maid in this remake of *Rebecca* they're doing." He turned to Laura. "Peter Weir, the director, said if I'd been ten years older he would have offered me the part of Maxim de Winter. When a guy like that says to you…" He must have noticed her fixed smile and stopped himself in mid conceit. "Sorry, you can read about me any day of the week. I want to hear what you two have been up to."

Sensing that I might not be able to speak for a moment or two, Laura pitched in. "Since his so-called retirement, your father's gained quite a reputation in these parts for solving other people's problems. Only this morning…" She went over to the cutlery drawer in the kitchen dresser and found Martin's plate among the teaspoons. "What do you make of that?"

He removed it from its polythene envelope. "Metal plate, four screw holes, sharp and shiny, D.I.Y stuff."

"Titanium," I said. "Orthopaedic usage."

He raised what Maggie used to call his Dirk Bogarde eyebrow. It started life being forced, now it seemed to come naturally. "Broken bones?"

He looked it over again while Laura explained how Martin and I had come by it. When she'd finished Jaikie said, "There's a number etched into the side of it. I can't make out if that's a one or a capital 'I' or if that's the letter 'O' or zero? Do you think I should have an eye test? I mean seriously…"

Laura took the plate and examined it both over the top of her glasses and through them, but still couldn't decipher what was inscribed.

"Not to worry," she said, putting the plate in her purse. "I've got something at the surgery that'll do the job."

"That's your disinterested face, Dad. I've known it for thirty years. But you must have some idea as to how it got there. A field, slap bang in the middle of nowhere? I see foul play, I see a body being buried, I see a leading role for me."

"As the body?"

"As the hero who sorts it out. As you, Dad."

Egocentric that he was, he was sometimes difficult to resist.

"Yes, well, that's where it gets tricky. Explaining its presence in Long Field, I mean."

Laura tried to be helpful, if not sensible, saying that patients often have the plates removed, especially if they develop real or psychosomatic aches and pains around the fracture.

"Then keep the plate as a souvenir," said Jaikie, nodding. "That's what I'd do."

"Take it out for a walk across Long Field? And drop it?"

"No need to be sarky, Dad."

"Don't worry, I did some sloppy thinking of my own. Came up with a pilot chucking it out of a window, it falling out of a balloon basket or a para-glider's pocket. None of them really works."

He and Laura were both disappointed, probably because I was leading them back to the simple truth. There was no viable explanation for the plate having turned up in Long Field.

Jaikie managed to smile. "I still see a leading role in it for me."

2

I was woken the next morning by something shattering on the kitchen floor below me. The red numbers on the bedroom ceiling told me it was 6.23. I fought my way into a dressing gown and went downstairs to find Jaikie brushing milk and muesli into a dustpan. As a rule I get Dogge to clear the worst of any spill for me, but with pieces of the broken china bowl mixed in that wasn't an option today

"Do the worst of it," I said. "I'll see to the rest later."

He smiled. "You mean Laura will?"

"Laura's not here."

"Early start, like me, eh?" He poured himself another bowl of muesli and his expression changed as he did so. "Or do you mean she doesn't live here?"

"None of your business."

"Su business es mi business, the Italians say."

"It's casa and it's the Spanish."

He shrugged. "Answer my question."

"She goes home most nights."

"Why?"

I wasn't keen to discuss my love life with my youngest son. "Bugger off to work. Have a nice day."

"Honestly, your generation is so hung up about the really important things in life. That *chilli con carne* last night was fantastic. Jump in, for Christ's sake, while you've still got the chance. Let's face it, you're not the easiest man to live with. Mum used to say that about you…"

"Really?"

"…and I love that husky voice. The height as well. Tall women do it for me. What is she, nearly six foot? And big faces, proper faces. Okay, so she's not a classic beauty, but in the right light she's Julia Roberts."

"I'll tell her that."

"Tell her this: Mum would have loved her. Mum would've said what I'm saying."

A car turned into Morton Lane and made its way slowly down towards us, headlights dipped. The driver must have seen the lights on in the kitchen and known that his passenger was up.

"There's Jamal. I'll phone you." He rose from the table, grabbed his satchel and turned at the door as if something had just occurred to him. "Heh, can you stake me two twenties? I'm sorry, but I haven't had time to cash any dollars."

I would have staked him a lot more than forty quid at that precise moment, just to get rid of him.

After breakfast I drove out to Chestnut Farm with Dogge for company and a metal detector I'd picked up at some auction on the pretext that it might come in handy one day. This was the day.

I found Martin Falconer behind his big barn repairing a fence to the acre or so of grazing land which justified his Christmas turkeys being called 'free range'. He stopped working and straightened up as I explained that the reason for my unskeduled visit was his wretched plate, once only four centimetres long in my mind, but growing longer by the day, and the look of boyish excitement on his face was almost touching to see.

"So you think there's something to it?"

"I don't think anything. I just want to run a metal detector over where we found it."

"I've been over the whole area, fine tooth comb..." He stopped dead and, ever the farmer, said, "How much will it cost me?"

"We'll talk money if and when it becomes necessary. Today's on the house."

We drove to Long Field, so called for too obvious a reason to dwell on. At its widest point it was no more than fifty yards across and on the far side there was an ancient woodland of beech and horse chestnut where Martin kept a herd of wild boar. Like his Christmas turkeys they were now famous and no local wedding, fete or birthday party was complete without one, "spit roasted over a charcoal fire to bring out the exquisite flavour", his brochure declared.

"I'm thinking of moving them on," he said gloomily and gave me a short lecture about bleeding canker in beech trees and leaf miner in horse chestnuts, both of which spelt the end of the herd's habitat. "And now I've thoroughly depressed us both, park up on the verge, mind the ditch."

He had taped off about half an acre on the other side of the hedge and banged in a fence post at the point where Jan Zawadski had actually spotted the metal plate. At first glance the place was more like a deserted crime scene than anything else, but the rest of the field had been drilled with wheat straw for thatching. He explained the reason for growing such an esoteric crop. A local thatcher had offered to re-thatch the farmhouse, which Martin's ex had claimed in the run up to the divorce, and he would do it in exchange for a year's supply of straw. The man was an absolute grafter, he added, getting by far the better end of the deal, but with a slipping thatch and rain coming into the top room, now wasn't the time to tell him.

As I opened the back of the Land Rover and reached in for the detector, Dogge snuck past me, leaped the ditch and ran off into the field. Nose down she began to quarter the area back and forth clearly interested in something.

"What's got into her?" Martin asked.

"She was trained as a police sniffer dog. Failed the exam. I'm guessing that's where you and Sharon hid the last consignment of heroin."

He shook his head as if I'd actually meant it. "Jan's dog goes barmy over this place. She found something, back in the Spring, and scoffed it. Threw up with a vengeance."

"And you'd like to think it was rotting human flesh?"

"Makes you wonder."

"I'll start the far side and work back. Don't raise your hopes."

I'd arranged to meet Laura and Jaikie in *The Crown* as near to eight o'clock as we could all manage. The plan was that Jaikie would be dropped off, Laura would make her way there on her bike, after a late meeting at the surgery, and we'd all go back to Beech Tree in the Land Rover after supper.

I arrived long before the agreed time. It's a habit I've tried to break over the years, with no success, but to my surprise my fiercest critic and most stalwart ally in the fight against being early everywhere had already arrived. Laura was seated at the bar talking to the young licensee,

Annie McKinnon, and a close neighbour called Jean Langan. Jean does a few bits and pieces at Beech Tree and that's as close as my father, who I should emphasise died in 1991, will ever let me get to calling her my cleaner even though the lady herself has no problem with the word.

When Jaikie walked in through the door it wasn't to the applause he always seems ready to receive, but to a chorus of gentle mockery. He could hardly have expected star struck wonderment from those present. Before coming to Winchendon we'd lived in a village in the same catchment area, so he knew many of them from the grammar school. A middle-aged, tweedy man called John Demise, recently widowed, had taught him Latin and Greek, yet such is our need for the Gods to walk amongst us that by the end of the evening he and Jaikie had almost reversed positions and teacher was deferring to student. However, before they parted company Jaikie put things right.

"Nice to see you again, Sir", he said.

The years concertinaed and he was back in John's classroom, conjugating irregular verbs, hearing the myths and legends which had so enthralled him.

"How's he doing?" I asked Laura as I watched him cope with his admirers.

"Jaikie is flourishing."

Pleased as I was to hear her speak with such confidence she hadn't really understood what I'd meant. Instead of asking me to explain, she waffled and said that Jaikie was tired and under pressure, but that's all there was to it. When I showed signs of arguing the point, she waved it aside and told me that I worried about my children unnecessarily.

A young woman I didn't recognise had just walked into the bar with a male friend, same age, mid twenties. The girl was tall and slim, with masses of shoulder length brown hair carefully disarrayed around a pale, bony face. She removed her black leather gloves and began to unbutton the long overcoat with its fake fur trimmings at the collar and cuffs. She paused and turned to her companion, he in a suit and tie off the peg but clearly hung up every night. They hadn't been expecting a crush and the girl thought twice about staying until she saw what all the fuss was about. Her face lit up and she called out to Jaikie. He went over to her and they embraced, held onto each other longer than they needed to, more than just good manners on his part or a display of submission on the girl's who I now recognised as Jodie Falconer, Martin's daughter.

"I'll grant you he can be self-regarding at times," said Laura. "I doubt if it's easy being famous, though. Anyway, the main reason I like him is he's a young version of you and as with all your children he's different." She added with heartfelt regret, "I see so much sameness these days, Nathan, I wonder how on earth the species will survive."

"Should that tell me you've had a rotten day?"

"I have had an *excellent* day. I'll tell you all about it over supper."

Jaikie came over to join us, leaning down to peck Laura on the cheek and laying a hand on my shoulder. He then announced that he was starving, having steered clear of reception food all day, but before supper he was off to wash his hands.

"I have shaken hands with a thousand people today, some of whom I wouldn't touch with a barge pole. Honestly, you don't realise how filthy people can be until you're obliged to touch them."

When he returned from the Gents, a journey which took him longer than he'd bargained for on account of being waylaid by several more neighbours, he opened his satchel and took out an expensive bottle of red wine he'd been given earlier in the day. He asked the waitress to uncork it and pour and as soon as she'd departed with our order he turned our attention to the titanium plate, asking Laura how she had got on today. She put on her glasses and took a post-it note from her handbag.

"The inscription on the side of the plate is AD07FI673", she said, passing the note to me. "AD identifies the maker, Ambrose & Dawlish in Corby. They've been making orthopaedic accessories since 1750."

She was clearly expecting enthusiasm from me but all I could manage was, "Good business to be in."

"What next?" asked Jaikie, taking up the slack

"I emailed them and after the usual blank wall of automatic responses, I sent another saying I wanted to place a large order." She snapped her fingers to indicate just how quickly a girl in the sales office had responded. "An actual person, with a real voice told me within two minutes that the rest of the serial number meant the plate had been made for The Chiltern Clinic, Amersham, Bucks in August 2009."

"That is brilliant!" said Jaikie. In common with the rest of his generation he was inclined to describe the simplest of achievements as 'brilliant'.

"I'm not saying I didn't feel dreadful doing it because I did," Laura went on. "I mean people are so gullible. Hah! I'm telling you two that! Nathan, you're an ex-policeman for heaven's sake, you depended on it, and you, Jaikie, an actor, you persuade people to suspend their belief for as long…" She paused and brought herself back down to earth with a sip or two of her wine.

"So, presumably you got in touch with this clinic?" I said.

"I phoned them, using my NHS credentials, and with no hesitation whatsoever this girl told me the number on the plate referred to a Patrick Scott, aged 24." She was talking only to Jaikie now, assured of his support. "He came to them as an emergency, via the ambulance service. A ski-ing accident, badly fractured metatarsal."

She pointed down to her foot in case he didn't know where the metatarsals lived.

"Did you get an address?" I asked.

"Well, no."

Regardless of me pointing out the shortfall Jaikie went into overdrive. "That is still one hell of a breakthrough, Dad. I mean this morning it was a plate found in a field, tonight we know who it belonged to." And then without a hint of irony, he added, "All you have to do now is track him down."

I beckoned the pair of them to lean in towards me. "Let me tell you where I've been today. Long Field with a metal detector. And I can assure you there isn't a body buried out there."

They lowered their voices to object, as if whispering might keep the myth alive.

"You sound very sure about that, Nathan."

"That metal detector is state of the art. It'll find a needle in a haystack."

"You weren't looking for a needle, Dad."

"The plate would have been held to the bone it was healing by four metal screws. I didn't find one of them."

Jaikie took a swig of wine to help him think. "Then we're back to pilots, balloonists, para-gliders, the bloody thing falling out of people's pockets?"

I shrugged. "I still can't tell you how the plate got there, but one thing's for certain: it didn't involve blood and guts."

Jaikie tried to stand the whole business on its head, saying that there being no apparent crime was highly suspicious in itself. More so, perhaps, than if an entire skeleton had been dug up. He pointed out that many a Hollywood success had been founded on far less and went on to name obscure films that fitted the bill. I let him exhaust his own argument which, by the time our food came, he'd just about done. I broke the silence which followed.

"Early start tomorrow, then?"

He nodded. "Jamal's picking me up at soppy o'clock. Five, I think."

I offered to get up with him, make some toast and coffee, see him on his way.

"I wouldn't want to spoil your beauty sleep," he said, smiling at each of us to emphasize that he'd put us in the same bed for the night.

We small-talked our way through the rest of the meal and finally Jaikie beckoned the waitress and asked her for the bill. When she returned with it he launched into a display of feeling his pockets, presumably for the dollars he'd planned to cash earlier that day. He frowned as if suddenly remembering that he hadn't done so and turned to me.

"Dad, I'm sorry…"

I held up my hand to spare him further embarrassment and reached for my wallet. He still hadn't got any money, then. Had he become like the Queen and never carried any or was there another explanation for his lack of cash? One for me to worry about.

3

At 5.30 the next morning Jamal turned into Morton Lane, switched off his headlights and pulled up at the other side of the five bar gate. A long silence followed, no sound from outside the house, nothing from within until Dogge went into her usual frenzy as she heard footsteps on the gravel. The house began to stir. Laura, who had indeed spent the night with me, in accordance with Jaikie's instructions, reached across and mumbled an offer to come downstairs and help me. I thanked her and told her to go back to sleep.

I put on a dressing gown and went up to the attic to check that Jaikie was at least alive if not exactly kicking. As I entered the room he threw back the duvet and knee-jerked out of bed, paused to get his bearings and managed to say, "Dad, Jamal." I took it to be a request for me to go downstairs and smooth ruffled feathers.

At the front door, wondering how to knock without making any sound, stood a mahogany skinned man, black hair, black eyes, mid-thirties. He opened his mouth to say something but smiled instead, shook my outstretched hand and followed me through to the kitchen.

"Tea or coffee?" I asked.

"No thank you, sir. We must leave as soon as possible. BBC Television Centre by seven. The M40. Terrible, terrible."

He adopted a classic at ease position, hands clasped behind his back, and smiled again. I took it to be a sign of his affable nature and as I tried to smile in return Jaikie entered in a cabaret act of dressing and drying himself all with a toothbrush jutting out from the side of his mouth. He spat it into the sink and apologised to Jamal. Still drying behind his ears he headed for his leather jacket, hung over the back of a chair.

"Breakfast Television today," he said to me. "You'll watch?"

"Sure."

On his way out he grabbed the satchel from me and I flashed back to the boy who was always late for the bus and had to be driven to school by his mother or me. It took us a year to cotton on that he was late on purpose, preferring to be chauffeured. He paused, looked me over and smiled much as Jamal had done.

"Real tough old copper, eh?" He could see that I had no idea what he was talking about. "The dressing gown, mate. Suits you."

I looked down at it. It was silk, it was lilac, it was Laura's. I went back upstairs and got dressed

It was an odd sensation, sat there a couple of hours later in Maggie's Dad's old rocker, itself a repository of our family history, watching my youngest son talk about the second world war as if he'd been in it, about Hollywood as if it were his second home, about himself with just the right mixture of modesty and confidence to make him likeable. The only trouble was I didn't know this man. I knew the boy behind him, the sixteen year old who had sulked and fought his way through school and when the time came had taken his mother's death harder than any of us. That vulnerable young man was still there, just below the surface, but before any of him could be revealed he was forced to give way to the news headlines. The presenter thanked him for his contribution, he thanked her for having him. Never mind sixteen, he was twelve years old again, thanking the parents of his friends for their tea-time hospitality. Impressed though I was by his good manners, I was finding it hard work being constantly wrenched from the present to the past and back again.

"He is so witty, so charming," said Laura. She took my hand. "You must be so proud of him."

"His mother would have been."

I must have sounded reluctant, though I hadn't meant to, It just came out that way. Nevertheless, I found myself wondering who he'd borrowed cash from that morning, Jamal or Laura. My money was on Laura.

I spent the rest of the morning repairing a downstairs window and blaming the fact that it didn't go well on my father. Laura said the reason I'd felt his presence these past few days was all too obvious. Jaikie was in England for the opening of *All Good Men and True* and the three of us - grandfather, son, grandson - were an unbreakable chain, no matter how we might have wished it were otherwise. My own view was less sophisticated. Dad was there to remind me of our mutual hatred for all things do-it-yourself.

My father was the hardest working man I ever knew, by trade a fishmonger who in the evenings cooked and sold fish and chips. Not burgers, pies, or chicken portions, but fish and chips. I turned at one point to see him standing at the door of our shop in North London, long striped apron, arms folded across it. He was annoyed with me. He wasn't a man given to fits of temper, that was my mother's weakness and one that I'd inherited from her, but there was Dad with his rarely seen anger directed at me. I'd fallen into bad company, he said, naming the two individuals with disdain. We were fifteen years old and had broken into the local cricket pavilion, with the intention of stealing recent delivery of beer, five hundred bottles of it. God knows how we thought we'd hide it from our parents who seemed to watch every move we made, but such was our faith in ourselves that we went ahead with the plan.

"That boy," he said to my mother, as if all of a sudden I didn't belong to him, "needs something to occupy his mind." He stopped short of saying he regretted the end of National Service or that a good war would teach my generation how to cope with life. Having suffered both he didn't believe a word of it. But here I was, nearly forty years later, wondering if that's what I needed now, something to occupy my mind. A decent murder, perhaps. Even as the thought occurred so Laura came weaving down Morton Lane. I abandoned the window and went to greet her.

As she leaned her bike against the wall she told me this was a flying visit, she had to rush back for more wrangling with the local Health Trust over money that she and her partners had once been promised, but now apparently weren't going to get. They wanted to build a new health centre to replace the shack they currently occupied, but recession, budget cuts and a U-turn in monetary policy were just three reasons for the Trust denying them the quarter of a million pounds it would cost.

Once in the kitchen she removed her helmet and shook out her hair. In his description of her, Jaikie had made no mention of her hair, so carefully cut and coloured, barley over grey she called it. He'd made great play of the husky voice and her height and I'd admired both before, of course, but when your son remarks on the physical attributes of the woman you're romantically involved with, you see them with a different eye.

"This is about Patrick Scott," she said. I must have groaned. "No, don't be like that. You'll feel the same way I do, when you know what it is."

I put my arms around her waist and slipped my hands under the belt of her skirt, pulling her close. It was probably all that bike-riding, but for fifty years old there wasn't much spare flesh to get hold of. She stepped back.

"Nathan, this is really important. I had a spare quarter of an hour this morning and with you being sniffy last night about me not finding an address, I did a search for Patrick Scott on the NHS data base. Guess what! I found several Patrick Scotts, yes, but none of them in their twenties with a fractured metatarsal!"

She paused as if expecting me to stagger with amazement, but I managed to stand my ground.

"Nathan, medical records are the holy grail of my profession. Not only have I breached confidentiality, I'm also committing a crime by passing on what I've discovered to you."

"Then I'm arresting you and taking you upstairs…"

"There is no longer any record of our Patrick Scott having been an NHS patient. All trace of him has been wiped out, almost certainly within the last few days."

I asked her to repeat that. She said I'd heard it the first time.

"There could be a dozen explanations," I said. "Maybe the Chiltern Clinic got it wrong. Maybe he's given them a false name, right back at the start when he broke his foot."

"I double checked with the Chiltern this morning. Three days ago they told me who the plate was for, the date it was used and for what fracture. Today, the girl I spoke to can't find any trace of it."

"You spoke to the same girl?"

She shrugged. "I asked for the records department and got put through to whoever was manning the phone."

I'm not given to hot flushes of intuition or bouts of ESP, much less to drawing inferences from misread paperwork, but what Laura had just told me took me back to Long Field the night we found the titanium plate. I'd had a hunch then that it was important but no evidence to back that up. I still had no proof of… anything, let alone that a murder had been committed, but if records had been removed from a government data base maybe all that was about to change. So what had happened in the last few days to make Patrick Scott disappear? We'd started asking questions about him.

Just after four o'clock Jaikie phoned and with a barrage of expletives told me that he was pig sick. The PR people and the Film Company had been at loggerheads all day and he'd been trying to referee their arguments. The film people should have had the final say on everything, but a new publicity girl, well over six foot tall, was so pushy, so domineering, she got her own way. She booked Jaikie to do an unskeduled interview with a journalist for a national paper, Richard Slater. He turned out to be a very nice guy but that wasn't the point. There was a plan, a running order, agreed upon days ago by all parties so the blonde bean-pole should have at least made…

"What time will you be home?" I asked.

"About nine. Will there be any food knocking about? Anything Laura-ish?"

I said she'd made a tub of chicken in a wine sauce, the same day she made the chilli, that I would defrost a couple of bags and do some rice. He was delighted. It meant he could steer clear of the reception food again.

It was just after nine when his car turned into Morton Lane. The headlights were on full beam, picking out threads of mist, turning them into a wall of light. The Mini stopped and I saw Jaikie get out. He'd obviously been asleep during the journey and stretched himself into life. He stooped to the driver's window and exchanged a few words with him, then turned and walked across to the cottage, entering through the back door in his usual fashion, as if waiting for the applause to die down.

"You look knackered boy," I said.

"I am. Bright side, though. Jodie Falconer's coming with us to the opening tomorrow. I mean there you are, you don't see people for eight years and all of a sudden…"

"You wonder how you lived without them?"

He dumped his bulging satchel, came over to the sink and started to wash his hands. I tore him off three or four sheets of kitchen towel.

"How many hands today?" I asked.

He shrugged. "Two, three thousand?"

"Jamal's gone, I see."

He turned and smiled at me. "Jesus, you don't get even the small stuff past an old copper. How d'you know?"

"Jamal turns the headlights off because he knows the road now. This bloke had them on full beam."

"The headlights and his mouth. I fell asleep round about Beaconsfield, thank God." He took out a bottle of wine from his satchel and offered it to me like a waiter seeking my approval. "His name's George. He asked if he could come in for ten minutes. He's had a hell of a day too. I said no and sent him up to *The Crown*. Was that mean of me?"

I shook my head. "What happened to Jamal?"

"Some rule about them needing so many hours off in order to work so many hours on." He nodded at the food. "Whatever that is smells fucking wonderful."

He looked round for Laura, concerned that she'd heard him swear.

"She's gone back to her place. All that stuff women do before a big night out."

He took two glasses and the corkscrew to the table and settled himself. I put a bowl of rice down beside the chicken in wine, leaned towards him and kissed him on the forehead. I wanted to ask him about money, why he hadn't got any, but as I drew breath to do so he reached up and touched my face.

"Good to be home, Dad."

The money could wait, at least until after the opening tomorrow.

I couldn't sleep and it was 1.56 in the morning and rather than lie there, watching the red light on the ceiling count down my life in seconds, each of them dragging way beyond its allotted time, I decided to go downstairs and talk to my other children.

It was a clear night outside, sharp and silent, ready to pick up the slightest sound and play it back ten times louder, in this case my leather moccasins scraping the path up to my office. Once inside, I switched everything on - lights, fire, computer, background music - as much to help me forget that I was alone as for their practical value. I sipped my tea and checked my emails.

The last one I'd had from any of my children was from Jaikie at the weekend with flight arrival times; before that Fee, a month ago, telling me how she was planning to move from Hokkaido's gentle town of Asahikawa, where she taught English to the Japanese, to hard-bitten Tokyo. She had met a man called Yukito who had offered her a job in so-called Electric City as he rebuilt his business after the appalling earthquakes. She was to be head of liaison between his gadget based company and his many customers in England, Australia and America. For a girl who couldn't speak a word of Japanese a year and a half previously, I thought it was going some. However, I hadn't heard since what had become of the job, the move or the man called Yukito.

If I was honest with myself I was hearing less and less from all of them these days and I wasn't quite sure how to explain that. Laura was a handy reason, of course. Since she and I had become 'friends', there was no need for my four children to keep such a close eye on me. In gloomier moments I was inclined to admit that as a family we were breaking up, perhaps into pieces that would never fit together again. Maybe the question I was about to put to them concerning Jaikie would spur them to repair the fractures, to start sticking their noses into each other's business again, just as they'd always done. But what was the question to be?

"Fee, hi!" I wrote as casually as I could. "Quickie, this. Do you know if Jaikie's okay? He's staying with me, pending UK premiere tomorrow of *All Good Men and True*. Any news on the job? Dad xx."

I could see from the four clocks on the wall what time it was in each of the places they'd settled in, places I hoped to visit one day. It was ten o'clock in the morning in Japan and eight the previous evening in New Orleans where Con had drifted ashore. Drawn by the lifestyle, the history, the abandonment of its people after hurricane Katrina, he had a new girlfriend, a terrifyingly beautiful creole called Marcie. They must have been at home that night since he replied within the hour.

"Jaikie's fine, man. Okay, so that bitch Sophie Kent dumped him, but he's living in Hollywood. Take his pick. Enough about him. We're off to Haiti for a couple of months, Marcie's ancestors and all that. How's Laura?"

I hadn't mentioned money, and certainly not the possibility that Jaikie was in trouble over it, so he didn't bite on it as a problem. Interestingly, though, there was no request for money from Con himself from which I deduced that Marcie was as rich as Croesus. If not that she had taught him shame. An hour later I received the following from Fee.

"Dad, job and move still in the pipeline. Don't worry, you'll be first to know. I didn't think anything was wrong with Jaikie, but now you mention it he was a bit distant when we last spoke. I'll find out more. Let you know. Fee. xx"

Ellie wasn't far behind, four in the morning my time, nine fifteen hers. She was working in Nepal and her email said simply, "What's this I hear from Fee? Jaikie's in trouble? More details before I text him. Ellie x"

It wasn't playing out quite how I'd intended. I certainly didn't want Fee badgering all and sundry about a problem that might not exist. I emailed her back to that effect, but it was way too late. According to her, if I'd thought that Jaikie had a problem, then he almost certainly did. Later still there was an email from Con. "Dad, sorry, didn't realise it was serious. I reckon it's classic depression. Sophie Kent. He was nuts about her. If he's peely wally (remember that saying, one of Mum's favourite?) she'll be to blame. Go head to head with him about it. Better still get Laura to. But for Christ's sake keep Fee away from Sophie, she'll kill the bitch."

Keeping Fee at a distance had suddenly become more difficult than it sounded. Her final email on the subject was "Listen, Dad, if it's as bad as it sounds, I'll take some time out and come home, sort Jaikie out while he's still with you."

From my own wish for us to be a family again, however far flung, and my kids' readiness to pick up an imaginary crisis and run with it, I had turned their brother into a depressive, his ex-girlfriend into a thorough going bitch, and received a threat from Fee to return home and sort it out. I could also, in idle moments, worry about a man called Yukito and Con's trip to Haiti, under the spell of a creole beauty called Marcie. But at least we were all talking to each other. I went back to bed and fell asleep immediately.

4

The next day began for me when the doorbell rang and Dogge let rip in her usual fashion. The red numbers on the ceiling said 6.43. I waited a few moments and then asked, "Was that the doorbell?" I wasn't sure who the question was directed at. Maggie or Laura, I imagine, each being conspicuous by her absence.

I pulled on some clothes and went downstairs to find that Jamal's replacement was a man in his mid-thirties, dressed in jeans and a sheepskin flying jacket, check shirt open at the neck. The top button was missing. No wife, no live-in lover to sew it back on. That aside, he seemed to believe that I knew exactly what he was doing here but when the opposite became clear he stepped forward and held out his hand. I shook it before I had chance to decide if I wanted to or not.

"I'm George Corrigan," he said. "Jacob's driver. He said he wanted me here at half past. I'm not sure if he meant half six or half seven."

"Half seven."

He slapped his forehead with his free hand, a theatrical gesture more up Jaikie's street than a common or garden driver's. He was carrying the weekend section of *The Guardian,* a strange accessory to bring from his car to my house unless he intended to read it, which meant he planned on staying for a while. I led him through to the kitchen and as I turned I caught him in the act of scanning the place like a pro. He stopped and smiled at me. I nodded him to a chair at the table.

"Coffee?" I asked.

"If you're making some."

He was a powerful man, just under six foot tall, with a zig-zag parting to the difficult dark hair and a skin leathery beyond its years, the result of long hikes against wind and rain, I fancied. The stubble squared off a striking face and certainly one that had been struck its fair share of times. In contradiction he had a full set of teeth, suggesting that he'd won most of the fights he'd been in. He also had a soft Irish voice, the kind I could listen to forever, although right now I wasn't too keen on what it was saying.

"There's a cracking piece about him in the paper. Thought you might want to see it." He opened out *The Guardian* supplement on the table and turned it towards me. "Mentions you. Thirty-seven murders? That is a lot of bad people."

"Maybe, but why should that interest anyone writing about my son? What else does it say?"

He gestured to the paper. "Keep it. Read it later."

"Tell me in a sentence now."

He leaned back and tried to get comfortable in the chair. "The usual kind of stuff journalists go for. Family, girlfriends, interests. Is it a problem?"

"You tell me. The kids were brought up never to talk to strangers and certainly not to journalists about their father's work. It was a condition of me keeping no secrets from them. More interesting, though, is why you're so keen for me to read all about it."

He gazed me with practised, unflinching eyes. "Am I?"

"Oh, yes. Perhaps it would help if you told me *what* you are, George."

"Jacob's driver," he said with the full body shrug of a much mistaken man.

He looked ex-Army to me, someone who'd found it difficult back in civilian life until one of the security outfits had collared him. I let it pass and as the coffee brewed I began reading the article. It was long and wrapped around a photo of Jaikie I'd come to know well during the past three months. It showed him in mud-covered action pose, machine gun at his far side, battle dress torn and bloody. The piece began with a synopsis of the film, went on to give a resumé of his career, then all of a sudden it got personal.

'Hawk is the son of a retired Detective Chief Inspector who, in the job, brought thirty-five murderers to justice, seventeen of them as the lead investigator. "Being retired hasn't stopped him poking his nose into other people's business," Hawk says. "Year before last he solved two nasty local murders. The Summer after that he found the killer of Teresa Marie Stillman." I ask if his father's involved in anything at the moment. "A farmer pal found this orthopaedic plate in one of his fields. The Old Man's certain it's off a body that's buried out there. All he has to do is find…"'

I stopped there, pushed the paper away from me and went over to the doorway through to the front hall. I yelled up the stairs. "Jaikie! Get down here!" Several moments of absolute silence went by. "Jaikie, foot to floor. Let me hear it."

It was a routine Maggie had established, otherwise the kids just turned over and went back to sleep. Another silence was followed by a couple of thumps from way up in the attic room.

Back at the percolator I poured Corrigan some coffee and pointed to the milk and sugar. Directly above our heads we heard the toilet flush, the taps turn full on, and a minute or so later Jaikie entered the kitchen, bleary and belligerent, a far cry from the charming film star who could wow anyone between the age of eight and eighty. He'd managed to haul himself into a pair of cut-off jeans and a sweater, no T-shirt, nothing on his feet.

"Dad, what the fuck…?"

I reminded him that way back in the mists of time we'd agreed that he would never talk to strangers about what I did for a living and he gradually twigged that breaking that agreement was the reason he'd been dragged out of bed. I pushed *The Guardian* round to face him, jabbing at the name of the man who'd written the article, Richard Slater.

"You didn't think any time, 'Why is this bloke asking about my father?'"

That brought on a frown, affronted ego I thought at first, but not so. He went over to get some coffee, poured in the milk - or cream as he'd begun to call it - then stirred it more than he needed to.

"Not just you, Dad," he said eventually. "The Others, Ellie, Con, Fee, Laura, the house, even the bloody dog. Like a fool I just answered his questions. He was so good at making me talk."

"And as usual you were reluctant to do so?"

I was hoping Corrigan would have felt the urge to chip in by now and reveal himself as something more than a driver, but I had to prompt him.

"George, you'd better start talking, but if I don't like what I hear, Jaikie's not going into London with you."

"Hang on a sec, Dad," said Jaikie. "Who the bloody hell is he?"

"That's what I keep asking and he refuses to say, but he isn't some hack driver." Corrigan turned to Jaikie and shrugged an appeal for sympathy. "Unless you're going to tell me Jamal carries a Glock 29 under his jacket as well, all pumped up and ready to go."

Jaikie couldn't resist it. "And there was I thinking he was just happy to see me."

It went straight over Corrigan's head but on the plus side our soft spoken Irishman handed me a well-used wallet in the front of which was a Met police warrant card. Jaikie was more concerned about him not getting the reference to a gun in his pocket and was on the verge of giving us Mae West's life story to make up for it.

"I thought everybody knew…"

"Jaikie, shutup and focus. This guy is from S.O.U. Special Operations, who deal with nasty stuff. Therein lies the question, George. What are you protecting my son from?"

Corrigan tried to relax and, now the Glock was out in the open, so to speak, he took off his flying jacket and hooked it over a chair. "They all get it now. Big stars. He'll be the fifth I've protected this year."

"Does Josh Hartnett get one?" Jaikie asked.

"Of course. Go phone him."

At a nod from me, Jaikie went back upstairs to get his mobile.

"Anything else I can help you with?" Corrigan asked, taking back his wallet.

"When were you assigned, Sergeant? Before or after Jaikie went to see this Richard Slater?"

"I rescued him *from* Slater. Jesus, he'd still be there talking but for me."

I was beginning to feel I'd overreacted, then remembered an old Desk Sergeant who once told me that was exactly the point at which he double-checked.

"So you never heard of a man called Patrick Scott?"

His eyes didn't flicker, face didn't move. "Should I have done?"

"Don't give me that shit, answering a question with a question."

"I have never heard of a man called Patrick Scott."

If it wasn't the truth, he was an exceptionally well-trained liar. I wanted to treble check but I knew it wouldn't make me any happier. Only when Jaikie re-entered the kitchen, talking on his phone to Josh Hartnett, reporting that a guy built like a concrete dustbin had taken over from his usual driver and was a member of the Met's S.O.U. did I begin to ease up a little.

It was one of those days you look forward to for months but the moment it arrives you long for it to be over and done with. Jaikie left for London with Corrigan at about 8.30 and I won't go as far as to say that I never expected to see him again, but I did run a few grim-ending scenarios through my mind to test their probability. I couldn't link any of them to the appearance of Patrick Scott in our lives, but the plate which had held one of his bones together couldn't be explained away as easily as I would have liked. All morning I fought the notion that because Laura had poked around in his records, they'd been wiped, but there was no other explanation. Then S.O.U. had stepped in and where they go trouble has usually been before, or will shortly follow. And Richard Slater bothered me. I'd read him over the years on all sorts of things, from capital punishment to cooking the perfect venison roast, but why he'd be interested in me was a mystery.

Eventually, I justified my concerns as the niggles of an old copper expecting the worst, preparing for a thunderbolt out of a bright blue sky. I was succumbing to an old weakness, seeing everything around me as a potential crime and everyone who crossed my path as parties to it. It must have made me lousy company and I apologised to Laura over lunch at her favourite London restaurant, The Mango Tree in Belgravia.

"It isn't so much the old copper who gets worked up as the man himself," she said so neatly. "Worrying, especially about your children, is your default position."

She went on to add that she didn't mind. She had come to London to see *All Good Men and True* and planned on enjoying it. Our itinerary was as follows: after lunch, an hour or so at the Tate Modern, then onto the Royal Overseas League where we'd booked a room for the night, change into our finery and then off to the pictures. It sounded like a good way to pass the time, but I still couldn't settle to it.

Paul Gauguin didn't help, either. Laura had bought tickets to a special exhibition of his work and, in odd moments during the past month, had briefed me on the man starting with his death at 54, an age close to my heart, shall we say. But as I stood in the Tate before those fabulous, primitive paintings, I couldn't get past their creator being a man who abandoned his wife and five children and fell out with most of his friends. Was painting his excuse for that? And, more seriously, how would he answer the charge of abuse against young Tahitian girls? Was their immortality as works of art a fair price to have paid? Back at the Overseas League we lay on the bed and talked it over, tried to make a case for the man who had punched his own wife in the face and drawn blood, then painted something as vibrant as The Swineherd, as sensuous as

Nevermore, as powerful as the self-portrait behind bars. We struggled and gave up, but somehow managed to doze off and sleep for over an hour.

We woke to find ourselves in our usual dilemma. I knew we were going to be late, Laura was convinced that we had plenty of time: two opposing theories working towards mustering in the lobby by seven o'clock to be picked up by a limo. Somehow we managed it, me in a DJ so old that I can't remember buying it, Laura in a blue silk dress she had bought for the occasion. It set off the silver jewellery she was so fond of, the long earrings, an heirloom necklace, bracelets and finger rings.

As we stepped out of the lift Jaikie was entering the building. He didn't wait for applause from those around him, but came straight over to us, kissed Laura left and right and told her how wonderful she looked. He embraced me without comment but then, as he held open the big mahogany door for us, he whispered, "You too, Dad. The suit. Still looks great."

Out in the courtyard, Corrigan had replaced the Mini with a stretch limo in the back of which was Jodie Falconer, dressed to kill, slim and sparkly, hair piled high showing more of her face than she usually would. She was nervous about a host of things. Top of her list was the fear that she'd somehow barged us out of the way. She deferred to us more than she needed to, even addressed us as Doctor Peterson and Mr Hawk until I threatened to call her My Learned Friend, Miss Falconer, Q.C. even though she was still a pupil. After a few failed attempts she settled on our Christian names.

The Odeon at Leicester Square proclaims above its entrance that it's 'fanatical about film' It clearly doesn't feel the same way about architecture, being one of the ugliest buildings in London, its facade finished in slabs of black granite. When Corrigan dropped us off outside we were hit by strobing light from cameras, calls to Jaikie from shapes and faces behind them, wanting to know who the new girlfriend was. He paused to be gracious, introduced her as an old schoolfriend, now a London barrister so they had better watch their steps. They wanted to know her name. He told them. Somebody asked what had happened to Sophie Kent. He pretended not to have heard the question.

We walked across the carpet towards the entrance, driven by the human sheepdogs of the PR company, prominent among whom was the blonde bean-pole Jaikie had moaned about the previous day. The cameras followed us, so too the voices, until another car drew up behind the limo and left us blinking in sudden darkness.

We followed Jaikie into the foyer where there were people to meet, hands to shake, names and faces to remember. He asked Laura if she and I could manage. She said that we'd try and looked round for the ladies' toilet. He then all but arranged an escort to take her there, but at that point the bean-pole did us all a favour and whisked him and Jodie away to meet people far more important than us. One of them was Richard Slater, a man with a bespectacled face that reminded me of a dozen others with its two clothes brushes of white hair either side of a bald dome and a bushy moustache trying to make up for the lack.

It struck me, as I waited for Laura, that just twenty years ago the foyer would have been overhung by a cloud of smoke but tonight all that remained of that indifference to dying were a few hardened smokers outside on the forecourt, shivering as they grabbed a last cigarette. I shivered with them, not from cold but from recalling how much the habit had cost me. My wife. And that's when I saw him. To me, with my practised eye and incipient paranoia, he stood out like a sore thumb. He too was waiting. Forty years old and dressed in a bog standard dinner jacket, white shirt and black tie he could have been mistaken for any one of ten thousand men in London that night, but he was putting on a show of impatience with a few too many clicks of the tongue and glances at his watch, all for the benefit of the SO14 officers who made up the royal protection detail. I counted six of them and they were ignoring him. Had he been standing alone in the foyer he would have been an object of suspicion, but a man waiting for his wife to come out of a toilet has instant credibility. He saw me watching him and gave me a smile of mutual forbearance before looking away. And in that moment I thought I might have got it wrong. This was a film premiere, for God's sake, not the starting point of a general strike, a revolution or a military takeover. So I left it at that, save for asking Laura when she finally emerged from the Ladies if there'd been many other people in there. Quite a few, she said, but she hadn't bothered to do a head count.

Once inside the theatre we were treated like aristocracy. Jaikie was a couple of rows in front of us and turned to point me out to the people next to him. They waved. I waved back. Five minutes later, and against all licensing laws I know of, I was brought a scotch with ice to calm my nerves. Laura said she hoped it wouldn't send me to sleep. I told her there was every chance I'd never sleep again. I was back at Jaikie's first school, watching him be a shepherd in the nativity play. He'd got his lines wrong and cried. There was nothing I could do for him then, there was nothing I could do for him now.

Then it started, this film I'd heard so much about. I'd been told the story several times but hadn't really taken it in. A young British Army Sergeant is taken hostage, along with two comrades, by a small band of Vichy French in Casablanca, November 1942. Being just after the allied landings at Safi, Port-Lyautey and Fedala, the collaborating Frenchmen try to use their hostages as bargaining tools to escape from Morocco, but one of them loses his nerve and shoots the captives. Drawn by whatever doubt, a young U.S Army Lieutenant who had witnessed the atrocity returns in the night to where the three Brits were killed. He finds the young Sergeant still alive, drags him through the dangerous city, and in doing so saves his life.

By chance the British Sergeant and the Lieutenant meet again in 1945 in Italy, just after the battle of Ravenna. Each has changed in his different ways, but this time it is the American who needs saving, though not from his enemies. Three years of war have left him dangerously unhinged and his own men plan to murder him. The young British NCO uses everything in his power, from subtle argument to brute force and saves his life.

At the end of the screening, the audience rose to its feet and applauded. The lead actors were introduced individually. Josh Hartnett and Jacob Hawk had heard it all before, in Los Angeles and in New York, but there was something about hearing it in London, they later told me, which made all the difference.

As the auditorium cleared, preparations were being made in the foyer for those involved in the film to be presented to the guests of honour, royalty from just down the road on The Mall. A girdle of onlookers formed and we were invited to the front of it. As the 3O14 faction prowled between government ministers, high ranking civil servants, army chiefs and the U.S. embassy mob, I resisted the urge to point out to those who didn't yet know that the tall one, fair hair, army cut, was mine.

The clatter of applause for the film and the performances resumed, led by the young prince and his girlfriend as they began to walk down the line. I saw Jaikie be introduced to them, step forward and laugh at something the prince said, a comment about army protocol. Jaikie turned to Jodie. She came forward, nervous but coping well in her role as the star's new love interest. The prince liked the look of her. There were more words, more looks, more laughter. And that's when I saw him again out of the corner of my eye, the man in the bog standard dinner jacket.

He came from way over the other side of the foyer, breaking the circle gently as he squeezed through it. He paused for a moment, walked towards the prince. The SO14 blokes moved. So did Corrigan. So did I. But as the man approached he veered slightly to his right. The prince wasn't his target after all. He stopped, drew something like a mustard jar from his pocket, unscrewed the lid, then threw its contents in Jaikie's face. Jaikie roared in terror and slapped both hands to his head. The sound was swamped by shouts and screams from those around. Within seconds the protection officers had the prince and his girlfriend out of reach, heading towards the exit, into a car and away. Only Corrigan seemed interested in the attacker. He drew his side arm, ran out of the building.

One of Laura's aunts described her niece to me as being superb in a crisis - it was everyday life she found so difficult to cope with. I knew what the aunt meant. My youngest son had just been attacked, sulphuric acid had been thrown at him by someone I could have stopped. Within minutes it would break up his beautiful face, eat it away, quite possibly blind him, and although I was right in front of him now and had taken him by the shoulders, I had no plan for the next critical thirty seconds. Laura had. She stepped out of her shoes and ran to Jaikie. She pushed Jodie and me aside, one hand each, and took hold of him. She dragged him by the arm, causing him to stumble, but she was strong enough to prevent a fall.

"Toilet!" she shrieked.

Strange, I remember thinking, even at a moment like that. She usually called it a lavatory.

"Move!" she said next and people in our path fell away.

"Paramedics!" she yelled at the bean pole who instantly reached for her mobile and dialled. I opened the door to the Ladies' toilet and in we went.

"Water!" she yelled and before the word was out of her mouth Jodie had the nearest tap running at full force.

Laura took Jaikie's head in both hands and forced it down into the sink, sideways on. As water rose up on the right hand side of his face, she dowsed the other side with water she was cupping in her free hand. As it drenched him we paused for the first moment since the attack. Laura saw where the acid had spattered Jaikie's jacket. It was still black, not bleached. She stooped and sniffed it, then said to Jodie, "Turn it off."

Laura pulled Jaikie upright and turned him to face us. The shock of the attack followed by being half drowned had reduced him to gasping for air. "Jaikie, it isn't acid," she said. "It's vinegar, cider vinegar I think. But it isn't acid."

Jaikie stared at her, eyes red and watery, then fell into her arms with relief. Our three minutes of hell was over. I turned and ran out into the foyer. The crowd of onlookers was breaking up, moving on, but the film people had stayed to see if Jaikie was alright. I yelled at one of the protection officers.

"D'you get him?"

"Who?" he asked.

"Man who threw it. Age forty. Caucasian. Five ten. For Christ's sake, who do you think?"

A colleague joined him, a thick-necked, early thirties man trembling with relief. "Thank Christ he didn't get the Ginga or the bird."

Odd how sometimes rage quickens you, other times it slows you right down. It seemed to take an age for me to turn and face this man and mutter, "What?"

"The prince," he explained. "It could have been the prince."

"Never mind the fucking prince, that was my Son." He tried to move away. I grabbed his arm. His colleagues didn't move to defend him. And he still hadn't answered my question.

"I said that was my Son! Does that make a difference?"

I was up close to him, but standing at a distance it seemed, watching myself, hearing myself insist on an answer.

"Well does it?"

Then I heard Jaikie, way out on the edge somewhere, calling, "Dad… Dad."

He'd emerged from the Ladies with Laura and Jodie to find me on the verge of ripping someone's head off. He hurried over, placed a hand on my shoulder and turned me towards him. I didn't see him too clearly but I heard him well enough. "Dad, you must have left The Map in your other jacket."

No one but Jaikie, Laura and I knew what he was referring to. The protection officer came into proper focus, more bewildered than terrified, yet pleased to have been spared the consequence of my anger. Jaikie's eyes were still streaming but he was smiling. I threw my arms round him and clung on.

The reception was held at the National Liberal Club in Whitehall Place, one of those rounded corner buildings which the Victorians were so good at. Subsequent generations had felt the need to ruin the ground floor and turn it into shops, a bank, a small Tesco's, but once inside and up on the first floor you can still get a whiff of Liberal tradition. It's helped by portraits of Liberal Party leaders all around the colonnaded main room, the most interesting of them being Jeremy Thorpe, cleverly concealed behind a massive pillar, along with the scandal which forced him to resign.

The celebration itself was a select and expensive affair, animated and congratulatory, some people even congratulating me when they learned that I was Jacob Hawk's father. First among them was Richard Slater who descended on me as if we were old friends, took my hand and shook it even though it hadn't been offered.

"You must be so proud," he said, a statement I was to hear over and over again in the next couple of hours. He introduced me to his wife. "Imogen, darling, this is Nathan Hawk, Jacob's father."

Imogen Slater was more restrained than her husband with a grounded sense of what was really important. "You must have been terrified when that maniac struck," she said. "Some jealous nutter, no doubt, but your companion, where is she?" She glanced round to see Laura being introduced by Jaikie to the rest of the cast. She stood taller than most of them. "Such presence of mind," Imogen Slater continued. "Such swift action…"

"Just thank God it wasn't the real thing," said her husband. "If it had been, if it had been…" He took another glass of champagne from a passing waiter and offered me one as if the drinks were on him. I asked the waiter to get me a double scotch in a tall glass with ice all the way to the top. Slater beckoned to a tall man in his early fifties whose immediate features were his large nose and oversized ears.

"Ralph, come and meet Nathan Hawk."

Ralph Askew, MP, was an old friend and a film buff, said Slater, adding with softly spoken regard that he was also Under Secretary at the Department of Energy.

"Hawk. Nathan Hawk, thirty-seven murders," said the old friend, now revealing a mouth with too many teeth in it. "I read Richard's piece about you in *The Guardian*."

"It was meant to be about Jacob," I said.

"That's Dickie for you, all too easily side-tracked. It's an honour to meet you, Mr Hawk." He shook my hand for a second time. "Thirty-seven? My God, most people in this country have never seen one dead body, let alone 37 who've been murdered. And as for that performance your son gave? Reminded me of a young Michael Redgrave, if you know what I mean."

I wiped away the fleck of spittle which had landed on my cheek. "How far back do you and Richard go?"

"Cambridge. Don't see as much of each other as we'd both like, but this film was a perfect opportunity to put that right." He lowered his voice as if to share a confidence. "I thought he might be able to get me through the door, to be honest. I've always been a bit of a film fanatic and my grandfather was in Italy during the war."

We had attracted some of Askew's friends and colleagues who were equally dazzled by Jaikie's performance and while I wanted to ask Slater why he'd featured me in an article about my son, I bore in mind that I'd already lost my temper once that evening. To do so a second time would smack of self-indulgence. Even so, as we chatted I began to see what Jaikie had meant when he said that Slater was so good at making him talk. He was asking, in his syrupy way, about me, Jaikie, Laura, the Others, questions which on their own were of no account whereas the sum of the answers might have formed a revealing profile. I fobbed him off with lies and under-statement.

"He never stops being the investigative journalist of his youth, do you Dickie?" Askew chided at one stage. "Mr Hawk came here to enjoy his Son's performance, not to be grilled by you."

Slater apologised and was soon drawn away by people who valued his opinion about the film more than I did. Our little group broke up as Askew and his crowd moved on to the next guest on their network, the next drink being offered. The waiter brought mine which I took downstairs and out into the stone canyon of Whitehall Place.

The chauffeured cars were lined up, so close together they might have been one grotesque, segmented creature. Most of the drivers were chatting by their vehicles, a handful were crammed into the back of a limousine watching a football match on a laptop. Corrigan's limo was the last in the line and he was on his own, stretched out on the back seat, asleep. I banged on the roof and in a split second he was up in a sitting position, fully awake, having drawn his side arm. He saw who was peering in at him through the smokey glass, holstered the Glock and got out. He gazed at me apprehensively, I like to think, but in the orangey darkness of that part of London I couldn't be sure. He offered me a cigarette from a crumpled packet and I shook my head. He lit one for himself and the smoke from it hung around us, no breeze to move it on.

"You told your boss what happened?" I asked.

"Sure."

I'd expected more than a one syllable answer. "And he said?"

"Pity you didn't catch the bastard."

I took a swig of the whisky, rattled the ice. "You knew the attack was on the cards, didn't you?"

It was there again, his trademark unflinching stare and after a stalemate silence he got back into the limo, cigarette and all, and I went back to the party for a top-up.

5

Next morning, or rather later the same one, I phoned Jaikie and left a message saying I hoped he and Jodie had recovered from last night's excitement and that Laura and I would be heading back to Winchendon after breakfast. As I spoke, Laura whispered that I should say again how wonderful he was in *All Good Men and True*, but I pretended I hadn't heard her.

The car ride home was subdued which, according to Laura, was hardly surprising. Laying aside that some jealous nutter had thrown vinegar in Jaikie's face, the film opening, the celebration party afterwards, had been a glamorous, glitzy event. The M40 at its best is a length of tarmac.

"Jealous nutter?" I said.

"That's what the morning papers are calling the attacker."

"That's how Richard Slater's wife described him. Why does that bother me? Who wants that attack made light of?"

Laura hadn't the faintest idea, she said. I reminded her that at least I'd been vindicated, that I'd been right to worry about Jaikie's safety, even though none of my grim-ending scenarios had included a mock acid attack. I added that I intended to keep him close by me for a week or two.

At Winchendon I pulled up outside Laura's house, a much altered Victorian clay tiled cottage standing three doors down from the church and very much in its shadow. A spinster's cottage if ever there was one. Laura's description, not mine.

I knew straightaway that it had been broken into. It had an affronted look to it, like that of an elderly woman to whom an improper suggestion had been made, then acted upon. In less floral terms, the place had been well and truly turned over. In the hall, shoes had been scooped from the cupboard and lay scattered on the tiles. The drawers in the hall table stood open, map books, gloves, keys had been tossed in all directions. In the downstairs cloakroom, the lid on the cistern had been removed and dropped, broken in half. Alongside it were pieces of frosted glass. This was the entry point. A small window pane had been punched in, a hand had reached through to the catch and in they had come.

In the living room the armchairs had been upended, a coffee table turned over and pushed aside, stereo and television toppled and pulled across the room. Books had been taken from the shelves in armfuls, then dropped in piles. DVD's had been frisbeed against the walls. Most of the ornaments on the mantelpiece and in the recesses had been broken.

"How dare they!" she said, for the third or fourth time. "How bloody dare they!"

Up in her bedroom a single forearm had swept her dressing table of all her make-up, perfumes and knick-knacks. Her clothes had been ripped from their hangers, her underwear taken from its drawer and scattered. She stooped and picked up a lacy favourite and looked at me. I shook my head, though I'm not sure what I was dismissing. Possibly the notion that any of this mattered in the great scheme of things. It was a mental platitude which I didn't really believe, so I didn't voice it.

"What's been taken?" I asked.

She went over to her jewellery box on the bed where its contents had been emptied out onto the duvet.

"Nothing, as far as I can see, not even gold rings, a pearl necklace…"

Having checked every room in the house we ended up in her cubby hole of an office under the stairs. Such papers as were there had been swept aside, pens and pencils tipped out of a clay pot. Her laptop had been taken out of its case and booted up.

"What was on it?" I asked.

"Everything or nothing, depending on how you look at it. I'll stop my credit cards, tell the bank…"

She'd fought it off up until then, but now gave way to the nausea which most victims of a break-in feel, the sense of having been stripped naked, violated, defiled. She flopped into the swivel chair at her desk and asked, "What the hell were they after?"

I'd no idea, but I was damned sure it wasn't her bank details. Even so she began the long haul of cancelling her credit cards and acquiring new ones while I phoned the local police station, hoping to speak to an old acquaintance there, Detective Sergeant Jim Kelloway. He was on holiday, back on Monday, said the Duty Officer but he'd get someone round to the house as soon as possible.

About half an hour later a car pulled up on the gravel. I went to the front door only to find that it wasn't a pair of uniforms walking towards me but George Corrigan. I must have smiled, though I certainly hadn't meant to.

"What's funny?" he asked.

"You just happened to be in the area?"

"You think S.O.U and local forces don't liaise?"

When Laura appeared he made a low-key attempt at being sympathetic. It was a monstrous thing to have done, he agreed, to have rampaged through her house like this, even though they didn't appear to have taken anything. In some ways that made it worse. Did Laura know anyone who might be responsible, a spiteful neighbour, an ex-partner, an aggrieved patient? She couldn't think of anyone.

He asked her for a guided tour of the place. It took about half an hour and occasionally I heard soft Irish concern oozing out of him above my head and when they finally entered the kitchen it was obvious that he hadn't been consoling her so much as quizzing her.

"Doctor Peterson says you've got a few ideas, based on an orthopaedic plate you found?"

I was keen to discover how much he already knew so I took him through the basics of finding the plate, naming Patrick Scott, and the subsequent disappearance of his records. As far as I could tell it came as news to him, though nothing to get excited about.

"Takes you nowhere, does it," he said. "Not to the attack on Jaikie, nor to the break-in here."

"Oh, I know who's behind that. You had this house turned over while we were in London."

I saw him calculate his options, all of them versions of outrage, denial or acceptance. In the end he appealed to Laura, as if being a doctor she might be able to give me something for my unwelcome opinion.

"Why would I do such a thing?"

"Somebody's afraid that a country GP has unearthed something significant about Patrick Scott. Maybe it's valuable and they want to use it, maybe it's damning and they want it buried alongside him. I don't care. All I want is for it to lead me to whoever killed him."

"If he's dead."

"Of course he's bloody dead. Something that was once inside his body, holding part of it together, has turned up in a local field. Don't you want to know where the rest of him is?"

Hands outstretched, he gestured round the overturned house. "So this is, what? A warning to Doctor Peterson, telling her to back off?"

"A warning to me as well. Or do you think somebody threw vinegar at my son to bring out the flavour in him?"

He smiled and turned away. "I'll get the usual forensic stuff done here, so if you could leave it as is for the rest of the day…?"

Laura nodded and I suggested that she spend a few nights at Beech Tree. She went upstairs to pack what she needed.

"You know, solving straight murders is one thing," said Corrigan, quietly. "This Patrick Scott business is quite another. You might be out of your depth here, Mr Hawk. The under-tow could drag you down."

"Don't go all tidal on me, George."

He smiled down at the floor, in restrained tolerance. "I expected a smart-arsed response, but this comes from the heart: you can't bring Patrick back to life so why not just leave him in peace."

"Or what?"

He winced as if the answer was obvious. "Or I can't guarantee your safety."

"That sounds like a threat. What next? I know where you live, where all your children live?"

"Not at all. Though I do, as a matter of course. Ellie, she works in an orphanage in Nepal…"

"What the fuck has that got to do with it?"

"…and Fee in Tokyo, Electric City. Con, New Orleans. To say nothing of Jaikie who I've grown really fond of."

Not for the first time in my life I was confronted by a man half my age, wanting to take his head and slam it down against the kitchen table before he realised what was happening. Corrigan wasn't just young, however, he was big and fit and well-trained. I'd wait till he turned to go, part the gathering red mist and punch him in the back. However tough you are a kidney punch feels like a sword running upwards through your torso...

"Don't even think about it," he whispered. He'd read my mind. "Your temper was always your undoing, the reason you were offered early retirement. Full pension, eh, even after striking a fellow officer?"

Never mind Patrick Scott's past, this S.O.U. henchman had been digging into mine. It wouldn't have been difficult. A few old colleagues would have been willing to tell the tale, some of them against me, most of them for.

I hadn't quite given up on the idea of a stand-up fight, but Laura entered the kitchen, her presence forcing me to see things more clearly.

"What's so special about Patrick Scott?" I asked.

"I don't know."

"You're just a messenger, eh?"

He turned to Laura. "I'm sorry about all this, Doctor. Truly I am. Call if you need me."

He handed her a business card, then took a pace backwards, and then another before turning and heading for the front door.

I spent the rest of the afternoon dwelling on the indignity of having been put in my place by George Corrigan. After several failed attempts to snap me out of it, Laura left for evening duty at the surgery. I tried to dissuade her. If her colleagues wouldn't indulge her on this occasion, when would they? She wouldn't hear of it.

Corrigan had offended me not just with his muted threats but his belief that whatever made Patrick Scott so important was beyond the scope of a detective with 37 murders under his belt. Important to whom, I wondered? I tried to give what little evidence I had a crime context and ran it against some old favourites. Big business and the attendant corruption, always a popular choice, but at this stage difficult to tie in with a muddy field in Dorton. A government *faux pas*, then, polite French for sexual intrigue, always worth considering and Corrigan was indeed a government employee. Terrorism. That would have been top of most people's list. Not mine, given its growing popularity as a handy panacea.

I kept coming back to the simplicity of the case. Whatever had happened to this kid, surely he had parents, siblings, a wife, girlfriend, a boyfriend who must at least have wondered what had happened to him? Or was I the only person in the world who gave a toss? And was that self-righteousness on my part genuine or a sign that I was getting drunk? I screwed the cap back on the bottle, returned it to the cupboard and rinsed out the glass, all my way of pretending that I hadn't drunk three double scotches in under forty minutes. I made coffee. None of it did any good. When Laura arrived home after surgery, she found me asleep in Maggie's Dad's rocker, in the pitch dark with the coffee brewed and forgotten.

"Where's Jaikie?" were her first words and for some reason they pissed me off. "Only I thought you said you'd keep him close by for a week or two."

"When he gets home I will."

She picked up the glass I'd used, still in the drainer, and placed it on the shelf where it lived.

"I'll make some fresh coffee," she said. "Not that it does any good, of course."

Jaikie and Jodie arrived back from London late that evening, driven by a fully rested Jamal. They were brimming over with the day they'd had, another round of back-slapping and pedestal hopping, questions from the press about being drenched in cider vinegar. Neither of them showed any concern that in just 24 hours the assault had gone from being a sinister mock acid attack to a schoolboy prank. Jaikie rambled on about how much people had loved the film, the script, the direction, his performance and how the reviews in the morning papers had been spectacular, especially one from Richard Slater. And that bloke, Ralph Askew, had phoned just before lunch to say how impressed he and his friends had been, so gripped, so moved, so thoroughly transported...

Jodie laughed. "Jaikie couldn't remember who Ralph Askew was."

"I still can't place the guy but according to Slater he's an MP, Under Secretary for some department or other."

"MP for Selingthwaite," said Jodie, filling in the blanks. "Under Secretary at the Department of Energy and Climate Change. They're old mates from uni, haven't seen each other for 12 years."

That jarred for some reason. "Those were his words?"

"Verbatim."

"Only 'we don't see as much of each other as we'd both like to' was how he described it to me. Does that suggest a 12 year gap? How did Slater get your number, Jaikie?"

"I gave it to him when he interviewed me," he replied, sheepishly.

"So now you've got his. Keep it. I might need it."

In the pause which followed it was Jodie who spotted that something closer to home was amiss. Laura hadn't been her usual self, offering praise and confidence to all who asked for it. She'd been quiet and still bore the marks, especially around her eyes, of a traumatic day.

"Laura, are you…?" Jodie began.

"I'm fine, dear, thank you."

"She's anything but," I said and told them about the break-in.

They were horrified, expressing their concern with rounds of hugging and distance kissing until Laura had had enough. She excused herself, saying she was thoroughly exhausted and did we mind if she went to bed. With my bedroom being directly above our heads, the kids and I decamped to the kitchen and tried to talk quietly. Jaikie poked around in the fridge for leftovers but with nobody having been here for two days there wasn't much to graze from. He made himself a cheese sandwich in the end, offered to make Jodie one, but the news about Laura had spoiled her appetite.

"What are you going to do about it?" she asked me.

Her faith in my ability to sort the problem out was flattering and a good deal more assured than my own.

"I don't know, hunt the killer down like a dog and in the last ten minutes chase him along the M4, kick box him all round Heathrow, cling onto the wings of the airplane he escapes in…" She smiled politely. "Something, I'll do something."

"You know, Dad, maybe the papers are right. Jealous nutter?"

"It isn't just about you," said Jodie, sharply.

He turned away from her and for the first time since they'd met up again I sensed an awkwardness between them, but quickly put it down to my cluttered feelings and soon our chat became more sociable, the talk smaller. As it veered off yet again in the direction of how brilliant Jaikie had been in *All Good Men and True* and he began to quote phrases from the morning reviews, I said it was time for me to hit the sack. Jodie rose from the table and Jaikie followed her lead.

"Dad, by the way, am I still insured to drive the Land Rover?"

"What makes you think you ever were?"

"Ah, that means you'll have to drive Jodie back to her dad's. Where's the key?"

"On the hook by the back door," I said, eventually. "Drive slowly. Will your father still be up, Jodie?"

"Definitely. Paper work."

While they went through to the living room to fetch her bag and jacket I cleared away the fallout from the cheese sandwich and as I did so, my selective hearing began to twitch.

"...I tell him now?" Jaikie whispered.

"Not now," Jodie hissed. "Enough on his plate."

"Okay."

"But you must, *must* tell him."

I'd been right earlier, then, all was not well in paradise. I guessed they were talking about money. Jaikie had borrowed from me and from Laura, though not in the last 48 hours. Perhaps he hadn't needed to because the film company had taken care of everything. Or perhaps he'd tried tapping Jodie and she'd asked him the question which I'd been avoiding: Why haven't you got any cash?

When the kids left I phoned Martin. As Jodie had said, he was still up and working. The monkeys from the ministry, the DEFRA jobsworths, were on his back demanding to be given chapter and verse on his turkeys, but when I finally got his attention he too was relieved that the attack on Jaikie had only been the work of a jealous nutter. I didn't set him straight, just told him about the break-in. He was suitably furious.

"Martin, the spot where Jan found the plate, have you still got it marked?"

"Wooden stake, right through its heart."

"I want you to dig a bloody great hole, six feet deep, twenty across."

I explained that I wanted it done before the police started poking their noses in, which wasn't likely but possible. He said he'd get Jan working on it right away.

"Is there anyone else you can ask besides Jan?"

"Have you got a problem with him?"

I said I hadn't, but since neither of us had seen him pick up the plate that night, it was just possible that he hadn't done so.

"That he put it there himself, you mean? Why would he do that?"

"Just allow me a few unreasonable suspicions."

"Right, I'll call Phil Mason, first thing. He's as thick as a brick but a good worker." He then tried to fake complete disinterest, but I could almost see the eyes sparkling with boyish delight. "Is it just a big hole you want, or are we looking for something in particular?"

"A skeleton, you bloody fool."

I couldn't bring myself to tell him that he wouldn't find one, but I wanted him to look all the same. Just in case.

6

I surfaced next morning to the sound of Jaikie downstairs talking to someone on his phone. The actor's voice was penetrating walls, rounding corners, going through oak doors even when he spoke softly. He was talking to Jamal who had sent him a text earlier saying he would be late, there had been an accident on the M25 and he was stuck between one junction and another. Terrible, terrible. I sensed pure delight in Jaikie's side of the conversation. Jamal, the fanatical time-keeper, thief of those extra few minutes in bed, had had his comeuppance delivered by a jack-knifed juggernaut.

I dressed and went downstairs and only then realised that Laura wasn't in the house, neither in bed behind me nor in the kitchen ahead.

"She's left a note by the kettle," said Jaikie. "Shall I read it to you?"

I didn't care for a simple message to be delivered with all the colour he would give it. I clicked my fingers and he passed it to me. The time on it was 5.30 a.m. and announced her intention to have Plum Tree Cottage up and running again by the end of the day. She knew I would offer to help, she said, but she would rather do it on her own. It was a job that needed tackling head on, without interference. The word interference had been crossed out and replaced by distraction. She hoped I understood but she would ring me throughout the day. Laura. Love to Jaikie.

It was lunch time before I couldn't stand the thought of her clearing up alone any longer. I walked Dogge round to her house, taking the cut through the churchyard, and found her crouched in the boiler house, torch in one hand, instruction manual in the other, trying to master the central heating.

"It's the same every year," she said, without looking up from what she was doing. "I forget how to forward the damn thing so it's back to the instruction book and…" I leaned over her and pressed the forward button. "…and then along comes a hero."

"Who would that be?"

"I forget his name. Some kind of bird, I think."

"Mr Dove from number fourteen?"

She smiled dutifully and stood up, knee joints clicking to her embarrassment.

"How've you got on?" I asked.

She beckoned with a crooked finger and I followed her through the back door into the house. In the kitchen, lined up and ready for a tip run, stood a dozen black bin bags, full. I glanced through to the living room and from what I could see the armchairs, the coffee table, the books were back in their places. I went to check.

"Jesus, you've done it." I said, in disbelief. "In eight hours."

"Plus inventory for the insurance company," she said, nodding at her laptop.

She explained that items beyond repair had gone into the bin bags, things that were still in one piece went back in their original places. Certainly she'd had a few pangs of sadness on the way, brought on by specific items. The china dogs which had sat on her grandmother's mantelpiece for fifty years and then on hers another twenty had finally been put down. She would miss their company, but on the other hand they weren't flesh and blood. A carriage clock which had stood on her father's desk had been smashed beyond repair, but there were far too many other ways of telling the time these days. A mirror she was fond of had gone, leaving only a pale impression of itself behind. Her mother had used the mirror to check her face, just before leaving the house. Laura did the same, but in recent years had begun to see her mother looking back at her, so it was time for a change anyway. I asked about the family photos. There weren't many but the few there had been she treasured: several of her younger brother, killed in a road accident at twenty-five, her parents in youth and old age, herself as a girl, then a young woman. They were all on disc, she said, so those here which had been ripped out of their broken frames could be replaced.

We stood for a while and in time we heard the central heating pipes creak into life.

"I began to feel cold when I stopped working," she said.

The house wasn't cold, it had simply been robbed of a particular kind of warmth.

"Where's Jaikie today?" she asked.

"At home. You haven't lent him any more money, have you?"

"No."

I smiled. "So you have lent him some."

"I should've been ready for that, shouldn't I. Fifty pounds, until he can change some dollars."

I looked round again at what she had achieved in so short a space of time. It was, as she'd promised in her note, up and running again but all too raw and recent to be lived in for a while.

"It'll take time to become yours again," I said. "You'd better spend the rest of the week with me."

She came up close, took my hands and put my arms around her waist. "Is that you at your romantic best?"

My phone trilled that I'd just received a text message. It was from Martin Falconer and said:

"Hole dug. Bodies found."

"Bodies?" said Laura. "Plural?"

I called Martin who told me that he'd found the skeletons of two foxes which must have been ploughed in last winter. At least it explained why the dogs had been so interested in the place.

"No human remains?" I asked.

"Sorry, mate, no."

We arrived at Beech Tree as Jaikie was returning from a hike along the Winchendon Valley, delighted to have been on his own for an hour or two. Nobody had followed him there, wanting to know if he and Jodie were an item, if Sophie Kent really was history. It was refreshing, invigorating, liberating, he went on, it had taken him back to those halcyon days when he was an ordinary bloke, out for an ordinary walk, with an ordinary dog...

The lad was protesting too much, methought.

Meantime, Laura had found three tuna stakes in the freezer and together with vegetables she'd been given by one of her patients was turning them into a five star meal. As we sat down to eat it Jaikie said for no reason whatsoever, "Dad, d'you remember that bloke Jack Blundell?"

"I do, though I never had the pleasure of meeting him."

Jaikie explained to Laura that 15 years ago when Fee was determined to Save the World, to feed the poor and hungry, she met an ageing tramp in Thame and invited him to live in a rusty old caravan at our previous house. Maggie and I had no idea that he was there, though she did say she thought the kids were eating more these days. Stuff that was in the fridge overnight for tomorrow's lunch kept disappearing. So did an old jacket of mine and a few T-shirts.

"How long did he stay?" asked Laura.

"Only three weeks," said Jaikie. "Left in a bit of a hurry one evening, halfway through a cottage pie Mum had made. He casually asked what sort of man our father was and Ellie, aged eight at the time, said he was a policeman sort of man. Jack put down his knife and fork, packed his carrier bag and thirty seconds later was gone. We never saw him again."

"When did you find out?" she asked me.

"Two years later."

Jaikie smiled. "Dad was always slow on the uptake. He bought Mum this set of casserole dishes…"

"Her thirty-ninth birthday…"

"One day, Con laid the lids down on the floor and walked across an imaginary river using them as stepping stones. All of them broke. Mum stuck them together and swore us to secrecy. Christmas Day, Dad takes off the lid to the sprouts and says, "Maggie, this lid's been broken." She confessed to having dropped it. It took him another year to realise they'd *all* been broken, by which time he could hardly lose his rag."

I wanted the family stories to end right there and apologised to Laura for the two we'd already had. "They're like dreams," I said. "Your own are fascinating, other people's are plain boring."

"I'd hardly call what Ellie did boring," said Jaikie.

Indulgent as ever Laura asked him to elaborate.

"She swallowed Mum's engagement ring. Our GP said that if she didn't throw it up within an hour they'd have to wait for nature to take its course."

Perhaps drawn to the medical implications, Laura seemed interested. "And did she?"

"Half an hour later she threw up like a real pro and there it was."

I wish I could say that it was a eureka moment but it was more a case of Jesus Christ why didn't I think of that before. It must have shown on my face.

"What's wrong, Dad?"

"I may not know the who and why of this murder yet, but I think I know how they disposed of his body."

Laura stopped loading the dishwasher and came back to the table.

"I said it didn't involve blood and guts, right? That's exactly what it *does* involve."

As we drove to the Zawadskis' house I asked Jaikie to phone Martin and tell him to meet us there. Martin wanted to know why.

"Just be there!" I yelled at the phone.

The place had once been two cottages in a terrace of eight and was small enough now so God knows how any family could have lived in the originals. Victorian and built of stone with slated roofs, their main advantage had always been their closeness to the office, standing as they did overlooking the valley half a mile from the main farmhouse. We parked on a cinder lay-by behind a secondhand Audi and a BMW, tokens of the upward aspirations of Jan's neighbours.

The night was cold, remarkable for being the first one of an approaching winter and our breath seemed to drift from our mouths as if trying to drag us away from our purpose. I knocked on the door and set off the Zawadskis' German Shepherd. The front door opened six inches and Katya Zawadski peered out into the darkness, concerned to see three people on her doorstep at this time of night. Doubtless in her family history a visit at this time of night was never friendly. This one wasn't exactly affable. She relaxed when she recognised Laura and removed the safety chain in a fluster of embarrassment at her initial suspicions. Jan had come up behind her by now, having taken the dog into the kitchen, and he recognised me from the night I'd been combine harvesting in Long Field. I stepped over the threshold, shook his hand and some of the tension caused by our arrival fell away.

Jaikie, for once the only person in the room nobody recognised, introduced himself as my son and gave them his professional smile before turning it more gently on the two little girls who were descending the open stairs to see what the fuss was about. Both were in their pyjamas, one of them clinging to a soggy piece of blanket, the other clutching a tattered teddy bear. Jaikie waved to them, Katya turned and spoke with a soothing voice in a mixture of Polish and English.

"Back to bed, my darlings."

"I woke them," I said. "Forgive me."

She was a tall woman, a fact made all the more apparent by the low beamed ceilings. Her blonde hair was tied back in a pony tail, fully revealing her face, straining it a little. Her eyes were pale blue, intelligent eyes, seeking an explanation as to why we were there. Her husband removed a couple of soft toys from the sofa, dropped them into a basket and Laura and Jaikie took their places. Now that I saw him in more detail I can only describe his looks as Eastern European, a smooth, square face with untrusting eyes betraying a nervous disposition. Over my shoulder he spotted the headlights from Martin's pickup pulling up outside and went to greet his boss.

"What's all this about, Nathan?" Martin asked. The dog in the kitchen, hearing another strange voice, barked again. Jan called in Polish for her to be quiet.

"Actually, it's her I wanted to talk to you about," I said. "Mr Falconer told me that you and he were in Long Field with her, one day in Spring, and she threw up."

Jan frowned and looked to his wife for a translation. Her English was good, but throwing was still something you did with a ball.

"She was sick," Martin said, miming the act of vomiting. "We thought she might have found something in the field and eaten it."

"Did you see what it was?"

"She was fifty yards away, Nathan. She came running over to us afterwards, clearly feeling a great deal better. As one does."

"When do you feed your dog, Jan?"

"Morning, evening."

"And this particular day, did you stick to the routine?"

"That day was no different," said Katya.

"What do you feed her?"

"Dog food from the internet. We buy 50 cans each time, much cheaper."

"Always from the same place?"

"Ever since we got her."

Behind me on the sofa I could sense disquiet from Laura. "Nathan, if you're saying what I think you're saying…"

"I think the titanium plate was in a can of dog food. Jan fed her that morning and when she got to the field she threw it up."

The implications were becoming obvious, but we avoided putting them into words, perhaps out of regard for the Zawadskis whose pet dog, to put it bluntly, had eaten some of Patrick Scott. If it hadn't been so gruesome it might have been laughable. Jan was catching on, but frowning in disbelief.

"She was sick in one place," he said, "We find the plate in another."

"By then you'd drilled, you'd raked, you'd rolled and God knows what else. Moved it. Fetch me a can of the dog food."

He went through to the kitchen, allowing the German Shepherd to enter the living room. Jaikie looked at her warily, the Hollywood part of him wondering if eating human flesh had altered her in any way. Had she developed opposing claws, perhaps, could she blow up a building or be the getaway driver in a car chase? When he finally stroked her she became just another family pet with a bark worse than her bite and a healthy respect for Katya's instruction to go and lie down.

Jan returned with a can of dog food. It was called Fivestar and the label on it boasted of its health giving properties. At the bottom the name of the company who produced it was given in small type. The address was in Tilbury, East London.

We drove back to Beech Tree in silence with Jaikie and Laura trying to resist all thoughts of Patrick Scott's disposal, but inevitably they kept returning to the details, as did I. Had his body been butchered into manageable chunks, or had he been left in one piece and processed along with other carcasses? And what of the blood? Had that been let in some other place? And the entrails? It said on the can of Fivestar that it contained everything 'your four legged friend would find in the wild including meat, heart, kidney, tripe and bone'. There were no additives, it stated in bold type. Little did they know. And who had turned their back when this horrific act was carried out? Who else, apart from the murderer, knew that Patrick had been fed to the dogs?

As we sat in the kitchen, having exchanged the bare minimum of words, Jaikie looked down at Dogge and asked, in a fiendish whisper, "What does he feed you, little one?"

It brought us back to earth again and Jaikie was surprisingly objective, saying that with Patrick being transmogrified we'd never find a body, surely an essential starting point in any inquiry. He warned that Patrick's fate, to be crushed and cooked by some small time pet food manufacturer, was still supposition, at least in terms of due process. Since renewing his friendship with Jodie he'd begun to bandy the odd legal phrase about.

"That's why you and I are going to visit their factory tomorrow. Unless you've anything else skeduled?"

"No, no, I'd like that."

He went to fetch my laptop from the living room and brought up a Google map of the area we were talking about. The address on the tin was Shoreline Industrial Estate and as Jaikie zoomed in on the plant itself it gave off nothing but innocence. It was an ordinary factory on the edge of a 20 acre site where the main venture was re-cycling. Close by were other businesses which hadn't survived the credit crunch. A packaging manufacturer, a gravel supplier, an engineering plant. Their buildings were to let and even from the perspective of a Google street map they seemed forlorn, desolate, hopeless.

I looked across at Laura. I would have Jaikie close by me tomorrow, but not her. She and her colleagues were due to hear the final decision of the local Health Trust with regard to funding but even I couldn't be in two places at once.

7

When I came down for breakfast, Jaikie was already there with my laptop open, researching dog food. With the blast furnace of a stomach he was known for in our family he slurped away at a bowl of cereal while describing some of the illegalities of the trade. He offered to show me YouTube proof of what had been called meat bi-products, but I declined to view it. Most of it, he said, was veterinary waste, regularly dumped at the gates of rogue manufacturers and used in upcoming batches of their product. Things had changed, he assured me, at least in the UK. Pet food companies were now regulated to the point of paralysis.

"Anything more on Fivestar?"

"They sound like a decent company. Started life as a family business, late 1940's. Two brothers. Now run by a direct descendant, William Stringer."

We left the house at seven, having wished Laura all the best in her last ditch attempt to squeeze money out of people who didn't want to give it to her. The traffic up on the main road was hissing through fine drizzle with its uncanny knack of making people like me feel morose and taciturn. Actors are different, being eternally optimistic and terrified of silence. We'd been driving no longer than three minutes when Jaikie said,

"Dad, what do I say to people if they recognise me? I mean seriously…?"

"What do you usually say?"

"Hi!"

"Then say Hi!" He nodded, gratefully. "You may even get a chance to say it to George Corrigan. He's three cars behind us."

For some reason it cheered me up, especially when Jaikie followed it up with, "Can you lose him, Dad?"

"It's a twenty year old Land Rover, but I'll try."

I turned off into a lane which ran from Dorton back down to Winchendon and soon afterwards Corrigan made the same turn, switching off his running lights in the hope of being unnoticed.

The land to either side of us was farmed by Martin Falconer though not owned by him. It belonged to a man called Forester, a relic from the days when farming was a law unto itself. The rules and regulations of the past 50 years had robbed him of his livelihood, he moaned, and as a result he'd allowed any land which he didn't rent out to fall into disrepair. Come the height of winter, a tributary of the River Thame would bring down topsoil from higher ground which would settle as a black, unyielding sludge in the dip I was heading for. I slowed to a crawl and the Land Rover took the eighteen inches or so from the previous year in its stride. As I climbed the hill on the other side Jaikie looked back to see Corrigan's dainty little Japanese hatchback reach the quagmire. He must have thought the car could handle it, but as it hit the deepest point the engine stalled. He tried to restart it, but in vain.

"Call him, Jaikie."

He got out of the Land Rover, turned to look down at Corrigan and called effortlessly across the intervening pasture, "Hi, George, how's it going?"

Corrigan had wound down the driver's window and now stuck his head out but he didn't answer. Jaikie relayed a message from me.

"Dad says flash your headlights if you can hear." Eventually, reluctantly, the lights pulsed. "The man you need is Martin Falconer. After he's pulled you out, do us a favour. Keep an eye on Doctor Peterson."

I remember Tilbury from childhood. My mother's sister lived on Canvey Island with a man called Santiago who worked in the docks. It sounded so romantic: docks, islands, tall-masted ships from all over the world, and yet it never lived up to that promise. The island didn't have waves crashing on its shore, or mysterious creatures roaming its hinterland, and although in keeping with childhood memory it never rained there, I don't recall the sun shining either. Not that it mattered because Aunt Auria made up for any disappointment, being carefree and witty and, unlike her older sister, blessed with an even temper. My father maintained that he came away from a day spent in her company feeling… better. At ten years old I wasn't sure what he meant, never having felt anything but good, but I know now.

Londoners say that if you stand on any Thames bridge on an average Saturday night, you will smell three things above all others: diesel fumes, marijuana and chicken tikka. I've never put it to the test, but any one of them, or a mixture of all three, would have been preferable to the stench given off by Fivestar Pet Products in Tilbury. It hit us from half a mile away, intensifying as we approached, and as we got out of the Land Rover neither of us would have been surprised had we needed to hack our way through a physical form of it.

I parked in the visitor's car park, noting that the staff one was almost full, a sign of the firm's prosperity. We hurried across to an elderly brick building which a century ago had been a stable for dray horses and now housed the offices of Fivestar Ltd. Jaikie was still concerned about being recognised, or perhaps about *not* being recognised, but either way he'd stepped neatly into the role I'd assigned him. We were directors of a firm called County Fare who supplied all manner of top class goods to garden centres, farm shops, country fairs and the like.

The middle-aged lady at reception, Mrs B. Lanfranco according to the name tag on her blouse, listened politely as I explained that we were looking to add a quality range of dog food to our list and wondered if Mr Stringer would be interested in supplying it. She invited us to take a seat in a small jungle of potted palms and with us safely at a distance, she swivelled round in her chair and spoke quietly on the phone to her boss's secretary. I picked out one or two phrases which gave me confidence. "Two gentlemen", for example, and "business proposition" and best of all "seem genuine". I put it down to the Land Rover she'd seen us arrive in, the Countryman anoraks we were wearing.

A few minutes later William Stringer himself appeared at the glass door which led to a small suite of offices. He was a far cry from the skin and bone carcass I'd expected to meet, being four stone overweight with a large, drooping face obscuring the neck he'd once had. His eyes were small and quick and what little remained of his hair was slicked back with a coloured gel. He was quietly dressed and loudly spoken.

"Gentlemen, Bill Stringer, I gather you're interested in one of our products."

The handshake was strong and pudgy, and after the introductions he invited us to follow him back through the glass door, first asking Mrs B. Lanfranco to rustle up some coffee.

His own office was as unfussy as the rest of the place with a desk, a few chairs and a middle-aged secretary through a glass partition, working at a computer. The side wall was dominated by an oil portrait, Andy Warhol style, of a can of Fivestar, with another of the brand's cat food hanging at a respectful distance. Stringer gestured for us to pull up two working armchairs to his desk.

"You decided to just drop in on us, rather than telephone ahead?" he said.

"We're in town visiting suppliers, thought we'd come and see what you're all about." I made an expansive gesture. "Business seems to be thriving."

William Stringer enjoyed being stroked and gave us a well rehearsed appreciation of his own achievements. Eight years ago it had been a matter of survival, he said. His father, God bless him, had allowed the business to run down but with hard graft Bill Jr. had set it back on its feet again. He'd re-vamped the production process, re-tooled the entire operation, and was now at a point where the place was running 24/7. And he wasn't the only one who worked hard here, he quipped as Mrs Lanfranco, brought in the coffee. Every member of staff, from the factory floor to the boardroom, had played their part.

"It's true, it's a damn good workforce," he repeated once Mrs Lanfranco had departed. "My policy is simple. The harder somebody works, the more I pay: weekly wages, Christmas bonuses and free dog food." I'd been nodding my approval all the way. "So, how can I help you?"

I told him that if we liked what we saw, and I'd every confidence that we would, then I would place an initial order for two thousand cans of Fivestar and take it from there.

"Like what you see?" he asked, a little warily.

"A quick look at the process itself, if someone could spare the time."

He smiled. "You've come to see us on an ordinary working day. To catch us out. I like your style, Mr Hawk."

He pressed an intercom button and asked his secretary to phone across to the shop floor and arrange for Derek to show two visitors round.

The factory itself, set at a slight distance from the offices, was a modern building, concrete sections over a steel framework, insulated panels for a roof. It had a neatness to it, an efficiency, even a cleanliness which I hadn't expected, given the nature of what was being produced here. The hum and clatter of machinery was softened by innocuous music, orchestral versions of once popular songs.

Derek Jones was the shift foreman, a Jamaican in his fifties who told us that he'd been with the company through thick and thin, good times and bad times. Where would we like our tour of the place to start? You choose, I said. He took us to the chiller, a refrigerated room where a forest of incoming carcasses, hanging on a moving rail, was checked along with its offal for quality. I gathered that most of what was here today was the remains of old dairy cattle, past their prime and too tough for the supermarkets or the school meals service. The trimmed carcasses were hauled on handcarts, piled high, through to the hub of the operation where they were placed in one end of a huge cylindrical tank. When full, the tank was closed off and then revolved slowly as blades inside it rendered down the contents. It was the same principle as a kitchen blender, Derek said, and from there the product was never touched again by human hand. It was pumped from the tank in near liquid form to one of several vats, the size of small swimming pools, where it was microwaved. When cooked it was piped straight to a conveyor belt, an exact amount was poured into each can and allowed to set in its own natural gelatine before having a lid attached. At no stage was anything added, Derek assured us. As it said on the can it was exactly what a dog would find in the wild, turned into canine spam.

Back in his office, Stringer's bonhomie had been replaced by a business-like frostiness. His secretary was standing beside him and had clearly discovered that we weren't who we'd pretended to be.

"We've looked up County Fare on the web, Mr Hawk," said Stringer. "We can't find you."

"That's because we don't exist," I replied.

My no nonsense reply was intended to faze him but appeared not to. He walked to the door and opened it.

"Gentlemen, I am an extremely busy man."

Jaikie made a move to leave, but I caught him by the arm.

"I'm sorry I had to go through this charade, Mr Stringer, but…"

"Marie, phone the police will you. Tell them we have two intruders and I would like them removed."

"That would do more harm than good," I said.

The secretary turned at the door in the glass partition and waited for her boss to respond.

"That sounds like a threat, Mr Hawk, if that is indeed your name."

"Nathan Hawk. I'm a retired police officer."

"Call it by its proper name, Dad," said Jaikie. "You're a private detective."

"And you are his son? Only I've an uncanny feeling we've met before."

Jaikie was ready with his smile. "Oh, really? Where do you think we…?"

I cut him off. "A young man called Patrick Scott has been murdered. The only clue to the crime was found in a tin of Fivestar dog food."

Stringer let go of the office door and it closed of its own accord. He came towards me slowly, trying to make sense of what I'd just said, and in the face of their immediate disbelief I took him and his secretary through the events which had led to our being there. They listened attentively, with Stringer breaking off just once to pull out a handful of tissues from a box on his desk and dabbing the sweat from his forehead. By the time I'd finished he'd managed to compose himself and agreed with George Corrigan, a metal plate and my supposition weren't much to go on and if I were to claim, to a newspaper or anyone else, that Fivestar dog food was at the heart of a murder investigation he would take legal action.

"Mr Stringer, I've no plans to tell anyone anything about your dog food." He looked at me, aware that I might have played this kind of game before and certain that my discretion would come at a price. "All I want to know is have you had occasion to sack anyone lately, someone who didn't respect the company's work ethic or, indeed, someone you simply fell out with or became uneasy about. Between, say, August 2009 and the Spring of this year?"

"There hasn't been anyone," he replied immediately. "I've been running this business since my father's death and I have not had to fire a single soul. People have left, certainly, but they've always given me the appropriate notice…"

He stopped, raised a hand to his chin and stroked it hard as if to reshape it. Failing to do so he recalled with a hint of bitterness that there was somebody.

"I didn't sack him, he sacked himself, Charles Drayton. Worked here for ten years. Rose to be shift foreman. He walked in here one morning and told me to stuff the job. Walked out again."

"Did he give a reason?"

"He said he'd won money on the lottery."

"When was this?"

Stringer turned to his secretary.

"November the 19th 2009," she replied from memory.

"Presumably you've still got his address, Marie?"

She'd be only too happy to forget it, she said, but didn't think there was much chance of that. "34, Clark Road, East Tilbury."

I wrote it down on a small notepad on Stringer's desk and tore off the page. Stringer was smiling as if, in spite of everything, the last laugh would be his.

"What's funny?" I asked.

"There's a kind of poetic justice at work, if poetry can apply to a business such as ours. The last I heard of Charlie Drayton he had cancer, just about everywhere."

I didn't really get the joke but I thanked him for the coffee and we left. As we pulled out of the car park Jaikie said admiringly, "So that's where I get it from. That was quite a performance, Dad."

Number 34, Clark Road was the last house in the street and stood slightly apart from its neighbours overlooking the bleakest of farmland and beyond that to the Thames Estuary, softened at the edges today by a winter haze. The smell here was more traditional, the familiar one of ozone and recently treated sewage and it was difficult to believe that just twenty miles down the coast from here stood Southend where, as a boy, I'd swum in the sea with my father.

The house itself was a fifties build, chucked up in the post war rush but still in one piece in spite of its construction and exposure to the elements. It stood alone on a large elevated plot, a castle of its kind, surrounded by the scrap of a lifetime, consisting in the main of old cars, trucks and trailers. It wasn't all rubbish, however. Fifty yards away, outside a brick-built workshop, stood a red 1960's MG Sports. The tarpaulin which covered it had been hauled back and weighted down by a couple of rocks. Examining the car were two men, most likely a father and son, the one to want it the other to sign the cheque. I didn't pay them much attention, to be honest. I should have done.

In my time as a police officer I must have knocked on thousands of doors but never before has one been opened by a Catholic priest. He was a man in his late twenties, dressed in a dark suit with a roman collar and carrying a shoulder bag. His face was tense and drained of colour, the result of shock I would have said, but he managed to nod a greeting at us before turning back to the woman who'd followed him to the door. She was in her seventies, small and wiry, her white hair coiffeured to hide its sparseness.

She said goodbye to the priest and thanked him. He told her it had been no problem, he'd been happy to hear Charlie's confession and if he required anything further, she should call. He gave extra weight to his departure, and himself a little courage I fancied, with some words about us all needing to make our peace with the Lord, then he walked off down the path and got into a Fiat, two sizes too small for him. As he drove away the woman watched him, lips pursed against his sanctimony.

"Barely out of nappies," she said. "What does he know about sin? If you've come about the MG, those two have beaten you to it."

Bucked by Jaikie's compliment about my acting skills, I went straight for it. "I was hoping to speak with Charlie, Mrs Drayton."

"What about?"

"I guess he hasn't mentioned me. Nathan Hawk? I heard about his illness, decided to pop round and see him but with the priest and everything..."

She looked me over, moving slightly to get me in profile as if that might jog her memory. Finally she decided that she'd neither seen nor heard of me before, folded her arms and leaned against the door jamb.

"He's not seeing people today."

Reluctant to concede but short of ways to get past her, I turned to Jaikie. He laid a filial hand on my arm.

"Mrs Drayton, I've never seen Dad so upset as when he heard about Charlie. I said 'Look if he meant that much to you, if you really were that close, why don't we jump in the L and Rover..."

And just as Jaikie was about to go over the top I was blessed with one of those strokes of luck which every investigation deserves. Beyond Mrs Drayton, way back in the gloom of the hallway, I caught sight of a figure in white, ghostly for a moment until I realised that this must be her dying husband. He wore cotton pyjamas, the jacket unbuttoned, revealing his body which had been hollowed out by the cancer William Stringer had been so pleased about. As his flesh had shrivelled, so his skin had been drawn around his bones, so tightly that at any moment it might be pierced by a jutting rib or an axe-like shoulder blade. The cruellest change had been to his face. His cheeks had been gouged out, chemo-therapy had left him with thin wispy hair, his eyes were slow and staring, seeing little. He was the reason the young priest had been upset.

He came towards us, using the wall to stay upright and even as I wondered how best to take advantage of him being away from his death bed, it seemed as if some all-powerful puppeteer cut the strings above him and he collapsed, joint by joint, ending up slumped against the hall table. Hearing him fall his wife turned and hurried back to him. I followed while Jaikie, with well-mannered uncertainty, brought up the rear, closing the front door behind him.

"Charlie, what are you doing!" she screeched. She grabbed at her hair with both hands, trying to control her fear. "You bloody old fool."

"Let's get him back into bed," I said. "Jaikie, take him under his arm."

Between us we lifted him to a standing position and hauled him along to a room at the end of the hall. It had been set up as a last-but-one resting place and had the smell of imminent death to it, an airless heat overladen with disinfectant. A bed in the centre had a cylinder beside it, oxygen I assumed from the mouthpiece hanging on the headboard. Within reach there was a table on which stood a large enamel bowl, a flannel draped over the side of it. There were towels, ointments for infected skin, painkillers, a dish of sweets. On the wall opposite hung several framed posters advertising past events of the MG Enthusiasts' Club interspersed with enlarged photos of the family. I counted three children from the dozen or more set around an elaborate carving of Christ on the cross. He was looking pretty rough as well.

Mrs Drayton pulled back the duvet and straightened the sheet while Jaikie and I stood holding her husband. He caught sight of us in a mirror but was way beyond caring who we were, being more concerned about where he was heading almost certainly within the next week.

We manhandled him into a sitting position against the pillows his wife had plumped up. His trip to the hall had exhausted him, but after a few sips of water he said to me, "Was it... your boy?"

His voice was thin and tremulous but the words were clear.

"Who, Charlie?" I asked quietly. "Who are you talking about?"

"He doesn't know what he's saying half the time," said his wife.

Drayton looked at me with eyes that had come back to life for a moment as he searched my face for reasons why I might be paying him a visit. He repeated his question. "Was it... your son?"

I shook my head and he closed his eyes with some relief and within half a minute he appeared to be asleep. His wife sighed and pulled the duvet up around his chest, then led us out of the room thanking us all the way. The act of helping to get her husband back into bed had turned us from malicious snoopers into kindhearted confidantes.

"He's never mentioned what he did?" I asked as soon as the chance arose.

From the way I'd put the question I might have been asking about one of his hobbies. Mrs Drayton knew I wasn't.

"Something dreadful to a young lad, that's all he'll tell me. Sometimes I wonder if it's even true, but it worries him so much it must be…" She broke off and looked at me, not doubting my integrity but concerned about my religious sensibilities. In the end she laid them aside. "That bloody priest knows all about it, but he won't tell me either."

I smiled in support of her disdain. "You know, Mrs Drayton, I heard somewhere that Charlie won some money on the lottery. When all this is over why don't you treat yourself?"

She chuckled, though not with any joy. "I would if there was any of it left. Old bugger spent most of it buying up cars. How do you throw twenty-five grand away in under three years?"

"Will he know it was me who called, once he's rested?"

"Maybe. He has good days and bad days. Today was bad. Tomorrow? Why don't you pop in and see?"

"I'll do that."

We saw ourselves out and as we walked back to the Land Rover I turned to glance over at the red MG Sports. The two men who'd been checking it out when we arrived had replaced the tarpaulin and gone.

When we reached home there was no sign of Laura so I phoned her immediately. She would be with us in thirty minutes and although news from the Trust was as expected, being a resounding no, there was a fresh glimmer of hope from elsewhere. I asked her to elaborate but she refused to do so over the phone in case it sounded fanciful. Face to face I might just agree that all was not lost. Did Jaikie like Chinese takeaway? In common with his siblings, I told her, Jaikie would eat anything she put before him.

She duly arrived with a Chinese and as we dug into it she told us about her day. The Health Trust had said no to any part of the quarter of a million she and her practise partners needed. No surprises there. However, things had taken a bit of a turn in the last few hours. The Trust was made up of seven people. Running the whole affair was the Chairman, Non-executive. Below him, prompting him at every turn, constantly rustling papers and trying not to meet other people's gaze, was the Finance Director, Executive. To his left sat one of two women on the board, the Director of Service Improvement, Executive…

She paused to apologise, assuring us that these people were superfluous to her story. The only name that mattered was that of Doctor Michael Wilson, Non-executive, a tanned, white-haired man in his early eighties. None of the others liked him and Laura hadn't been too keen on him herself to begin with. He was forever arguing the toss over minor points and doing so just for the sake of it, but after the day's wrangling was over and they'd said their frosty farewells he'd caught up with her in County Hall car park and told her to meet him in a pub.

"Which one?" I asked.

She thought that was pretty irrelevant too until I pointed out that where a man likes to drink tells you most of what you need to know about him.

"Elderly, Tory and monied. *The King's Head,* Ashendon," she said. "Mind you, George Corrigan was there and he's none of those things, but that's also superfluous."

No it wasn't. It meant that he'd been keeping an eye on her just as I'd asked him to.

"So, since Doctor Wilson promised it would be to my advantage, I followed him there at a steady twenty miles an hour and once in the bar, with a gin and tonic in his hand, he spent half an hour trashing the other members of the board before he got down to business."

He told Laura that the whole application process had been a farce, start to finish. There had never been that kind of cash available in the Trust so why they'd wasted time behaving as if there were was beyond him. Bloody bureaucrats. Jobs for the boys. Old codgers, scared of losing their grip, wanting to feel useful in their dotage.

I was beginning to like him, if only for his jaundiced view of humanity. That aside, he thought he knew where Laura could raise the money she needed and advised her to approach a charitable trust called Argent Sans Cordes. Wilson had a very English way of pronouncing it but said that it was run by a group of European businessmen who consider cases like Laura's and if they like a project, if they think it serves the community, they look favourably upon it.

"Or in Doctor Wilson's less pretentious language," she modified, "the buggers sometimes cough up."

"In return for what?" I asked.

She raised a forefinger to let me know that she'd been ready for the question. "Absolution, for having picked our pockets in the first place, Wilson said."

She took a business card from her bag and passed it to me. The main name on it was Argent Sans Cordes, but running a close second was that of Julien Raphael, Investment Facilitator.

"Investment Facilitator?" I said. "Sounds better in French, probably."

"You've already made up your mind about him?"

"On the strength of his poncy office, yes. I know that corner of Bloomsbury Square."

"Doctor Wilson suggested something else," said Laura. "When I meet up with Raphael, he thinks I should go alone, without my fellow partners. 'Those boring old sods will do more harm than good'. Quote."

What struck me about Wilson's suggestion wasn't the money which Argent Sans Cordes was theoretically willing to part with but the amount of work they must have done to get the elderly doctor on side. Had he come willingly, I wondered, believing that he was helping a rejected applicant? Or had he been coerced? People still need money in their early eighties and he was certainly new to them or he would have known how to pronounce their name. And I didn't like the suggestion that she went to see Raphael alone.

"What do you know about Wilson?"

"He used to have a practise in Long Crendon. Passed it onto his son who threw it all up and went to work in Botswana."

Not for the first time since Jaikie had been staying at Beech Tree, he and Laura ganged up on me with Jaikie leading the charge.

"Dad, that's your imminent disaster look, as Mum used to call it."

"From one of her pet sayings to one of mine. If it sounds too good to be true…"

"Dad, she can't just thumb her nose at a possible two hundred and fifty grand, sitting there in this Argent Sans Cordes, waiting to be used."

I asked if either of them had considered a link between this possible pools win and the murder of Patrick Scott. They hadn't, but what on earth could the connection be? I reminded them that records had been wiped, Jaikie had been attacked and Laura's house had been broken into and whatever those people were looking for hadn't turned up. Was there just a chance that they'd decided to change tack and try buying it?

She laughed. "From me? Do I have it?"

"I've no idea but you must be onto something and Patrick Scott is the key to it."

"All because I started asking questions about him?"

"They think you know more than you're telling."

She stood up and took a few awkward steps, going nowhere. "You're frightening me, Nathan."

"Good, because you're usually the one who's got their head screwed on."

"Dad…"

"Julien Raphael hasn't made an offer yet, Laura. He's dangled money in front of you and, like the sucker he takes you for, you're reaching for it instead of asking yourself who he is and why he's suddenly appeared."

She sat down again, perched on the edge of the chair, muttering that she wasn't keen on being labelled a sucker.

"Then you won't like this either," I said. "Today Jaikie and I met the man who got rid of Patrick Scott's body. He thought I might have been Patrick's father and was heartily relieved to learn that I wasn't. I can't tell you if he killed him, but I do know he got paid twenty-five thousand pounds for turning him into dog food."

"And told everybody he'd won it on the lottery," Jaikie added.

She nodded slowly and reached across the table. I laid my hand on top of hers, keeping us both calm. "A fortnight ago, the two of you were trying to persuade me there was a case to investigate. I didn't really want to know. Now it's the other way round. I believe this kid has been murdered and you two, three if you include Martin, have lost perspective. Your quarter of a million pounds is trumping my dead body, Laura, and this Julien Raphael knew it would. He's banking on you being prepared to do anything to get your surgery built. Can you honestly telling me he's whistling dixie?"

She didn't like the sound of that but acknowledged that there was a vestige of truth in it.

"So what now?" she asked, frostily.

"Like I keep saying, the next move is where it gets tricky."

I explained that I no longer had an army of old friends and ex-colleagues to call upon in times of need. Most of them had retired, leaving me without people to run names and faces through police meat grinders. As recently as last year I would have phoned Steve Yates, spent half an hour chewing the fat, wishing the old days had never passed, and then asked him to run Julien Raphael's name through the Interpol data base. 24 hours later he would have called me back with chapter and verse. Right now, though, Steve was criss-crossing the States with his wife on the Harley, living the biker dream at 55 years of age. I looked at the business card again, hoping it would tell me something new. It didn't.

"Go see him and take me with you, but be absolutely clear in your mind about our purpose. We're not after money. We want to know what his connection is to a young man who ended up as dog food."

I'm not sure how heavily she edited my words but enough to offer the possibility that while I could obtain whatever information I was in search of, she might also be able to get her funding. When I made to argue the point, she dismissed it as understood.

With the mention of food, albeit dog food, Jaikie had started digging around in the fried rice for leftover prawns.

"What about Richard Slater?" he said.

"What about him?"

"A journalist of that standing has a legion of contacts, an army of researchers, they could provide the info your old cronies used to. And he's just dying to be my new best friend."

It wasn't a bad idea and without being too fulsome I thanked him for it. He responded by asking what we were doing tomorrow and although I hadn't banked on him becoming my side-kick, I invited him to join me on another trip to Tilbury. Hopefully we'd catch Charlie Drayton on one of his good days.

8

Jaikie must have been up half the night, though he denied it, putting together a research document about Argent Sans Cordes, gleaned from Google, maps, photos, testimonials, the lot. ASC was as Doctor Wilson had claimed the charitable window box of a group of European companies, Renault, BMW, Bosch being three names which leaped out, all intent upon putting back into the community some of the benefits which they had reaped. In general it was publicity written by docile admirers with limited vocabulary and one track minds. There wasn't a cross word to be found anywhere about the set up, often the case when money is given away without strings attached. And like any organisation from Church Roof Funds to NHS pyramids its governing body was cumbersome and top heavy with lobby fodder. These weren't Doctor Wilson's paid codgers, though, scared of getting old, wanting to feel useful. They were big name politicians, academics and media mouths.

Laura told us she had a quiet day planned, the high point of which would be making an appointment to see Julien Raphael at his London offices. She waited for me to pronounce.

"Any time you like," I said. "Just don't tell him you'll be bringing a friend."

She went back upstairs to shower and Jaikie proved again that he wasn't just female eye candy by asking an intelligent question.

"What do we do if Corrigan decides to follow us again?"

"He won't."

He raised the eyebrows, more Jaikie than Dirk Bogarde this time.

"He's tailing Laura, like I asked him to," I said.

"He's on our side, then?"

"Maybe, but what makes you think the good guys always play fair? Which is why I went up to *The Crown* last night and let all four of his tyres down."

It turned out that Charles Drayton was having the worst day of his life. A swarm of vehicles was buzzing around number 34 Clark Road, among them a police patrol car, a Doctor's car and a mortuary van, the drivers of which were huddled in a group discussing the meaning of life, no doubt. There were a few other cars, presumably belonging to friends and relatives, among them the Fiat I'd seen the young priest drive away in yesterday. One car was conspicuous by its absence. The Red MG Sports.

"What's all this?" Jaikie asked, as we drove past to find a parking spot.

"At a rough guess, he's checked out in the night."

It was a strange experience being introduced by Mrs Drayton to her children as another friend of their father. I'd only invented the relationship 24 hours ago, the shortest friendship I'd ever had, but nevertheless a fruitful one. I'd established that Drayton did get rid of the body and was paid handsomely to do so. I'd come today to ask what more he knew, fully expecting him to still be alive and able to tell me. His wife had expected the same.

"When the end came, it came quickly," she said. "Too bloody quickly, if you ask me. The specialist gave him another three weeks."

She showed us into her living room where her three children, all in their twenties, two girls and a boy, had spent the morning receiving old friends and neighbours. The room was furnished in the same style as the Draytons' back yard in that not a single piece of furniture matched another, having been acquired, just like his cars and trailers, one bargain at a time. The children gave the same impression yet the one thing they did have in common was the nature of their grief: restrained, dignified and genuine. Whatever their father had been up to in his spare time, his family clearly loved him. They'd been building up to his death for three months now, one of the girls told me, but when it finally came it still hit them like a ton of scrap.

"When did he pass?" I asked Mrs Drayton.

She didn't like the word 'pass' anymore than I did. "Die, you mean? About two this morning, the doctor reckons. I took him in his tea at six, luke warm, three sugars, there he was gone."

"Do you think I might go and say goodbye?"

"Help yourself."

I went into the dying room on my own. Jaikie had decided against accompanying me, real death being a very different proposition to that on a film set. The heat had been turned right down to a point where I shivered and seeing Drayton laid out on the bed, covered in a hospital night gown out of the ark, threw me back to an elderly relative who had also died in a downstairs room. My great grandmother Mabel Hawk who, when she finally let go, looked far better at 94 than Drayton did at 65. But the whiteness was there. The white wispy hair, waxen skin, bloodless hands and fingernails. As with Mabel, Charlie's eyes were closed and to that extent he looked a damn sight more peaceful than he deserved to. His corpse had been kissed on the forehead by the elder daughter, a smudge of scarlet lipstick said as much.

I lifted the makeshift shroud. The spindly, emaciated form had nothing new to tell me, it simply confirmed what I already knew: morphine notwithstanding, it must have been a painful death. His upper arms were a blue black mass of needle marks, his mouth was dry and crusty, just as it had been when I first saw him. I checked out the cylinder and the mouth-piece, all intact and set in their place. I went over and twitched the curtains at the window. It was double-glazed, closed and locked. Whoever had hastened his death, and I believed that someone had, they'd left no calling card, no trace of their visit. At least not on the strength of my cursory inspection.

I went back to the living room where the family had been joined by the young priest I'd met yesterday. He'd been unable to give Charlie the last rites, but at least he'd heard his confession, he said, and now followed it up with something grating about the importance of family and friends at such a time. We continued to trot out the patter of condolence, with Jaikie being rather good at the one size fits all when it comes to the recently departed, so long as you stick to generalities: in Charlie's case his courage, his determination, his pride in his children.

When the priest stood up to leave I said it was time we made tracks as well. Mrs Drayton saw us all to the door, suffering more banalities from the man of God, even as he backed away down the front path. She sighed with relief when the front gate closed behind him, then she turned and thanked us for our help yesterday, me for being a friend to Charlie. It was a pity that he hadn't rallied before he died, she said, been more himself for a few hours and able to talk over old times with me. I asked her if he'd said anything, late yesterday perhaps. She knew exactly what I meant. It wanted to know if he'd elaborated on the 'something dreadful he'd done to a young lad'. She shook her head.

I nodded over to the workshop where the red MG Sports had stood. "You sold the car, I see."

"That's the only good thing in all this," she replied. "They came back last night, those two who were looking it over yesterday. Two grand cash."

"Who were they?"

"Old friends of Charlie's. Don't know their names but they're always polite."

We shook hands and said goodbye and Mrs Drayton watched us walk down the path. Whether that was the good manners of her generation, or because something about my questions had made her uneasy, I couldn't say, but as the front door closed behind us, I said to Jaikie, "Where's that bloody priest?"

I knew full well where he was. He was two hundred yards away and about to get into his car and drive off. I hurried over to him calling out just once, "Wait!"

He turned, saw who'd yelled to him and leaned back against the driver's door, folding his arms.

"What can I do for you?" he asked, when I reached him.

"First things first. Me calling you father goes against the grain. What's your Christian name?"

"Robert."

"Okay, Robert, yesterday you took Charlie Drayton's confession. You came out of that house white as a sheet and we both know the reason why. You're one of the few people who knows what happened to Patrick Scott…"

He held up a hand. "And now you expect me to flout the sanctity of the confessional, Mr Hawk?"

"He got rid of a body. He threw it into a dog food processor. All I want to know is did he kill him as well and if not who did."

"Canon Law forbids it and comes down from a higher power than either of us."

"Canon Law's three hundred years old, Robert, and it isn't absolute. This boy has been murdered and you can help me to catch…"

He shouted me down. "I suggest you take your request for me to break the seal to the relevant authority."

He went to open the car door and I grabbed him by one shoulder, turned him and shoved him back against the bodywork. I stepped right up close, into his space and stared at him but the black magic of physical threat didn't seem to be working. Without taking his eyes off me he said, with all the smugness of a man who knows that God is on his side, "Would you kindly remove your hand."

Priest or not, I had a sudden urge to take his head and slam it down on the bonnet. Trouble was, over the centuries these blokes had been massacred in their thousands for what they believed in, so slapping one from East Tilbury wasn't going to get me very far.

"So you didn't ask Charlie for permission to discuss the crime?" I said. "Like you should have done?"

He seemed surprised that I'd picked up that scrap of Canon Law on my way through as a police officer.

"No, I didn't."

"You admit there was one to discuss?"

He smiled and told me with renewed insolence that I could try any trick I liked to get him to reveal what had passed between him and Charlie, but he was not about to risk excommunication. Canon Law 1388 paragraph 1. Perhaps I knew about that as well? And that's when the red mist began to gather, in spite of us being in a public street, in spite of my son standing right beside me about to witness his father commit an act of violence. On the fringe I heard Jaikie's voice.

"The guy's just doing his job, Dad."

It's always been an excuse I've loathed, but I considered it for a moment before rejecting it. That's when Jaikie must have seen the warning signs. He stepped forward, reached into my inside pocket and I watched as he took out The Map, unfolded it and spread it on the roof of the Fiat.

I really should explain about The Map. It's an imaginary one of the world, bequeathed to me just before he died by an elderly career criminal with whom I shared a particular character flaw. In certain circumstances, usually after undue provocation, we both had - and I still have - a tendency to boil over. So far so ordinary in anyone's world. However, just as with Roy Pullman, my problem had always been that for the following five minutes I had absolutely no idea of the damage I frequently caused. To combat this, whenever Roy felt the anger rising he would reach for The Map and, with all the precision of a mime artist, spread it out and place his finger on what he called 'a far more agreeable place'. He would go there in his mind and be unreachable, sometimes for over an hour.

I released my grip on the priest who must have thought he was witnessing some kind of pagan ritual as Jaikie took my hand and set my forefinger down on The Map. He looked at where it had landed and turned to me.

"Winchendon," he said.

He folded up The Map, replaced it in my pocket and walked me back to the Land Rover.

The drive home was a subdued affair, each of us silent for our separate reasons. I was first to break it, just as we emerged from the underpass at Hanger Lane, though there's nothing to be read into our travelling from darkness into light. I muttered my thanks to Jaikie. They were brief and simple. He'd stopped me weighing into Robert the Priest and thereby adding more trouble to my CV. Jaikie nodded and gestured to a garage up ahead where he and Jamal sometimes bought coffee. I changed lanes, someone behind me hooted. Far from annoying me me I found it rather comforting. I was back on familiar ground.

We sat in silence for a while, drinking the halfway decent Americanos in this mixture of petrol station, corner shop and coffee house. Jaikie had taken a caramel slice as well but was having difficulty eating it with the plastic fork provided. As he abandoned etiquette in favour of his fingers, I suddenly heard myself say, "Do you think I'm being paranoid over this case?"

It must have sounded like a trick question which is why he took his time over it. Finally he said there must be an easy joke in there somewhere but he'd leave it for another day. Meantime, no, but why had I asked?

"I think these bastards are closing in. Charlie Drayton dying ahead of time is their latest move."

"You think he was murdered?"

"I'm bloody sure of it. We went to see him yesterday, today he's dead. As an actor, surely you know: it's called timing."

I took a few sips of coffee, wishing I'd bought a slice of caramel shortbread as well. He offered me a chunk of his own but he'd mauled it fairly comprehensively by then. I could see his fingerprints in the chocolate glaze.

"Thing is, from one angle it feels like a crime I've invented, drawn out of thin air, but if that's the case why are so many other people interested? This Julien Raphael hasn't turned up out of the goodness of his heart. He'll want something for his money. As for Ralph Askew coming back into Slater's life all of a sudden? For film tickets?"

"Does happen, Dad, people just turn up."

"After 12 years, bang on cue! And now he's got a line straight through to you, me, and Laura."

"What the hell's he after?"

"Christ only knows, but MP? Under Secretary? It took someone with access to government records to wipe out any trace of Patrick Scott. Who's to say they didn't get rid of the man himself?"

"But Dad, all these guys are just… blokes."

It would've been my own reaction, 30 years ago, so I brought him up to date in terms he understood, pointing out that the bad guys didn't necessarily come at you all muscle and good looks with a hoard of extras in tow. More than likely they came in ones and twos with a talent for fading into the wallpaper. Look at the people we already had who fitted that bill. Corrigan from S.O.U.? Not exactly Josh Hartnett. Slater, a reporter, but not one you'd confuse with Robert Redford in that film…

"*All the President's Men*," he filled in.

"And Askew, for Christ's sake? You couldn't even bring the guy to mind."

He laughed. "I still can't, but maybe that's what you're saying, he doesn't stand out."

I nodded. "So you don't think I'm way off beam"

"No. Two murders. Trouble is we're the only people who know about them, apart from the killers."

"Half an hour from now it'll be three. Either that or he'll laugh like a drain."

It was actually 40 minutes later when I parked the Land Rover outside Thame nick and asked at the desk for Jim Kelloway. He'd returned from a holiday in Sri Lanka, three days previously, and was sporting a Bournemouth Tan which set off the shock of white hair and sharp blue eyes. Here was a man due for retirement in a couple of years time, looking to leave behind the pallid grey of police work and reinvent himself as something more colourful than a Detective Sergeant in the Thames Valley Police Force, even though he hadn't a clue what that might be. He was dressed as sharply as ever, a new jacket from a tailor in Colombo. The man had made him two sports jackets, a suit and half a dozen shirts, all for about four hundred quid. He lowered his voice.

"He does leather jackets as well, guvnor. Send him that one, he'll do a carbon copy, only new."

I said I'd think about it and once we'd dispensed with some mild swooning over Jaikie from the girls in the office, and we'd been shown photos of Kelloway swimming in the Indian Ocean with his granddaughter, visiting an elephant sanctuary, leopard stalking and God knows what else, I told him the story of Patrick Scott. He knew about the break-in at Laura's but that was all, so I took him through the rest of it and he listened without a murmur of doubt, even when it came to my theory about the dog food. When I finally reached the death of Charles Drayton with the accent on it being three weeks before its due date, he paused, took out his iPhone and started to wrestle with it.

"I know just the man you need," he said. "Knew him at North Finchley. Bit off the wall like yourself and our generation. Artisan." He paused with the iPhone. "These bloody things, you think you've got the hang of them, a day later it's all a mystery again."

"Would you like me to…?" Jaikie began.

Kelloway passed him the phone and said, "Alan Baker. His details are on there somewhere."

He turned back to me and said that he'd get in touch with Baker that evening, catch him at his ease. And I was right. Charles Drayton's death, expected or not, should go down in the books and Alan was our man. He was a real lad, which was police shorthand for him being a womaniser, but in all other regards he was dead straight, worked like a bastard, and if there was something there he'd find it.

"You're the first person I've told about the dog food, outside the family," I said.

"Sounds like a damn good way of getting rid to me. In our day the disposal of choice was to bury the body in some new motorway, but times have changed." He added in response to

Jaikie's inquiring look. "We've run out of concrete, son. Feeding to pigs would be my own choice. They'll eat anything."

As usual there was a film to go with the theory.

"*Snatch*," said Jaikie. "Guy Ritchie film."

Kelloway leaned back in his chair and spread his hands. "What can I do?"

It was a genuine question, not a declaration of uselessness.

"See if Patrick Scott was ever reported missing to police and who by. I don't think you'll find anything, but…"

"Why not?"

"Because George Corrigan, much as I don't trust him, will have checked. If he'd found anything he'd have asked questions of me, Laura, Martin Falconer, Jan Zawadski, uncle Tom Cobley an' all. He hasn't."

He nodded and made a few notes on a tear-off pad and I was glad to have captured his interest. He had a reputation for laziness which I thought was more of a pretence than anything. Secretly, he was the kind of copper who was anxious to make one big splash before retiring, to leave the job as a legend not an also ran. Contrary to popular belief, they do exist. I thanked him and, as he reached out to shake Jaikie's hand, he turned and picked up the notepad.

"Sorry about this, Jaikie, but would you mind? For the wife."

Jaikie smiled. He'd heard all the variations there were on an autograph being for someone else. "What's her name?"

"Evelyn."

Jaikie wrote 'To Evelyn, with very best wishes' and signed off Jacob Hawk. For some reason, which I'll never be able to understand, it made Jim Kelloway a very happy man.

Darkness had fallen by the time we drove out of Thame nick and with it, unsurprisingly, came a general sense of foreboding not helped by the all too recent murder of the one man who knew the name of Patrick Scott's killer. Why that in turn should've made me realise I hadn't spoken to Laura all day I've no idea but I suddenly had the urge to do so, even though we'd be with her in ten minutes. I asked Jaikie to phone and see if she had any plans for supper or should we get something from Waitrose while we were in town. His short burst of local fame had made him cocky again.

"Shouldn't I ask first if she's okay?"

"You can ask her to reel off the Kings and Queens of England, if you like. I just want to hear her voice."

He tried her number only to find that her phone was switched off and as a result we were both edgy as we turned into Morton Lane, with Jaikie having re-dialled several times during the journey, saying to me on the last attempt that her mobile was as dead as Charles Drayton. The limbo persisted right up to the five bar gate, even while Jaikie opened it for me to drive in and park. Then Dogge came belting towards us and I relaxed. Only one person could have let her loose, there being a knack to opening the back door when it swells up in Winter.

"Where've you been?" I asked, more anxiously than I'd meant to.

She laughed. "Checking up on me? I took your dog for a walk, down over the valley beyond Chestnut Farm. We had a stalker. George Corrigan."

I smiled. "Bloody Irish, they're everywhere."

"We didn't talk much. It's difficult to chat with someone who's fifty yards behind you. How was Charles Drayton?"

"Deader than your phone. My old friend from the dog food days, I shall miss him."

She reached out and patted my hand. "Time is a great healer."

Sip by sip over the next couple of hours I mourned the passing of Charles Drayton, the one viable link I had to Patrick Scott's murder. Over supper, Jaikie tried to give my gathering bleakness a voice.

"Dad reckons Drayton was pushed over the edge. If he'd lived, even for another day, he might have told us the name of Patrick Scott's murderer."

"Assuming that it wasn't him," she pointed out. "Are you *sure* Drayton was killed?"

I told her I was but in keeping with the rest of this case I hadn't a sliver of proof to confirm my suspicions. I'd searched Charlie's dying room and found nothing I could use. The rash of needle marks on his upper arm were the perfect cover for someone to shoot God knows what into him while their companion, in another room, counted out two thousand pounds for the red MG Sports. And all Mrs Drayton knew about them was they were old friends of Charlie, and were always polite to her. Today, however, they'd been downright bloody rude, murdered her husband, paid her a fraction of what the MG was worth and brought the hunt for my 38th killer to a dead stop.

It was three in the morning when I finally accepted that I wasn't going to fall asleep. It wasn't the coffee, it wasn't the scotch and it wasn't Laura snoring gently away beside me. It was my mother's voice, repeating one of her treasured truisms. One door closes, another opens, she would say in times of disappointment or loss. My father's eyes would rise to the ceiling as he held back from belittling her optimism. She said it about my very first girlfriend ditching me. What have doors got to do with a broken heart, I wanted to know? You'll see, she said, you'll see. One closes another opens.

She was right, of course, it's the way with doors, though as far as catching Patrick Scott's killer was concerned I couldn't yet hear any creaking hinges or feel a draught around my ankles. Partly to avoid more truisms from my mother, I went downstairs and put the kettle on. Tea. More caffeine. As I waited for it to brew I went over to the dresser, took out the metal plate from its place of safety in the cutlery drawer. It was still all I had, the only thing I could actually touch, that gave me a link to the victim. It couldn't even be classed as evidence. At the risk of sounding like a broken record it was a metal plate four centimetres long, one centimetre wide, with four countersunk crew holes in it. And the two people who'd persuaded me that it once belonged to a man called Patrick Scott who'd been murdered within the last couple of years, were upstairs fast asleep. That didn't seem fair. I went upstairs to wake them.

Laura wasn't as put out as I'd thought she might be. I needed help, I told her, and she was out of bed in a trice, turning the tables and making me feel guilty. She wasn't on duty that day, she said, she could catch up on sleep if she needed to. What was the problem?

"Kitchen?" I suggested, feebly. "Jaikie's coming too."

She put on the lilac dressing gown, tied it securely at the waist. I carried on up to the attic and prodded Jaikie. From the outset he was downright obstreperous.

"Wassup?"

"Rise and shine. Need your help."

"Jesus, Dad…"

He tried to block me out by dragging the duvet up over his head and twisting himself into some pre-historic shape. A minute later and short of air, he flung back his temporary shell, pitched himself forward onto his feet and looked at me. I handed him yesterday's T-shirt and jeans and after some under-breath swearing he followed me downstairs. He fell into Maggie's Dad's rocker and laid there, body in a straight line at a forty-five degree angle to the floor, hands clasped on his chest. It had been the full blown performance of a semi-conscious, belligerent, and much put upon man. Laura was already seated at the table, fresh as a daisy. She'd even run a brush through her hair, probably for Jaikie's sake.

"So, how can we help?" she asked.

I was still hold of the metal plate, for some reason, and now held it up to the light, turning it as I did so.

"Tell me what you see when you hear the words Patrick Scott. Describe him for me."

Laura clearly didn't see any point to the exercise but played along. "I imagine him to be six feet tall, dark brown hair, boyish face. Doesn't smile easily but that's part of his stillness, not because he's miserable. Glasses. Trendy, round, steel rimmed. Short sighted."

"It's Harry Potter," muttered Jaikie.

"Yes, yes, I suppose they are rather similar."

"What do you see, Jaikie?"

He rolled his head to get me in his eye line. "A cylinder, six inches high, full metal jacket, with a soppy label on it."

"Before he was dog food," I said.

He took a deep breath and closed his eyes. "I see the kid everyone picked on at school. Shorter than average and already losing his hair. Works behind the counter at a gym, or somewhere. Nice enough bloke, it's just that nobody wants his company. What do you see?"

"Nothing."

"Nothing will come of nothing, speak again," he said, involuntarily. "King Lear to his youngest daughter."

"Zip it. Nathan Hawk to his youngest son. I see nothing because I've taught myself to resist mental previews of murder victims. They're always wrong and wind up getting in the way.

Besides, ordinarily after a couple of days I would have known more about a victim than anyone, apart from his mother. I'd have known what he looked like, what colour his skin, hair, eyes were. How tall he was, how much he weighed, if it was fat or flab. How many teeth were in his head, how many bones he'd broken, whether he smoked, drank or did drugs, what he'd had for dinner the day he died. I'd have known where he lived and who with, what he did or didn't do for a living, how he spent his free time, who his friends and enemies were. I would have known most of his secrets." I paused, not expecting a round of applause but hoping for more enthusiasm than Jaikie and Laura showed. "Am I making any sense or do you think it's the coffee talking?"

Laura held out her hand for the metal plate. I slid it across the table to her.

"You're saying that in Patrick's case we still know bugger all," said Jaikie.

"And somebody's gone to a lot of trouble to make me feel that way. Records wiped, an attack on you, Laura's house being turned over. Even Corrigan suggested that I step back. Who told him to do that, I wonder? The same people who murdered Charles Drayton to stop him confessing?"

"So why the four o'clock call?" Jaikie asked.

"Well, having said we know nothing I'll now say there's no such thing in a murder inquiry. We three know *something* about this boy. We've missed it, that's all."

"Did you ever visit The Chiltern Clinic?" said Laura, prompted by the metal plate I presume. "For a description, I mean. Somebody there might remember him."

"The Chiltern's the last place I can go. Alarm bells rang when you phoned them, if I walk in there they'll lock the place down."

"That doesn't alter the fact that at some point he broke a metatarsal. The people who made this were quite adamant."

"Ambrose and Dawlish from Corby," said Jaikie, closing his eyes for a moment. "AD07F1673."

"Memory man, eh?"

"Helps when it comes to lines." He sat up properly at last. "You said after a few days you knew how a normal victim spent their free time, Dad. Well, Patrick Scott went ski-ing, didn't he. What does that conjure up, Laura?"

She smiled. "St. Moritz, Claviere, Cesana, Scotland even. You?"

"Aspen, Colorado. Lake Tahoe. Kirkwood in California."

"Yes, well, like you so famously said, Jaikie, all I have to do now is track him down. Anywhere in the world where it snows so that shouldn't be too…"

Again, I wish I could say it was a eureka moment, a dazzling piece of deduction, but it was another case of why the hell didn't I think of that before. That sudden chill around my ankles was the draught from a distant door opening and Patrick Scott was standing the other side of it.

"That first time you phoned The Chiltern, Laura, what did they tell you about the plate?"

"I can't remember exactly. Probably something like…"

Jaikie was word perfect. "We were in *The Crown* and the girl on the phone had told you 'the number on the plate referred to a Patrick Scott, aged 24. He came to them as an emergency, via the ambulance service. A ski-ing accident, badly fractured metatarsal.' Then Dad moaned about you not getting an address."

"Say you break a bone in any of those places you mentioned. St. Moritz for example. Where would you be taken?"

She answered as if it were all too obvious. "The nearest emergency point. Celerina, top of the Cresta run."

"And from there to a hospital? One nearby or a day's journey away?"

"Nearby," she said, catching on. "So why take Patrick Scott all the way to the Chiltern Clinic from St. Moritz?"

I slapped the table and they both flinched. "Because he wasn't in St. Moritz or anywhere like it. He wasn't somewhere that boasted real snow. He broke his foot in this country. Ski-ing, yes, but on a dry ski-slope."

Jaikie laughed. "You mean Bracknell, Esher, Brentwood?"

"Those places may not have the ring of Aspen, Colorado but it doesn't make him any the less dead."

I beckoned him to the table and asked him to do a Google search on my laptop for dry slopes within a 50 mile radius of The Chiltern Clinic. They both wanted to know where that would get us. I reminded them that we had a rough date for when the accident happened, August 2009, we had a name for the victim. If necessary I'd approach every one of those slopes till I found what I was looking for.

"Which is?" said Jaikie.

"He'll have paid to use the place. Debit card, credit card. We can prove that he did exist. See, I told you we knew something."

Delighted though they were it didn't stop Jaikie pointing out that if the nameless, faceless 'they' we were probably dealing with could wipe the NHS database, which was no doubt linked to that of the Chiltern Clinic, the records of a tin-pot ski-slope would have been no problem. It was a good point.

"Unless, like us, they heard the word ski-ing and assumed foreign climes," said Laura.

"Jaikie, give them to me alphabetically," I said. "Phone numbers."

I walked over to the wall phone by the back door, took it from its cradle and turned to see them both smiling, Laura to herself, Jaikie right at me.

"Dad, it's four thirty in the morning. Maybe leave it a few hours?"

9

As with all theories which are dreamed up in the middle of the night, when they seem crystal clear, this one had clouded over by nine o'clock the next day. Sleep was the great problem solver, according to my mother, but now I looked again at the list of ski-slopes which Jaikie had printed out, I wondered how I could be sure that Patrick Scott had visited any one of them, or that they, in their turn, had kept perfect records.

Nevertheless, getting in touch with them was now essential if for no other reason than to eliminate possibilities. Fair enough, but as a serving police officer I would've had a team to do the donkey work, the texting, phoning, emailing. Here I had only Jaikie, who would worry that people recognised his voice, and Laura who had a full time job anyway. There were twenty-seven slopes within a fifty mile radius of The Chiltern Clinic. I'd expected more. If we broadened the trawl to take in London the number would rise almost certainly, though not to unmanageable proportions.

After breakfast I divided the list into three and gave Laura and Jaikie a script to work from. Without saying as much they were to be members of the human resources team at County Fare. An employee of the firm called Patrick Scott claimed to have broken a bone in his foot in August 2009 and was using it as a reason to take time off for physio appointments. If this accident was real, fair enough, we'd support him, if not we'd think again. There were several possible responses ranging from the most likely, no, never heard of him, to the one we were looking for, yes. In case of the latter they should hand over to me. For anything in between they should lie.

It was routine and tedious work, as far as I was concerned, but my new recruits soon began to get a kick out of being gently deceptive. If I had any criticisms at all it was that Jaikie gave it a little too much Hamlet at Elsinore and Laura veered towards asking the person on the other end where it hurt. By the time we'd reached number seventeen on the list, with nothing positive to show for it, I was beginning to lose heart. Just after a break for coffee, though, all that changed when I was put through to the manager of The Snow Centre at Hemel Hempstead. He picked up almost immediately telling me that his name was Kevin Stapleton. I began to parrot the script and got as far as the name Patrick Scott at which point he said, "Don't tell me he's turned up."

His response threw me but I quickly regained my balance. "Well, in a way, yes."

"He either has or he hasn't. Which is it?" He was excited, but my refusal to answer quickly made him suspicious. "Who am I speaking to?"

He was in a cleft stick now and knew it. He couldn't go back and deny knowledge of Patrick, but for reasons best known to himself he wasn't prepared to talk further.

"I don't discuss the people who use our facility," he said. "Thanks for your call."

The line went dead. Jaikie and Laura finished their own calls and turned to find me already on my feet, reaching for my leather jacket and momentarily wondering, though God knows why at that particular moment, if Jim Kelloway had got a point and I should invest in a new one.

"You off somewhere?" Jaikie asked.

"Hemel Hempstead. The manager there knew him, assumed from me asking about him that he'd turned up."

"Can I come?" Jaikie asked.

"Stay here and find out for me if Ralph Askew's grandfather was in Italy during the war. That should be easy enough. Not so easy is whether Ralph is a film buff or not." I paused at the door, unhappy to admit that I might have been wrong about someone. "Any problem, get onto George Corrigan."

To speak the truth about Hemel Hempstead is to run the risk of offending anyone who lives there, so I'll be brief. I know it for having the most tortuous traffic system in Europe where six roundabouts are chained together in one. I've been unable to avoid it over the years with it being en route to the M.1. motorway and that just about sums the place up. It's one of those southern towns famous only for being on the way to somewhere else. It was the case a hundred and fifty years ago with the Grand Union Canal, London to Birmingham, it's the case today with the motorway to Leeds and the main line railway to Scotland. All three carve the place into chunks rendering it disjointed and characterless, its double barreled name giving it no more charm than, for example, Leighton Buzzard or the unthinkable Milton Keynes. I said I'd be brief...

My only interest in Hemel Hempstead that morning was The Snow Centre. It is a pale imitation of the real thing in every respect, an indoor parody of The Alps with home made snow. A wallscape depicting a sunny part of Switzerland runs the entire length of one slope, trying to create an atmosphere, but it remains tantalisingly unreachable.

Kevin Stapleton had the air of a man who'd spent too long sitting tight and hoping for a better offer, presumably one that took him to the real thing, the ski slopes of France, Italy or Switzerland. He must have known that time was running out. He was in his late thirties and there would be younger, more attractive, less forgettable men who would be chosen ahead of him. Should he go or should he stick it out in Hemel? While he made up his mind he was running a successful business here, with satisfied customers and contented staff, but he was hardly brimming over with joy. Not that I'm an expert on the latter. He was losing his black hair rapidly. There were strands of it on the shoulder of his jacket. He was putting on weight. The said jacket didn't quite fit anymore.

He took me into the mock après-ski bar where we stood at the window alongside proud mothers watching children as young as five descend fearlessly, return to the summit on the ski-lift and do it all again. After a few pleasantries with regular customers he ordered me an orange juice, himself a diet coke, and took me to a corner table. Though not surprised to see me, he was hardly the most welcoming of hosts and with it being half term they were busy, so the sooner we got whatever it was over and done with the better. He spoke as if he knew that at the heart of my questions lay more than just a broken bone and my first thought was that he'd always known that Patrick's accident would return to haunt him. But as I pressed him for answers I sensed more to his hostility than a possible insurance claim against the company he worked for.

"You said on the phone that you knew Patrick Scott," I began.

"I said no such thing. I said..."

"I know what you *really* said, Kevin, but you gave yourself away. You knew him."

He noticed that I'd used the past tense. I told him I'd done so on purpose because Patrick was dead. He took time to absorb the news, wondering no doubt if a man could die from a broken metatarsal or complications arising therefrom. Deciding that it was unlikely he allowed himself to react to the news.

"What did he die of?" he asked.

"Somebody murdered him."

He mouthed the words 'fucking hell' and I went on to explain most of the events which had brought me to this apology for Switzerland. I'm not sure he heard much of it.

When I stopped talking he said, "You sound like a cop."

"Used to be. Can't seem to shake it off. An unsolved murder comes my way, I jump in."

He responded quietly, aware that news of a customer being murdered wouldn't go down well in this bar. "They didn't catch whoever killed him?"

"D'you know, Kevin, you are the first person I've met who acknowledges that he actually existed." He took it as a compliment, for some reason, until I added, "I'd like you to think about that."

"Why, does it make me a suspect?"

I spluttered a little. "What is wrong with your generation? Everything's about you, you, you. I said the first person to acknowledge him, not the last person to see him alive."

He shuffled his chair closer to the table and leaned forward, lowering his voice even further. He told me that Patrick was a regular there at Hemel, a strange, neurotic sort of guy but he liked him. Had reason to be grateful to him. They'd had a new ski-lift put in and it kept breaking down. Patrick was the man who could fix it in twenty minutes. He was an engineer of some kind, always had a new invention on the go, something he said that would Save the World.

"He used those words?"

"Quite often. Is it a problem?"

"No, but it's a long time since I heard anyone express the desire to do so. I've missed it. When he broke his foot...?"

"August 15th, 2009. I looked it up after you phoned."

"You called an ambulance?"

He nodded. "A private outfit we use. Cambry's. They came within minutes, took him... wherever. I never saw him again."

At least I was narrowing down the time scale. The accident took place on August 15th 2009. Charles Drayton quit his job on November 19th the same year. Five months during which, at some point, Patrick Scott was killed and turned into Fivestar.

"Did he come here alone, or with friends?" I asked.

Stapleton looked at me with mistrust which he tried to pass off as curiosity.

"Why d'you ask?"

"No reason. Or there wasn't, till you asked me why I'd asked. Who did he come with?"

He took a few surreptitious deep breaths and appeared to consult his diet coke before responding. "You tell me he's dead, I guess it doesn't matter anymore. He came with a girlfriend, Belinda Hewitt."

"Was she here the night he broke his foot?"

He nodded. "I haven't seen her since, either."

"And you wish you had?" In response to my old-fashioned look he turned away, mouthing the words 'fucking hell' again. "Don't blame yourself, I have a nose for these things."

I was disappointed, though. I'd begun to hope that Patrick Scott's murder would turn out to be an interesting one with a chance of it involving government lackeys, civil servants, press, big business, cover-ups and yet here it was in danger of boiling down to a love triangle gone haywire. When I put this to Stapleton he smiled for the first time since we'd met. Wonderful teeth, as white as the snow beyond the window.

"You could not be more wrong," he said.

He'd slept with her once. He knew it was inexcusable, another man's girlfriend but besides being this captivating, flame haired beauty Belinda was also a very persuasive creature.

"Is that the polite way of saying she was gagging for it?"

He winced at my crudeness. "Not at all. They were here one evening and they had a row. Patrick just got up, walked out, drove home, leaving Belinda to cry on my shoulder. I took her back to my place in Apsley."

He shrugged to make what had clearly followed understandable.

"Bob's your uncle, Fanny's your aunt?" I said.

"If you must."

"Do me a favour. Poor boy, backed into a corner where some divisive woman forces you to screw her? You think I've never heard it before? What had they been rowing about?"

"She thought he was involved with some girl called Henrietta. She was the real love of his life, according to Pat."

"You mean according to *Belinda*, according to Pat."

He shrugged. "Fair enough."

"I suppose you never met this Henrietta?"

"No, I didn't."

"Just Belinda."

He was beginning to resent my style and accused me of making it sound as if they'd had a lurid affair lasting God knows how long and not the one night stand it was. If I'd finished my questions, he had work to get on with.

"Couple more," I said. "Where did Patrick live?"

He looked round the bar. It was filling up. He waved to a couple of newcomers and I waited for him to give me back his full attention.

"Where did he live?" he repeated. "No idea."

"Kevin, your worst fear right now, based on what you already know about me, should be that I raise my voice and all these people here learn that one of your punters was murdered and you'd been screwing his girlfriend."

He was the one to raise his voice, in a strangulated sort of way. "I don't know where he lived. Ask Belinda."

"Okay, where does *she* live?"

"I don't know that either, but she runs an antique shop, Not the real pricey stuff, more home decor and ornamental."

"Where?"

"Golborne Road, West London. Off Portobello."

"Number?"

"No idea, but it's called, wait for it... Belinda's."

I smiled at him. My own teeth are pretty good, considering what they've been through, but I drink far too much tea and coffee I'm told.

"When I find her, shall I give her your love?"

Back at Winchendon, the workforce had had a fruitful afternoon too and couldn't wait to tell the boss all about it. Unlike most new recruits, however, one of them was keen to make a three act drama out of the essentially routine work, the other was putting the finishing touches to an apple and blackberry pie.

"You want the good news or the bad first?" Jaikie asked.

"You choose," I said.

He had difficulty with that. "Well, I guess it depends on your definition of either. One man's crappy performance is another's Olivier Award."

"Ralph Askew," I said, sharply.

"That's the bad news. He told you the truth. He is a film buff, he's even on the board of bloody BAFTA. And his grandfather was in Italy during the war. We found him on a regimental database."

To their bewilderment, I said that wasn't bad news, it was excellent.

"We thought you wanted us to come up with something damning," said Laura.

"You have done. Askew told me at the premier of *All Good Men* that Richard Slater was a means of 'getting him through the door'. If he's on the board of BAFTA…"

"He wouldn't need help getting cinema tickets," said Jaikie. "He was probably given a fistful."

"If Askew was the bad news, what's the good?"

"Julien Raphael," said Laura. "He phoned to ask if I'd send him the plans for the new Health Centre, before we meet."

"He sure is keen to spend that money. You know, I wouldn't mind seeing these famous plans myself."

She nodded across the kitchen to her briefcase. "Help yourself."

I took them up to my office to scan them into my computer. The 40 page document comprised surveys, drawings, reports, permissions, promises, recommendations and every damn thing you can think of to keep pocket Hitlers in work. And still the Trust had denied Laura and her colleagues funding. I printed off a copy for Raphael and then put a dab of glue on the top right hand corner of pages 18, 19 and 20, placed the document in an A4 envelope and sealed it.

10

It wasn't a day for visiting antique shops, whatever your purpose. The sky was as leaden and full of threat as only a late Autumn sky in London can be. The weather was reflected in people's mood and pace. Those on foot hurried to get indoors, those in cars snarled at each other. I had a minor confrontation myself on the Shepherds Bush roundabout with a kid in a Peugeot but it was such a lousy day neither of us wanted to stop, get out and take it any further.

Belinda's shop was easy enough to find. It was set in a mid-Victorian terrace, the original building flat and square in design but oddly beautiful for all that, even on a day like this. When I entered, the brass bell on a copper arm rang and a middle-aged woman looked up from her den in the corner. She'd been reading a book and must have reached an important point in the story if her barely concealed irritation was anything to go by. Even so she bade me good morning and asked if she could help. I said I wanted to look round. She smiled, told me there was more stuff upstairs and went back to her book.

As Kevin Stapleton had said, the place was more suited to interior designers in search of accessories, to historify modern penthouse flats, than to serious antiques collectors. My father would have called it a junk shop and refused to go near it. Times had changed beyond his belief. There was hardly a price tag below two hundred pounds and that for the type of stuff he would have thrown out forty years ago.

It wasn't all brass fenders, pine furniture and gilt mirrors, however. In the centre of the shop, stood a dozen wooden replicas of Easter Island statues, arranged in a circle, as if to repel marauders from all angles. Their grim faces were no more inviting to a potential buyer than their prices. Each of them was marked up at more than a thousand pounds and as I was gazing back at one, trying to fathom the appeal, I received a text message from Jim Kelloway. It simply said, 'Guv, no report of a Patrick Scott missing on the Police National Computer. JK.' The news itself hadn't surprised me: officially Patrick still didn't exist. And I'm not saying I'd expected kiss, kiss, and a smiley face from Jim, but an implied offer of more help wouldn't have gone amiss. It seemed that the deeper I delved into this case, the more isolated I became. Was that my imagination or was there a grain of truth to it?

I finished my browse and went over to the lady and her book. The den she was in was fenced off and pokey, no doubt with a cash tin down out of sight and an alarm straight through to the local nick: two tin cans and a length of string, by the feel of it. The pin board behind her was covered in business cards, taxi cab numbers, a few newspaper cuttings about the shop, and the inevitable family photos. Again she stopped reading and smiled up at me.

"See anything you like?"

"Plenty." I nodded at the snapshots, specifically at a photo of her holding a toddler in her arms. "Yours?"

It was routine flattery but she smiled appreciatively.

"Grandson."

I held back from saying that she didn't look old enough because, frankly, it was far from the truth, but I did ask if Belinda was around.

"She's taken the day off."

I turned away and called upon the spirit of Jaikie to deliver my disappointment. "The first day I travel into London for over a year. Will I ever learn? I should have checked."

"I could call her, but it'll only go to message."

"Or I could just drop round?"

The years may not have been kind to her face but they'd made her into a wily old bird. "If you know the address."

I nodded, and played the only card left in this particular hand. "Does she still live on the boat?"

I pointed to one of the photos on the pin board. It was of a red haired young woman in T-shirt and shorts, sitting at a table on the roof of a narrowboat.

"She does," said the book lady. "She's a regular water gypsy these days."

"You mean she moves about, she might not be there?"

"She'll be there today alright. Her father's coming back from Turkey, been away a whole month. She likes to be there for him."

"They were always close."

A remark too far, maybe. For all I knew they might have hated the sight of each other and Belinda have a dozen other reasons for wanting to be there when he arrived home. That aside, the Grand Union Canal is 137 miles long but this particular photo pinpointed exactly whereabouts on it the boat was moored. In the background I could see the re-vamped Paddington Station. Belinda was tied up in Paddington Basin.

"I'll call in," I said.

"You want me to phone, see if she answers?"

"No, let me surprise her."

There was nothing antique about Paddington Basin except the water itself which smelled a thousand years old. The whole area either side of the canal had been ripped apart and turned into a pastiche of its former self. The tow path and surrounding walkways were a mixture of brand new granite cobbles and machine tooled paving slabs. On the far side of the canal stood the back wall of Paddington Station, on the near side rose the new offices of Marks and Spencer. The firm had evidently subsidised the re-jigging of the area and in return now had something mood enhancing for their staff to look out on as they continued to flog the world its underwear.

I'd parked up in North Wharf Road and walked down to the basin. It was nearly lunchtime and people were out and about. The stationary, gawping ones were late season tourists, those on the move were office workers heading towards the plethora of cafés and bars farther down. All the big names were there, Costa, Subway, Starbucks, trying to push out their smaller competitors who still seemed to be making a decent living, but then at £2.60 a cup minimum that wasn't surprising.

There were no more than a dozen narrowboats moored on the stretch I could see and for a moment I considered calling out Belinda's name and waiting for a response. I didn't have to, she was expecting me. The book lady had obviously phoned ahead to warn her and, as I approached, she emerged through the cabin door and stood in the rear well of a boat called *Scorpius*. Dressed in jeans and a thick Scandinavian cardigan several sizes too big for her, she was tensed up against the drizzly breeze, arms folded, hands hidden, and even from a distance I could tell that Kevin Stapleton was right. Belinda was a natural beauty and her hair was just one of the features which made her so. My mother would have called it titian, if she liked the woman, ginger if she didn't. She had the pale skin which often goes with that colouring and what most would consider to be a perfect face, slightly tapered, with a nose Jaikie would describe as 'proper'. It was her lips that said most about her. There was no twitching with nerves, no pouting for effect. At her age, and with the kind of questions I was about to ask her, there should have been. She called out to me.

"Hallo, there! Who are you?"

"I'm Nathan Hawk."

"Chrissie at the shop said you knew me."

"Ah, Chrissie the Reader?" I was all smiles and it was getting painful. How the hell did Jaikie manage it? "I've come about Patrick Scott."

She closed her eyes and lowered her head. "Oh, dear. You'd better come aboard."

They aren't called narrowboats for nothing. This particular example was six feet ten inches wide and fifty feet long and try as you will there isn't much you can fit into 349 square feet of living space. At the far end, the pointed end, was the bedroom evidently and just this side of it the bathroom. I didn't use it, imagining it to be much like that in a caravan we once owned. Maggie and I had tackled a few holidays in it with four children and the horrors came flooding back.

The kitchen was next, compact and fuelled by bottled gas. The living area, in which we were now both standing, was half the size of my garden shed, with walls that sloped inwards, giving the impression that at any moment they would fall in. Belinda invited me to sit down on what she referred to as a sofa. I perched on the edge of it while she went through to the... galley to make coffee. She lived here on her own, she said in answer to my enquiry, but didn't feel lonely. Her father had a boat round the corner in Little Venice, called *Sweet Lady Jane*. The name said more about his taste in rock music and hankering after the sixties, than about history, or even his taste in women, she added with a laugh. *Jane* was twice the size of *Scorpius* but he used it as both home and office. He had an open offer to go back and live in the flat above the shop but reckoned that she needed it more than he did. Probably true. She stopped babbling only when she brought the coffees through and placed them on top of the gas fire. As she settled herself on a floor cushion opposite me the spectacular hair fell around her face as if to curtain off her emotions.

"I just know you're going to tell me something dreadful," she said.

"What makes you say that?"

"You're a policeman so you've either come to tell me that he's turned up or that he's dead."

"Neither. I'm looking for him." I smiled again as reassuringly as I could. "And I thought I'd junked the policeman look ages ago."

Policeman or not it had been unprofessional of me to offer hope by implying that Patrick might be alive, and the trouble with an opening lie is that the follow-up has to be bigger, the one after that bigger still.

"How did you find me?"

"Kevin Stapleton."

She nodded, unsurprised by the source of my information, but for all her acceptance she was still curious to know how much detail he'd gone into.

"But he didn't give you the information you needed?"

"He said he knows and likes Patrick, but not as well as you do." Present tense, further confirmation from me that he was still in the land of the living. She opened her hands towards me, inviting questions. "I know this sounds cheesy, Belinda, but what sort of bloke is he?"

"He's a one off," she said, without hesitation. "I mean I know you need a really high I.Q to be one, but I think he's a genius."

It was another of those words like 'brilliant', dying on its feet from misuse by people who apply the term to football players, dress designers and chefs when the only ability they need is to kick a ball, sew a hem or read a recipe.

"180 plus," I said. "That's the beauty of it, at that level it can't be measured, but you can still fall in love with it."

She laughed. "Is that what I've done? Fallen in love? It's the last thing I wanted to do I assure you. Clever men are not the best people to throw your cap at. They're difficult, temperamental and selfish. Those are euphemisms for cruel, unforgiving and egomaniacal, but once you've come under their spell, there's no going back."

"You sound as if it happened against your will."

She shook her head. "I knew exactly what I was doing. I might have backed off if people like Kevin Stapleton hadn't persuaded me not to."

"Matchmaker, eh?"

"He wasn't the only one." She tossed her hair back and screwed it into a loose knot. "Once my Dad took a liking to Pat, that was it. Sat me down one night, gave me the facts of life;

the real ones that asked who I'd rather be talking to in forty years time, Patrick Scott or Kevin Stapleton?"

"I agree with him. Were you and Kevin ever an item?"

She smiled. "I assume he's told you about our one night stand?"

"Only insofar as it applies to a woman called Henrietta. Have you ever met her?"

Mention of the name made her pause, not so much to invent as to dredge up a prepared response to this intrusion into the conversation. This competition?

"I don't think Henrietta ever existed. He made her up to get me jealous. More fool me, he succeeded."

"Why would he want to do that? Or are we back to the cruel, unforgiving egomaniac?"

She was quick on the defence. "He's not like that all the time. Mostly he's insecure, vulnerable, easily damaged."

"Maybe that's what you fell for?"

"No, but it made me tread warily. I was all for telling him about me and Kevin, for example, so we could start afresh, no secrets. Dad reckoned it was all too easy to hurt someone with a truth like that, then blithely ask for their their forgiveness. Why risk losing the person you love with some girly confession?"

"Especially since you'd already cleared the first hurdle. You'd got your boyfriend past your father."

"Funny, because they didn't get on to begin with," she recalled with affection. "They grew on each other. Like Dad said, Pat was so interesting, so downright clever."

"Ah, *that's* why you fell for him."

"You won't pin me down, Mr Hawk," she said with a laugh. "I fell for everything."

She reached out for her coffee, took a sip of it, then gestured for me to ask more questions. In answering those I'd already asked she had brought the man she clearly loved back into her life and that had been comforting.

"Kevin thought you might know where his parents live?"

She crawled over to a locker beside the door and took out a neat bundle of papers.

"I used to have their address on my phone but every time I searched my contacts, it would come up and I'd go mental all over again. The fact that he just walked out on me would…" She'd found their details on an old Google map print out. "Here it is. Gerald and Marion Scott,

Rushfarthing House, Clarebourne. It's one of those little villages in the no-man's land before you reach Milton Keynes."

"At which point you turn back?"

She acknowledged my aversion to Milton Keynes with a smile and I copied down the address in the notebook I still carry.

"When he disappeared my life kind of halted. Business has been okay, it runs itself, but I haven't felt like making new friends or pitching into a new relationship."

"How did you meet?"

"He came into the shop one day looking for prints for the walls of his new flat."

"Where was that?"

She pointed to my notebook. "At his parents' house. He kept coming back, bought paintings, old maps, lithographs, far more than he could possibly have needed. One day I asked how big this flat was. Not very, he said, and asked me out to lunch. That was it."

"Do you have a photo of him?"

She thought for a moment and frowned. "No, I don't, not even on my phone. That's weird, isn't it?"

"I'm not a great one for photos myself."

"My Dad's got one," she suddenly remembered. "He'll be back from Istanbul today, I can ask him."

"When's he due?"

She glanced at her watch, even though it couldn't give her an answer to my question. "Any time between now and midnight. Flying in via Amsterdam. Peculiar people the Dutch. Take off and land when they feel like it."

"All that funny tobacco. When did you last see Patrick?"

"October 31st, day before I went up north on a buying trip. I was hoping he'd come with me, I needed a driver, but he'd broken a bone in his foot a couple of months earlier. It was on the mend but he hadn't looked after it properly."

"When you say you needed a driver…"

"Never passed my test. Chrissie came with me in the end. We did auctions in Leeds, Manchester, Newcastle, Edinburgh, Glasgow."

"Did you call Patrick while you were away?"

"Twenty times. Called his mobile <u>and</u> the house, left messages to no avail. His parents were away too: Cuba, of all places. Do you know what I think?"

"No, but I can tell you were hacked off with him."

"I think he waited till we were all safely out of the way and then disappeared into the sunset."

It was an explanation that I'd listed and then struck out. "Did you have any inkling beforehand that he might do that?"

"No, but then people who are left behind never do, I gather."

"You've thought about it since? Any explanation?"

"Not really, no. I was just trying not to face the obvious."

"All the more reason why someone should have reported him missing."

She raised a hand. "Someone did. Me, the day after I returned from the north. Buckingham Police Station. November 12th. 2009."

Her answer took me by surprise, being a direct contradiction to what Jim Kelloway had told me an hour previously. I said, rather feebly, "Are you sure?"

"Of course I'm sure. He was my boyfriend."

If his disappearance had been reported to police, it meant the details of it had been removed, probably at the same time his NHS records were scrubbed. I was just about to come clean and help her 'to face the obvious', as she'd put it, when there was a knock on the cabin roof and Belinda's demeanour changed completely. The distressed beauty, who perversely had enjoyed reliving the agony of being dumped, became in a flash the child who'd just been told that Daddy was home. She leaped to her feet and rushed out of the cabin, up onto the towpath. I heard snippets of the exchange between two people, one of them Belinda squealing and wanting to know what he'd brought back for her. I peered out through the window, a genuine porthole, and up on the cobbled walkway she was embracing a man slightly taller than herself dressed in a long, dark overcoat and leather gloves. They clung on in silence and then separated to look at each other. He said something along the lines of 'what a welcome' and suggested dinner that evening. She wanted the Palestinian near the shop, he was fed up with Arab cookery, preferred somewhere Italian. And then she remembered me. I heard the name Patrick and saw the man close his eyes, just as his daughter had done with me initially. A family trait.

He stepped aboard and she handed him down his suitcase. She entered the cabin ahead of him and I rose to greet him. If it had seemed crowded with just the two of us there it now felt like a ghetto.

"Nathan Hawk," he said, when the handshaking was done. "D'you know, that name rings a bell."

He removed his overcoat and barely turned to look at his daughter as she took it from him, being far more concerned about where he knew me from. I put him at 50 years old, dressed in a tailored suit over a white shirt and grey silk tie. Beneath that he was clearly fit and athletic. And vain. The lines in his face had been dowsed in anti-wrinkle cream which had left behind a lacquered finish. The bastard still had a full head of hair, though, most of it bottle brown. He sat down on the sofa which obliged me to retake my place beside him putting us closer to each other than either of us cared for.

"Belinda says you've come about Patrick," he said, quietly. "I can't imagine what it feels like. Your only child just… disappears out of your life."

"You know his parents?"

"I went over to Rushfarthing House a couple of times." He glanced through to the galley where Belinda was making him tea and lowered his voice. "We had hopes of the two of them making a go of it. Wasn't to be."

"You liked him, then."

He nodded. "Very much. He wasn't afraid to be himself. Most kids these days are trying to be someone else, someone who doesn't exist - the thinnest, the richest, the most famous…"

"And they're off!" said Belinda, in the style of a race commentator.

Hewitt smiled. "Sorry. Hobby horse."

Belinda brought him his tea and placed it on the floor in front of him. He smiled up at her and, as she kissed him on the cheek, he reached into the magnificent hair as it fell in front of her. It was a more intimate gesture than I would have made to my daughters and her delight in it was more than either Ellie or Fee would've felt. She straightened up and wound her hair back into its loose knot.

"How was Istanbul?" I asked.

"Warmer than London. And doing better business, at least in my game."

He went on to tell me that ten years ago when he hit the big four zero he gave up his career in pharmaceuticals and went into something that interested him. Art. Buying and selling paintings. From drug dealer to art dealer, he quipped, adding that while most of the drugs he'd sold round the world cured people, so did paintings, sometimes more effectively. He wasn't making as much money now, of course, but he didn't need it.

"The Turkish art market is the latest to take off," he said with quiet excitement. He turned to include Belinda. "I bought two paintings this visit, one by a lady called Gizem Saka, another by a chap called Ozdemir Altan. They cost me an arm and a leg. I mean usually I just buy stuff I like, then wait for the painters to become famous…"

"Talking of pictures," I interrupted. "Belinda says you've got a photo of Patrick somewhere."

Confined though we were he managed to draw away slightly and stare at me with crystal sharp blue eyes, no bags under them, courtesy the anti-wrinkle cream.

"You've no photo of him?" he said. "A man you're trying to find? His parents must have given you one, surely."

"I haven't met them yet."

He found that equally puzzling. "Well, when you do, go easy on them. One of the reasons I stopped visiting was that I couldn't bear their hope. They believed, and still do I imagine, that Patrick will just walk back into their lives one day with a reasonable explanation for his disappearance. Life will carry on as before."

"And you don't think that's going to happen?"

"Do you? It's been a year, for Heaven's sake, without so much as a postcard."

"You said hope was one reason you didn't go back. Were there others?"

He glanced up at his daughter as if to check some conclusion they'd drawn at the time. "Gerald didn't want us to. He was afraid we might bring a touch of reality to things."

Belinda laid a hand on his shoulder. "Why don't you go dig out that photo, Mike?"

Children calling their parents by their first names was a vanity I'd always disapproved of, for no reason other than it smacked of disrespect, but in Belinda and her father's case it felt downright inappropriate. He smiled and she helped him on with his overcoat. He paused, one arm in a sleeve.

"If you've not met Gerald and Marion, it isn't them you're working for. Who, then?"

"A well-wisher."

He accepted my evasion with a nod and left.

When Mike Hewitt returned from his own boat with the photo it was quite a moment, one that had been creeping up on me for a month now, but when it arrived it still packed quite a punch. All of a sudden there he was - clear, imposing and memorable, the young man who'd been demanding so much of me, largely against my will. He was sitting with Belinda at the table on the roof of *Scorpius*, reading a paper. *The Guardian* strangely enough. He was a gangle of a man, tall and long boned, with curly fair hair and something old-fashioned about him. He wasn't as strange a looking boy as I'd imagined, in fact some would say that he was rather good looking. Belinda Hewitt was no doubt one of them. He'd been caught on camera just as he turned to it, the expression on his face one of passing irritation. When asked to smile for the shot he'd done no such thing. In fact he'd challenged it.

"Who took the photo?" I asked.

"I did," said Hewitt.

"Taken when you hadn't known each other long. He's on his guard."

Hewitt smiled his appreciation of my deduction. "He took some getting to know, did our Patrick, but once I did…"

I knew what Hewitt was talking about, It had taken me an age to get to know Maggie's Dad, reserve on both our parts, but eventually we became the greatest of friends. As for Patrick being clever, never mind a genius, that didn't show. Then again I'm not sure what cleverness looks like.

Back at Beech Tree, Jaikie had been in touch with Richard Slater who'd been so thrilled to hear from him, so flattered, so overjoyed, so everything a grown man should have grown out of. Even Jaikie had found it cloying but had persevered with my request for information about

ASC Slater had heard of the organisation, though not of Julien Raphael, but he would certainly ask Ralph Askew if the name meant anything. Ralph was his friend the Under Secretary at the Department of Energy, Slater reminded Jaikie for the two hundredth time. And Cambry's did deliver a patient to The Chiltern Clinic on August 15th 2009, Laura added.

After I'd told them about my own day I asked them to look at the photo of Patrick Scott, to examine it for thirty seconds and then write down their immediate impressions. They agreed to do so and, with a smattering of classroom humour, sat at the table with pens and paper while I showed them the snapshot. Just as had happened with me on board the narrowboat, he became real as opposed to an idea which had grown out of my need to go combine harvesting in the dark. They wanted to talk about that, his sudden humanity, but I made them concentrate on the job in hand.

Laura's immediate response was that Patrick clearly felt uncomfortable at being the centre of attention. She couldn't resist adding a medical observation. "If he carries on slouching like that he'll end up with back problems."

"He's ended up with more than that," I said.

Jaikie's summary was much as I'd expected. "Skinny sod, a poor man's Matthew McConnaughey without the presence."

"Oh, I think he's rather attractive," said Laura.

"And Belinda Hewitt, who is even more beautiful in the flesh than in the photo, thought the sun shone. So, possibly, did another girl called Henrietta."

"Look at that jutting bottom lip," said Laura, with the same delight she reserves for Martin Falconer. "Sulky, volatile, mercurial. Clever, though."

Jaikie thought he must have missed something, took the photo back and re-examined it.

"Everyone seems to think he's clever," I said. "Belinda, her father, Kevin Stapleton. Mind you he was a moody sod as well, inclined to flare up, mouth off and storm out. So I have to ask: instead of being chopped up for dog food did he just walk out one day and never look back? People do."

Jaikie smiled. "Second thoughts, Dad?"

"Not my style I know, but for all her beauty and all her distress there's something about Belinda Hewitt which isn't quite as irresistible as people would have me believe."

They wanted me to elaborate, of course. I declined to do so. I was back in the realms of insight, intuition and gut feeling. I hear those words tossed around in everyday conversation and I recoil, yet even as I do so I can't completely deny their validity. I'll leave it at that, especially where Belinda Hewitt's concerned. Suffice to say that I felt something about her was... unsafe.

11

I wanted to visit Gerald and Marion Scott alone mainly because homes where a child has gone missing are the most soul destroying places in the world. Everything has been put on hold in expectation of the loved one's return, or end-of-the-world news that they never will. And although the mechanics of daily life are reduced to their rightful essentials and nobody cares if dinner is late, a bill unpaid, a car unwashed, those involved in the loss suffer a crippling mixture of hope and despair in which every extraneous sound, every shadow across the wall, might be followed by the subject of their anguish just breezing in. Mike Hewitt had found the Scotts' hope unbearable and had asked me to go easy on them. I didn't plan to. My intention was to leave their house having told them the truth about Patrick, insofar as I knew it, and I didn't want Jaikie looking over my shoulder while I did that.

However, he was insisting that he accompany me and in light of my reluctance was giving me his beaten dog performance, the one where the victim quietly agrees to do anything you say but thinks you're a grade one bastard for saying it. I tried the 'stay and take care of Laura' angle but it didn't work because we both knew George Corrigan was nearby. I'd pointed out the signs the previous evening and it wasn't just a matter of the odd fag end in the ditch, or a half finished sandwich in the spinney the other side of the lane. It was the top button of his check shirt. I'd found it under the kitchen window as I went to the gate for yesterday's post. Its fate was never to be sewn back on

In a *volte-face* of principle I finally agreed to Jaikie coming with me, justifying the change of heart as a chance to ask him a few questions, such as why Jodie hadn't been near us lately. Did it have anything to do with the money he owed Laura, Corrigan and Jamal? Not to mention me. He still hadn't cashed those dollars, still had no money in his pocket, but as with all returning children he'd grown comfortable with me paying for coffees and the odd lunch on the road. Shame no longer entered into it. There'd been no further displays of forgetfulness on his part, just an understanding between us that I knew something was amiss.

Belinda Hewitt had been right about Clarebourne where the Scotts lived. Set in a no-man's land of similar villages it had been untroubled for hundreds of years, and then some Civil

Servant, charged with conjuring up homes to live in, had hit on the village of Milton Keynes and turned it into a city. Ironically, this might well be Clarebourne's salvation, the fact that all too close to it lay the ugliest experiment in social manipulation that Europe has seen since the Third Reich. People would steer clear of it.

Rushfarthing House lay at the end of a single-track lane, broken and pot-holed by winter. The house was a curiosity in itself, being of Georgian design and set in twenty acres, and it gave the impression of being a hideaway, built by a monied family to house an embarrassing relative perhaps. Why else would it be so tucked away? The rusty iron gates hung on two stone pillars and stood open, not as a welcoming gesture, but to accommodate the Tesco delivery van which had arrived minutes before us. As I pulled up beside it, a woman whom I took to be Marion Scott, was thanking the driver and now turned her attention to Jaikie and me.

"Can I help?" she asked, as we got out of the Land Rover.

She looked ready for battle, dressed in a sheepskin body warmer, gardening gloves on her hands and brandishing a pair of secateurs.

"I was hoping to speak with Mr Scott," I said. "Is he home?"

She thought about the question while she looked us over with suspicion, then said, "I don't know."

The delivery van was driving off by now and, hearing its departure, Gerald Scott emerged from the house holding an electronic handset. He pointed it at one of the stone pillars and jabbed at a button, twice, three times but nothing happened. He questioned the device as to why this was, apparently expecting an answer, and walked towards the gates, still clicking away. Not until he was within ten feet of it did the mechanism creak into life and the two gates began the arthritic process of closing on each other. Gerald Scott turned and walked back to the house, pleased with himself.

"I think it's just the batteries," he said to his wife and brought us into the conversation with, "It's a bit of a toss up. Spend thousands on a system we can operate from inside the house or make do with what we've got. Who are you?"

"They've delivered the groceries," said his wife.

Having just seen the Tesco van leave, he knew that wasn't the case and gave us his full attention. It was an interesting face, boney and delicate. The eyes were quick, blue grey and far younger than the rest of him. What gave his age away - mid seventies - was the paper thin skin with its road map of veins just below the surface.

"My name is Nathan Hawk," I said. "I'd like to talk to you about Patrick."

He looked across at his wife. "He isn't here at the moment. We expect him back, shortly. If you leave your name and a telephone number…"

"Are you from the papers?" she asked.

"No, I'm a retired policeman."

"You say that as if it might give me confidence?" said Gerald, expecting his wife to appreciate the sarcasm. He pointed at Jaikie. "Who's he?"

I told him that Jaikie was my son but that didn't soften Gerald either. As far as he was concerned we were bad news, here to make capital out of the tragedy which had left him and his wife in a paralysing limbo for nearly a year. I stooped and picked up one of the boxes, nodded for Jaikie to grab the other.

"Kitchen?" I said to Marion.

Inside, Rushfarthing House was empty, not in any literal sense, in fact we must have passed a small fortune in antiques on our way through. But every piece lacked an… attachment to the room it stood in and the kitchen was as forlorn as any, with breakfast dishes still scattered across the vast pine table, dead flowers in the centre of it, a couple of baited mousetraps on the floor.

I settled the box of groceries on one of the ladder-back chairs and Jaikie placed his on top of mine. When the Scotts entered, Gerald tried to get beyond the politeness we'd shown and return to his annoyance, his anxiety, that we'd come to ask questions about his son.

"Right, well, thank you," he said, eventually. "Busy day. You'll want me to open the gates again."

"Mr Scott we need to talk about Patrick."

"No."

"You're being hasty, Gerald," said his wife. "These gentleman might know things."

Gerald doubted that very much and for a moment or two I mistook his wife for the half of this marriage with its feet still on the ground.

"When did you last see him, Mrs Scott?"

"Oh, please, call me Marion."

"When did you last see Patrick, Marion?"

The question bothered her, as if it had come straight out of the blue, and hadn't been asked five seconds previously.

"Monday," she said.

"Monday the 20th of October, a year ago," Gerald modified. "Just before we went on holiday."

Marion looked down at the shopping, then at the secateurs still in her hands. If we hadn't been there she might have voiced her dilemma but, given our presence, Gerald spared her the need and took both secateurs and gardening gloves from her and laid them on the table. She mouthed her thanks and began to unpack the groceries, examining each item before deciding on its place. Jaikie tried his best to help and she smiled at his willingness.

"Do you know my son?" she asked him.

"I know his girlfriend, Belinda."

The frost on Gerald thawed a little. "Ah, the lovely Belinda. We haven't seen her for some time. Do you remember her, Marion?"

"Yes, of course I do."

Clearly she didn't which was why Gerald went on to describe her. "Quite a beauty. Red hair, Botticelli's Birth of Venus, that sort of thing."

Marion smiled. "What is it with men and red hair? Mine is grey."

I wasn't sure if it was said in playful regret, or as a simple statement of fact. Whichever it was, Marion Scott must once have been pretty, rather than beautiful, but time and gravity had played their downward tricks on her face. The eyes were bagged, the cheeks gouged, the skin on her neck turkeyed. She wore no retaliatory make-up and, like her husband, she dressed in the plainest of clothes which had survived way beyond their natural lifespan.

"So you haven't seen Patrick for a year?" I asked.

"If that's what my husband says, I'm sure it's true. But that's Patrick for you. Bee in his bonnet and off he goes." She took a box of eggs from Jaikie and turned to the fridge. "That doesn't mean to say…"

She paused as if the simple act of placing the eggs on a rack combined with thinking about her son required more of her than she could give.

"Doesn't mean what?" I prompted.

"That he's lost. But if he were to be, could you find him?"

Jaikie glanced at me, wondering how much of a lie I was prepared to tell.

"I'd need to know certain things about him," I said.

"Are you one of these private detectives?" Gerald asked, clearly not a fan of the species.

I nodded and side-stepped. "I gather Belinda's father came to visit you."

Gerald nodded and turned to include his wife. "Mike Hewitt, dear. Good looking and well-mannered, was your verdict." It meant nothing, so he gave her more. "He bought and sold paintings, took a particular fancy to the one of your father on the stairs? Said he knew the artist's work?"

That struck a chord and she was delighted. "So he did. He too thought Patrick was lost. Why does everyone believe that?"

"People are worried," I explained. "When was Mike Hewitt here?"

She looked at me, trying to keep pace, unwilling to accept that it was a losing battle. I tried to help.

"Belinda's father, Mike Hewitt?"

"Oh, last Tuesday," she replied.

She turned to her husband who said, "I think you'll find that it's longer ago than that, dear. He stopped coming about the same time as Belinda."

"A year ago?" I said.

"But it was definitely a Tuesday," his wife insisted. "I remember because Mrs Brennan was here…"

"The cleaner," said Gerald.

"…she comes on a Tuesday."

I was nodding a great deal, not because I agreed with anything - there wasn't much to take issue with - but a show of acquiescence can bring you closer to a goal in a fraction of the time spent frowning or, God forbid, shaking your head.

"Belinda told me that Patrick lives in a flat here," I said. "May I see it?"

"If it will help you, I think you should," said Marion, with a sudden burst of purpose. She realised that she'd made a decision without first deferring to her husband. "Is that alright, Gerald, if you take Mr…?" She faltered at the name, having thought she would remember it.

"Hawk," I said.

"Hawk, Hawk, Hawk," she muttered, trying to commit it to her crumbling memory.

"Subfamily *Accipitrinae*, dear," he said, gently.

I've been called many things in my life, but this was the first time anyone had broken into Latin. Gerald pointed to the doorway through to the hall and I followed him, first suggesting that Jaikie stay and help Marion finish unpacking the shopping.

The stairs were a wide, bannistered sweep which turned halfway up and then rose to a landing off of which were half a dozen bedrooms behind heavy oak doors. On the walls hung oil paintings, mainly portraits, including the one of Marion's father which Mike Hewitt had admired. He was an academic, Gerald told me, in fact Marion came from a dynasty of zoologists and had lectured in the subject herself. Her speciality had been *siphonatera*, better known to the man in the street as the common or garden flea, a creature she still held in high regard.

A second, narrower flight of stairs took us to the attic flat. It comprised just three rooms built into the roof space: a bedroom, a living room and a small kitchen and, just as Belinda Hewitt had led me to believe, every wall was crammed with prints, maps and lithographs bought from her shop. In all other regards, however, it was a pretty anaemic place for a man in his early twenties, uncomfortably clean and well looked after. Patrick's mother came up here every day, Gerald said, to check that the place was ready for his return and if something needed doing Mrs Brennan would see to it. As a result the dishes and cutlery were stacked on the drainer, the carpets were hoovered, clean clothes were folded on a freshly made bed.

Gerald followed me round, hands deep in his pocket, as I strolled this crow's nest to see if it had anything useful to tell me. Whatever it might once have revealed had been removed, not by Marion or Mrs Brennan but by Gerald himself, or so his confidence that I wouldn't find anything suggested. Even so, once I'd made my brief sweep of the place he was keen to go back downstairs, anxious that in his absence his wife might have told Jaikie more than he wanted us to know. I perched on one of the stools at the breakfast bar and Gerald waited as patiently as he could.

"So, have you never wonder what might have happened to him?"

"Of course I have," he said, quietly irritated. "Do you really think I took the disappearance of my only son in my stride?"

"How did you cope?"

He removed his hands from his pockets and laid them on the counter, fingers splayed. "I gave myself a fresh explanation every day as to why he'd gone, until I couldn't bear it any longer. The speculation was exhausting, reducing me to a feeble old man. So I stopped."

"Belinda was the one who reported him missing."

"Yes, to be honest I thought he'd gone up north with her, but apparently not."

I'm not sure which of us was steering the other away from the obvious truth that Patrick was no longer alive, but we were avoiding it like the plague.

"You liked her? You thought she was good for him? Along with her father, you thought they'd make a go of things?" He nodded. "Did Patrick see a future for them?"

Gerald nodded. "He once told me so."

"Then why do you think he left without a word?"

"We were in Cuba at the time."

"I know where you were, Mr Scott, and it has nothing to do with the point I'm making."

He stared at me, offended by my implication that perhaps he hadn't asked the right questions, of himself, of Belinda, even of the police.

"I told you, I've a hundred explanations for why he disappeared, all of them leading me right back here to this very room where I last saw him. I came up to say we were off to the airport, October the 22nd a year ago. It seems like twenty. You've clearly never had anyone go missing on you, Mr Hawk. Oh, no doubt as a policeman you've overseen your fair share of disappearances, but that isn't quite the same. When your only child... leaves, it's absurd to say that a piece of you dies because that isn't what happens at all. That essential part which is them doesn't die. It lives on, in the sharpest of relief, only somewhere else where you can't reach it. And while you picture it fifty times a day, this other life they might be living, you know you'll never be part of it. That's the hell you go through and I wouldn't wish it on my worst enemy."

He stopped, turned away and headed to the door. He'd spoken movingly to be sure, but I knew no more about his son now than I had done when I'd carried the shopping in.

"What sort of lad was he? Was he sociable, arty, sporty? Did he have any particular interests? I mean I know he liked ski-ing..."

"He was a rather reserved lad, as a matter of fact. Didn't have many friends."

"He had a couple that I know of, apart from Belinda," I said. "A chap called Kevin, a girl called Henrietta."

He didn't like that for some reason. "If you're suggesting that he was two-timing Belinda…"

"Friends, I said, not lovers. So you've never met this Henrietta?"

"Certainly not."

"I suppose you're going to tell me that he wasn't very clever either, even though I've been told he was a brilliant engineer."

He gestured to the door but I stayed put and tried to soften a little.

"Please don't think I can't appreciate the jam you're in, Gerald. Your wife."

"I can manage so long as people respect her right to fade in her own particular way and my right to stand by her while she does so."

"You'll keep him alive and on the verge of returning home, until she's forgotten him?"

He paused for a moment. "That isn't a crime."

"Not one you can be charged with, no, but what about the young man who lives in that world you can't reach? I think you and I both believe that he's dead. I think he's been killed. If you like I can take you through my reasoning, I can describe the dreadful things that were done to his body…"

"I'd rather you didn't," he said, sternly.

"You'd sooner go on pretending it hadn't happened? It's not an option for me, I'm afraid, so I'll ask you again, only this time the real question. Why do you think your son might have been murdered?"

He shook his head in an end of tether show of despair. "I really don't have the faintest idea."

"I don't believe you. You've kept far too much back, from the police, the press, from me today. You've disinfected this flat till there isn't a trace of him. And you want me to believe that it's all for love, the altruism of sparing your wife the agony of losing her only child? Well, I think there's another reason…"

"I want you to leave now."

"…I don't know what it is but at least one other person has been killed to stop me finding out. His name is Charles Drayton. Does that mean anything?"

He gestured once again to the open door and this time I fell in with his wishes and we made our way downstairs. On the main staircase I paused at the stone window and looked out over the gardens to the rear of Rushfarthing House, across the village rooftops of Clarebourne and onward into the cold haze of the horizon. The only thing which broke the view was a web of pylons fanning out from the changing station at Steeple Claydon, carrying electricity to Aylesbury, Buckingham, Milton Keynes and beyond. In the garden itself there was little colour, of course, with it being October, nearly November. The outbuildings, of stone like the house itself, were in reasonable repair, though the paths leading up to them were punctured by weeds. Set in the patio right below us was a swimming pool, accessible from the French windows no doubt. It was looking sorry for itself. However much water had been emptied at the end of the Summer, the rains of late September had filled it up again. A Winter cover had been applied but the central dip showed the water to be as green as pea soup. Gerald saw me notice it.

"Patrick's the only one who uses it now," he said, returning us to the charade of his son still being alive. "I shall open it up again in the Spring, if need be. It'll endorse the proposition that he might suddenly appear. You won't tell her anything to the contrary, will you Mr Hawk?"

Downstairs, Marion and Jaikie were getting on famously. They'd finished unpacking and she'd taken him through to the living room, a room furnished with baggy sofas and other furniture which Mrs Brennan had little regard for if the cuts and bruises on the table legs, the dresser and bookcases were anything to go by.

Jaikie had been telling Marion Scott about *All Good Men and True* and she'd struggled to get a grasp on it. It was a film and Jaikie was an actor. Those two facts she could cope with. Where she came unstuck was over the story being set in the last war, seventy odd years ago and Jaikie being only thirty. He'd tried to help her, saying it was a kind of reconstruction, a snippet of history retold for the present day. The frowning began when she asked about the events which had befallen him in Casablanca in 1942 and he came up against her superior knowledge of history, locked away in her memory and now under attack. What she'd always accepted as fact was being retold to her as fiction and unable to separate the two she'd become distressed and tearful. I've never known Jaikie so pleased to see me walk in through a door.

Marion herself turned to me and went off at another, brighter tangent. "Is this the man you told me about?"

"My father, Nathan Hawk."

"Subfamily *Accipitrinae*. You didn't say he was an actor."

"I'm the actor."

"Right…"

She looked at her husband to see just how badly she'd got things wrong and he smiled, benignly.

"Mr Hawk and his son are just leaving, dear. Where did I put the handset for the gates?"

She smiled. "Ah, so I'm not the only one who forgets things."

"It's been a pleasure meeting you," Jaikie said, giving her his smile.

She remained seated, took the offered hand and gazed up at him and for a moment her life became simple and straightforward again, untroubled by the havoc in her mind as she flirted with a young man she liked the look of. "Likewise. I do hope we meet again."

She suddenly tensed up, raising a finger for us to listen to something outside in the front garden. I'd heard it a split second earlier, the sound of the wrought iron gates being rattled, not as if someone were trying to force them open, more as if they were climbing over them.

Gerald excused himself from the room and it was obvious from the manner and speed of his departure that he was off to meet someone he didn't much care for. His wife was resourceful enough to know that a situation like this required cover-up and began to speak in a loud voice about the history of Cuba. Encountering her usual trouble with time scale she rambled back and forth between the slave trade of the 1600s and the government of Fidel Castro.

Inevitably, the conversation taking place in the kitchen began to reach us the more heated it became. There were three voices, including Gerald Scott's. His side of the argument was considered and unhurried but his visitors were fully intent upon getting answers to their questions. The younger man had a high-pitched, rasping voice and he might easily have been mistaken for a woman but for the occasional heavy thump on the table. His companion, older by the sound of it, was simply coarse and loud.

"Who are these people?" I asked Marion.

She stopped her brief lecture immediately. "I don't know."

I decided not to chase her down on the matter but moved closer to the door, in spite of a warning from Jaikie to take care. Through in the kitchen the younger man was now making the plates jump on the table in time with each of his points.

"You know what we want. You've known all along. Why don't you spare yourself more grief."

"I gave you the computer," said Gerald Scott, calmly.

"There was nothing on the bloody computer. Names, addresses, a glorified notebook."
I could picture Gerald's grandiloquent shrug. "Well, I'm sorry, that's all I ever had."
The elder of his two visitors rose from the table, scraping back his chair as he did so.
"Where did you put the car?" he asked. "They don't just evaporate. Have you sold it?"
"I've told you before, I've no idea what you're talking about."

"You do know the reason we're asking, I hope?" This was the younger man again. "People up ahead of us are getting impatient and here are you and your wife out here all on your own…"

"That sort of talk won't get you far!" said Gerald, recognising the threat.

"Nor will your cantankerousness. Last time we were here you said you'd have another look for a disc, you'd go through his things. Have you done that, or do we have to look ourselves?"

Gerald assured them that he'd searched high and low but still hadn't found anything. Through the gap at the hinges of the sitting room door and across the passageway I had a glimpse of the two men. Both were on their feet now, both had their backs to me, but even so I could tell from the way they stood, the way they interacted, that I knew them. First thoughts always shoot back over thirty years of being a police officer; every villain I ever nicked is lodged in my memory but these two weren't from those unhallowed ranks. They were later, possibly even recent. So where had I been and met two men, one with a squeaky voice and a heavy fist, the other his gofor?

They still showed no sign of turning round. Instead they were leaning across the table to Gerald who sat like an elderly cat, refusing to expend unnecessary energy while they continued to harangue him about a disc, a car and the possibility of another computer. His answer at every stage was the same. He didn't know what they were talking about and, from personal experience, I can vouch for that being the most aggravating answer of all, liable to bring out the worst in the inquisitor.

It was probably the constant reference to the car which led me to their identity and just as I realised it, the elder of the two men turned away from his companion and confirmed my suspicion with a perfectly etched profile. He was the elder of the two I'd seen in the distance at Charles Drayton's house in Tilbury. They'd been looking at the red MG Sports his wife had been left with and, according to her, they'd returned that same evening and bought it. I turned and went over to the French windows.

"Where are you off to?" Jaikie asked, rising.

"To get something from the Land Rover."

"Not the tyre lever?" he said, apprehensively.

"Something far more dangerous than that. Carry on with the history lesson, Mrs Scott."

As I stepped out onto the terrace I heard her pick up from exactly where she'd left off and she was still in full flood when I returned. I remember thinking what a fascinating place Cuba sounded, what a superb teacher Marion Scott must have been. However, her class of one was no longer listening. He was standing in my way.

"Two blokes, Dad? Let me help."

It was an awkward moment at which to be torn. I wanted to impress him with my ability to handle a situation like this but didn't want him to see me at my very worst, reducing two fellow human beings to a blubbering pile. He'd seen me lose my temper often enough, of course, but no one in my family has ever taken that seriously. I patted his cheek and declined his offer.

In the kitchen an uneasy calm had descended following Gerald's inability or, as the two men would have it, his bloody-minded refusal to help them. They were now planning to search the house, top to bottom, in spite of Gerald reminding them that they'd done so twice before, cellar to rafters.

"On both those occasions, we left everything intact," said the squeaker, "This time we might not be so careful."

It was an almost perfect cue, as I'm sure Jaikie would have agreed, and I muffed it. I'd meant to enter saying, 'More careful than you were at Plum Tree Cottage?' and halfway through the sentence I forgot which fruit tree Laura's house was named after. Or, to put it Jaikie's way, I dried. The two men straightened up and turned to me, not so much alarmed by my presence as bewildered by my opening blunder.

"Who the fuck are you?" asked the older of the two.

He was a smartly dressed slab of a man, grey suited over a navy blue shirt and tie. In its time his face must have been an impressive one but here, in its late fifties, it had developed unsightly skin markings, moles they used to be called but these days nobody's quite sure. His hair was still its original off brown, receding from a broad forehead more used to head-butting than to thinking. The eyes were narrowed beneath brows which should have been trimmed ages ago.

"Gerald, do me a favour," I said. "Go back to the sitting room, look after Marion."

"Why?"

"Just go!"

He didn't move a muscle apart from those in his jaw. "My house! I shall do whatever I please."

The squeaker smiled at me. "Everything going to plan so far, then?"

It didn't take Sigmund Freud to work out that he'd been at the mercy of his vocal chords since puberty. When other kids' voices had broken his had continued to whistle away at the same pitch as his sister's. At school, where no doubt he was weedy and underdeveloped in other ways, they'd given him no quarter. When he was old enough he hit the gym and the result today was a man of average height with muscles straining at every seam, not one of them part of the original blueprint.

"How can we help you?" he said.

"Tell me what you're looking for. I might be able to help *you*."

He was trying to work out where he knew me from but we hadn't got close enough at Tilbury for him to be sure. He reached out and gently karate chopped the table.

"We were having a private conversation, the details of which are none of your business."

The voice had aspirations to be posh and its owner could put a reasonable sentence together which meant that somebody had taken the trouble to educate him. I doubted if it was his companion who said, pure Sarf London, "Fuck off before you get hurt."

"I've got a few questions first." The squeaker looked at me, daring me to put them to him. "Who paid you to push Charles Drayton over the edge?"

He held out an arm to restrain the older man from launching himself at me.

"I refer you back to my uncle's previous suggestion," he said.

Uncle and nephew, then, not father and son as I'd assumed at Tilbury. Still a family business, though.

"Who paid you? And what's this disc you're so keen to get your hands on? Is that what you were looking for at Plum Tree Cottage?"

He lowered his arm. "You really are one for sticking your neck out, Mister…?"

"Hawk."

He nodded as if it meant something to him. "So nice to know the name of those whose bones you're about to break. One last chance, which I don't expect you to take for a moment, but manners, you know. Leave."

I was feeling in my pocket for the spray. I'd bought a batch of them from an internet site in The Czech Republic and given Laura one to keep in her car, stored the rest in the Land Rover's map locker. I'd omitted to tell her that it was illegal to either buy or own anything which contained *Oleoresin Capsicum* in the UK even though, in the States, the police use it on students regularly. I'd bought it to reassure myself that, were she ever attacked in the dark and dangerous streets of Thame, she'd be able to put up a crippling defence. So far she hadn't had occasion to use it. This, the device's first outing, was something of a gamble.

I was locating the nozzle, releasing it from its sideways on locked position, turning the small canister in my hand and settling my forefinger on the spray button when the nephew, having tired of waiting for me to respond, casually gave his uncle permission to beat me to a pulp. The uncle took two steps towards me, I drew and fired. A two second burst of brown liquid hit him right between the eyes.

It was the fact that I'd used such a delicate weapon on him that took him by surprise, juddered him to a halt. He stood wondering why I was counting down aloud. Five, four, three, two, one… and at that point my attacker roared with agony, bent forward at the shoulders the quicker for his hands to reach his eyes and start rubbing them. Big mistake. All that does, according to the accompanying leaflet, is deliver the contents of the spray to the mucous membranes even faster and while the eyes start to burn and the breath begins to shorten, so fluid pours from every hole in the head. The assailant is as neatly disabled as if I were to fire my old Smith & Wesson revolver at him. Yet still he kept advancing, arms flailing trying to grab me, missing me by yards, buckling by degrees until he fell to the floor.

The effect of the spray on the uncle gave the nephew a change of heart. For all his muscle-bound fitness he backed away, afraid of what was to come, certainly, but more terrified by the prospect of handling it alone. Lost for words, he scissored his arms as I shortened the distance between us then sprayed again like some vengeful racoon. The fluid hit him on the bridge of the nose, I counted out loud, and within five seconds he was screaming his head off. He called out for help. He thought he was going blind. He would kill me. He wanted water. Jesus

Christ, what had I done to him. He too kept rubbing his eyes when he'd have been better holding them open and allowing them to water. He stumbled and fell to his hands and knees, sapped of energy and the will to stand up again.

"Jaikie! In here!" I called.

Jaikie was already there beside me, drawn by the screams, and now wanting to know what I'd done to the two visitors. I showed him the spray, re-locked it and put it back in my pocket.

"Gerald, have you got any carpet tape?" I asked.

"Erm…"

"We've got half an hour before the spray wears off. Masking tape, gaffer tape, any tape?"

He got his amazement under control and turned to his wife who had entered in Jaikie's wake.

"Have we any tape, dear?"

"What have you done to them?" she asked, both amused and horrified.

The easiest course of action was to give all three of them a brief run down on the properties of *Oleoresin Capsicum*, the effect it had had on uncle and nephew, then look for tape.

Once uncle and nephew had been bound hand and foot with masking tape I was able to rummage through the younger one's pockets and discover that his name was Trader Gaffney, poor bastard. On top of a high pitched voice he'd been given a daft Christian name to cope with. He was aged 25, with an address on his driver's licence somewhere in Debden, the Essex end of the Central Line. I questioned him as best I could, given that he was lying on the kitchen floor with concentrated chilli broiling his face in the fluid streaming out of his eyes, nose and mouth. I asked what his association with Charles Drayton had been. There wasn't one, he said. Right, so had he been paid to bring Drayton's life to a premature end? If so, by whom? His response to that was to ask what the fuck I was talking about.

He begged me for water. I said he could have water in return for his first truthful answer. What were they doing there today? What did Gerald have that they wanted so badly? The question was met with a deep-seated, spluttery cough and some calling on Jesus, Mary and Joseph for mercy. A Catholic seam ran through the Gaffney family, I surmised. What had they expected to find on the computer Gerald gave them? I said, when the coughing and beseeching died down. Ask Gerald, Trader replied, but Gerald was already shaking his head in bewilderment. What car were they talking about? The MG? And who were the people he'd described as being up ahead of him? With his eyes tightly closed he asked again for water, as if to trade it for an answer. I went over to the sink and ran the tap. The uncle piped up.

"He ain't giving you water, Tray, he's taking the piss."

I stooped down to the uncle and reached into his jacket pocket. With his wrists bound in front of him, ankles taped all the way up the shins, the only part of him that was vaguely mobile was his upper body: head, neck, shoulders. Prone though he was, when I got within range he launched himself at me with the snarl of a Japanese fighting dog and bit me on the arm. He didn't catch the flesh but it did rip a three inch gash in the sleeve of my beloved leather jacket. I could have killed him.

"Give me that roll of tape!" I said to Jaikie.

We turned uncle onto his front and while Jaikie knelt between his shoulder blades I wound a length of tape around his head at mouth level. When I stood up again, Trader was already asking me to be reasonable and not do the same to him.

"His name is Jerome Gaffney," he said, panicking. "He's 58, unmarried, lives in Loughton."

I thanked him, rolled him over and taped up his mouth.

"Now what?" asked Jaikie with his irritating need to have life spelt out for him.

I took him to one side and told him that by close of play we'd have the Gaffneys in police custody, ready for questioning about Charles Drayton's death. With any luck forensic evidence, maybe even fingerprints from Drayton's dying room, would tie them to Charlie's premature end. In practical terms it meant throwing them in the back of the Land Rover and driving over to Tilbury.

"Alan Baker?" said Jaikie.

I nodded. "Jim Kelloway's friend. Jaikie, I shouldn't be doing this to you…"

It was a half-hearted attempt to say sorry and to thank him, all in one go, and maybe offer him a way out even though I didn't expect him to take it.

"Bit late for that," he said, looking down at the prostrate Gaffneys. "Which one first? Uncle or nephew?"

"Uncle. You take his legs, I'll take the arms."

12

I phoned Detective Sergeant Alan Baker from the M25, somewhere on the M25, in the molten lava of heavy traffic, which meant that I spent much of the conversation asking him to repeat what he'd said. The gist of it was this:

"Alan? My name is Nathan Hawk. I'm an old friend of Jim Kelloway?"

"I haven't seen Jim for must be four years. How's he keeping?"

"Fine." Haven't seen him? How about spoken to him? Didn't he get in touch one evening two weeks ago? Subject a murder, young man called Patrick Scott? "He said you were just the guy I needed."

Baker laughed, and yes I'd say that it was a womaniser's laugh, one always in search of the innuendo.

"Quite a few people agree with him. What can I do for you?"

"He said he'd talk to you about a death on your manor, Charles Drayton."

"Charlie, yes. No great loss to humanity, but painful way to go. Oesophageal Cancer."

"Two weeks ahead of time. Crucial fact. Didn't he mention it?"

"Who?"

"Jim Kelloway."

"It could be my filing system, or… when was this?"

And round we went until I was forced to accept that Jim hadn't been in touch with his old friend. Was that to be taken personally, I wondered? Had Kelloway made all the right noises that night I called in at Thame nick, only to dismiss my proposition that Drayton had been murdered as bad luck for Charlie Drayton but nothing to do with Patrick Scott?

"You think he was given a shove, then?" said Baker, making the first hopeful remark in our conversation. "He had enough bloody enemies, I know that."

"I not only think it, I've got the two blokes responsible tied up in the back of my Land Rover."

"Jesus Christ! Sorry, I didn't catch your name?"

"Nathan Hawk."

I cited a few of the cases I'd been involved in and gradually he began to take me seriously.

"Who are they, these two?"

"Jerome Gaffney and his nephew, Trader. Know 'em?"

He chuckled with sour delight. "We know 'em alright."

As I'd expected he was the kind of copper who had a special place where non-office work could be carried out and he gave me directions to it. It was a farmhouse off the B1040, three miles beyond East Tilbury. He'd make his way there right now and looked forward to meeting me.

Nobody in our vehicle spoke much during the journey, which was understandable in the Gaffneys' case. For the best part of an hour they did the sensible thing, conserved energy and gradually the seventy percent chilli factor, or more correctly the pain that went with it, began to wear off. It took longer than the leaflet said it would, but isn't that the case with everything?

It was one o'clock when we left the M25 and made our way towards the Thames Estuary and as we neared our destination it became clear why Alan Baker had chosen this spot for his non-office work. Thirty miles from the centre of London, we could have been on Exmoor, the Shetlands, even the west coast of Ireland, if isolation was the yardstick. This was deepest Essex, though, north side, the only place you get those square pebble-dashed bungalows, one small room either side of a recessed door, kitchen and a bathroom at the back. And, at the roadside, a domino rally of signs saying that Eggs and Potatoes are for sale, just about all the surrounding land is good for.

Coalfort Lane rose and fell, rose and fell, and after each peak we expected to see the river mouth stretching out way before us. When it finally appeared, Baker had told us, we would know we'd reached Fort Farm. I turned into it, through the open metal gate and pulled up beside a block-work pen, concrete floor, gully along one side to a drain, a place that once held animals. Not anymore. The land around us and down to the Estuary was arable, more potatoes I guess, and the farmyard itself was used as a storage facility. The house beyond, 1940s and rendered grey, was ramshackle: the onshore breeze whistled through broken windows and collapsing doorways.

I opened the tailgate and hauled the Gaffneys into sitting positions. Jerome was pleased that his unpredictability was a major concern to me, that I took extreme care as I unwound the tape from his head. The last twelve inches of it tore at his lips but he barely flinched. I handed him a bottle of water I'd bought on the motorway. He pretended not to care if he drank or not, then downed half a litre of it.

Trader wasn't so proud. When I removed the tape he thanked me, grabbed at the bottle with his bound hands and drained the rest of it. I told them to take a pee, over by the drain. Jerome asked how they would reach it. I told him to pretend he was in a sack race and jump. As he stood relieving himself Trader asked if there'd be any long term effects from the spray. I said that so long as neither he nor his uncle was asthmatic, had a heart condition or was pregnant, there was no real danger … other than me being willing to use it again. We didn't bother re-taping their mouths, simply closed the pen gate on them and said they could scream their guts out. The nearest human being was a mile and half away. And if Jerome bit me again, I would knock his fucking teeth out.

It was another half hour before Detective Sergeant Alan Baker arrived, along with a side-kick fifteen years his junior but clearly a willing pupil. The rain came with them, ahead of a rising tide, and the Gaffneys hunkered down into a corner of their pen to spare themselves the worst of it. They stood up when they heard the police van pull up beside the Land Rover. Baker walked over to me, hand outstretched and introduced himself.

"Good to meet you, Guvnor," he said. "This must be your son, yeah?"

He knew full well who Jaikie was, he just wondered what he was doing here. He turned to his side-kick.

"This isn't my son, thank Christ, though it often feels that way."

We chuckled dutifully as DC Neil Manning introduced himself.

Alan Baker had the cheap good looks of a ladies' man, and the meticulous preservation, a square face with steady grey eyes set against a pampered skin. Late forties, fair hair and a gold chain at his throat. There'd be more bling back home in the jewellery box, I imagined, not the kind of stuff you wear in a squad room unless you want the piss taken interminably.

He wandered over to the pen, zipping up his waterproof, leaned on the wall and looked at the Gaffneys much as a farmer might weigh up livestock before buying it.

"Jerome Gaffney," he said, eventually. "You and me met ten years ago. I was in Vice at the time. I don't think there is a Vice Squad anymore. Specialist Crime, they call it. Blurred edges, eh? Anyway, you'd turned your hand to money laundering, using that club in Chingford, remember?"

The uncle smiled. "I remember what a pig's ear you made of it."

Baker turned to me as he opened the pen and entered. "He's right, we fucked up and Jerome here got off. Jacob, look at that ship down there."

Jaikie was the only one present who didn't know why he'd been asked to look at the long container ship a couple of miles away, stacked high, making its way upstream, and as he turned towards it Baker swung his fist and caught Jerome's jaw with a perfect right hook and, without legs to move with, arms to balance, he fell ninety degrees, upright to zero, out cold.

"All things come to he who waits," said Baker, turning to Trader. "And you must be his brother's boy?"

Trader held up his hands, insofar as he could. "You've nothing on me, officer, no history…"

Baker smiled at me. "When they start calling you officer, you know you're halfway there. How d'you come by these two?"

I told him most of what I knew about Charlie Drayton's role in Patrick Scott's disappearance, how I'd seen the Gaffneys at 34 Clarke Road, ostensibly sizing up the Red MG Sports they'd bought from Mrs Drayton. She'd expected her old man to live another three weeks, but died that night. Baker turned and looked back at the Gaffneys.

"We knew they'd got into some heavy shit lately, they even did an English Channel drop three years ago - people, money, drugs - so none of what you're saying really surprises me."

"I'm glad."

"Keep me in the loop about the rest of it, will you. Your loop, I mean, because I doubt if S.O.U. will get stuck in. Meantime, if these bastards were in Charlie's bedroom the night he shuffled off, I'll get it out of them."

"What about Drayton's wife?"

He looked at me to see how far I was prepared to go, then said tentatively, "If it turns out she pulled the plug, not them, we play God and drop it. Agreed?"

We shook hands on it and Baker called out to his colleague.

"Neil, we're taking these two back to the ranch. They've been tipped off to us, Drayton's wife to my mobile. She remembers the older man calling the younger one by his Christian name. Trader. Name in a million, and a fucking stupid one too, but known to our brethren in Debden."

They loaded the Gaffneys into the van and Manning drove them away, pausing at the gate long enough for Baker to lean out and say, more to Jaikie than me, "Nice meeting you."

We didn't say much during the first leg of the journey home, though Jaikie wanted to. He was full of what we'd accomplished so far and, given that it was only two thirty, what might the rest of the afternoon bring? He must have mistaken my reticence for tiredness and eventually stopped blathering. We were about twenty miles from home when, as if to break our silence, the Land Rover began to cut out and threaten to die.

"What's wrong with it?" Jaikie asked.

"It started about four weeks ago, same night I went over to Long Field for the harvesting. You hear that, where it nearly cuts out? Does it more and more the warmer the engine gets."

"Didn't do it on the way here."

"We were talking, the radio was on, we didn't hear it."

He nodded and looked out of the window. "Might be time to think about a new one?"

I shook my head. "Take it down to Rodney, he'll sort it."

"Dad, there's only so much one man can do."

I didn't like his negativity. "Look, there can't be much wrong with it because it's easy to deal with. When it starts to play up like this, I pull over into a pub for coffee… Why are you smiling?"

"I'm not."

"I get a coffee, a bite to eat, let the engine cool down. An hour later it's right as ninepence."

"There's a place coming up on the left and we didn't have lunch. Maybe they'll do us some grub."

It was one of those new country pubs, designed to look a hundred years older than they are. Come the weekend they get overrun by two point four sized families from the suburbs but right now, mid-afternoon, mid-week, business was quiet, which suited me down to the ground. There were four couples still at tables in the restaurant, a handful of drinkers at the bar, even an old border collie curled up by the fake log fire. We ordered some food at the bar, two bowls of mussels, and took our drinks to a faraway table. After a couple of minutes, Jaikie said,

"You alright, Dad?"

"I'm sorry, mate, I just feel the day was hi-jacked by the Gaffneys. I'm not saying we could have played it differently but they weren't part of the original plan."

I started picking at a chip in a veneered table mat. Jaikie moved it beyond my reach.

"I didn't even ask how you got on with Gerald Scott," he said.

"Not as well as I'd have liked. He knows more than he's telling."

"Lying?"

"No, avoiding the truth and not just about Patrick's death, keeping it from his wife. Course, the irony is, the longer he's dead the more he comes to life, at least in what's left of Marion's mind. The price you pay for such a thorough deception."

"What was the flat like?"

"Clean as a whistle. Too clean. I'm not sure what I expected to find there. At least a man who wanted to know what had happened to his son. To hell with it!" I beckoned the waitress. "I'm writing it off as one of those days. Feels like you've achieved but you look back and realise you've got nowhere."

As I handed her my glass and asked for the same again, the waitress said she'd had quite a few days like that recently.

When the mussels arrived, re-christened *moules marinière* and accompanied by a basket of French bread, we realised how hungry we'd been and set to as if in competition. Jaikie, usually so untamed where food is concerned, has an irritating habit with mussel shells, inherited from his mother. Both would arrange them around the side of their plates, tucking them into each other and, unable to criticise them for being neat, the rest of us would make our feelings known by dropping our own shells into the bowls provided, as noisily as possible. Today, however, it wasn't anyone's finicky treatment of mussel shells that was getting to me.

"Why can't I just leave it at that!" I said. "One reason? While Gerald Scott struggles to cope with a wife losing her marbles he'd like me to believe that his son wasn't clever, didn't have friends, enemies, secrets, something worth killing him for. And why has nobody been rattling the gates of Rushfarthing House, trying to find out what happened to this kid? No neighbours, no press, no self-righteous television crews?"

"There've been quite a few people, according to Marion," said Jaikie.

Under the weight of a day which hadn't gone the way I'd intended I'd slumped a little into my chair and now struggled back to a full sitting position.

"Names?"

"Ah, well, the names eluded her, or rather boiled down to just one…"

"Which one?"

"Edward Rochester, I'm afraid." He shrugged as if I knew what he was getting at. "He's the hero out of *Jane Eyre,* Dad. I guess he got lodged in her memory as a girl and every time she needs a name and can't find one, she falls back on his."

"What did she actually say?"

"Friends of Patrick used to visit all the time and carried on doing so long after he disappeared. First time she mentioned Rochester, though, he was young, second time middle-aged, then he was tall and good looking, then short, fat and ugly, so she was definitely referring to more than one person."

"Are we talking mates, enemies, people he owed money to, what?"

"They had 'mutual interests', she said."

I slapped the table. "That could be anything from aardvarks to zulus."

"She told me something else." Ever the ham when allowed to be he paused for dramatic effect. "Something she wished she hadn't. She said Rochester was clever. He wasn't as clever as Patrick and she thought that's why they fell out. Competition. Jealousy. And by this time I didn't know if she was all there or daft as a brush."

"Marion used those words? Competition? Jealousy?"

"Yes. Patrick was always inventing things as a boy. He put together the mechanism that opens those bloody gates, for example…"

"Maybe, but he didn't invent it."

He smiled. "Great minds, Dad, and I pulled her up on it. What did he actually *invent*, I asked her. Long pause. Wheels began turning. She couldn't remember, she said. But you know what? I think she remembered fine."

"Maybe today hasn't been wasted after all," I said.

I pushed the Land Rover keys across the table and signalled the waitress for another drink, my third, and but for its effect on me I might have raised the subject of money when it came to paying the bill. I might even have done it in Jaikie's style, slapping my pockets for non-existent cash, hoping that he'd take the hint and come up with an explanation. It would've meant doing it right there at the table, in front of an audience, the waitress, the chef who'd by now recognised Jaikie and come out to get his autograph. His name was Darren and, for some reason, I can't forget him.

Even though Jaikie still wasn't insured to drive the Land Rover we both agreed that it was the lesser of two evils, the greater being some zealous traffic cop breathalising me and finding me wanting. He drove home slowly and I nodded off round about Chinnor, didn't surface until he pulled up under the big beech tree. My first words were, "Have I been asleep?" shortly followed by, "How was the engine?"

"How was the engine?" I asked.

He ran his forefinger across his throat. "Two hundred thousand miles, Dad? You're going to have to put it out of its misery."

I shook my head. "Nonsense. They live forever."

Laura was in the kitchen putting together a meal for later that evening so I guessed Jaikie must have phoned her on the way home while I was resting my eyes.

"How did it go?" she asked.

"We've either learned sod all or the most important thing we ever will about Patrick Scott."

"Which is?" Laura asked.

"I don't know. His parents are currently concealing it."

"The day wasn't wasted, Laura," said Jaikie, washing his hand at the sink. "We caught the guys who killed Charles Drayton."

It was true but sounded both momentous and trivial at the same time. I slumped into the rocker as he gave Laura the straight to video version of Trader and Jerome with the accent on the violence, especially the part played by *Oleoresin Capsicum* and Alan Baker. There was little regard, however, for the fact that when it came to a courtroom we still wouldn't be able to prove if Patrick had disappeared of his own free will or someone else's. When I pointed that out, he defended our day again.

"For God's sake, this morning we knew nothing of his background. By midday we'd met his parents, seen the house he grew up in, you even poked around in his flat. Okay, we were hampered by his mother who's losing her marbles at a rate of knots…"

"What does that mean?" Laura asked.

"Early onset dementia?" I offered.

She wasn't keen on that diagnosis either, no doubt considering us unqualified to label others in such a way.

"You say they know something important," she said. "Do they know their son is dead?"

"He does, she doesn't," Jaikie replied.

"He's trying to keep it from her," I added. "All very noble, wouldn't you say?"

"Well, yes, unless…"

She stopped breathing, horrified by the thought which had crossed her mind. It had had crossed mine earlier too.

"Unless Gerald had something to do with his son's murder? People do. Rarely, but they do."

Jaikie smiled. "Define rarely."

"Every ten days one child in the UK is killed by a parent. It's a snippet I picked up along the way and can't put down."

Feigning relief, he dried his hands and asked Laura if he could help with supper. She gave him a cauliflower to deal with.

"I can't help feeling that all this is… larger than it seems," I muttered, loud enough for them both to hear. "Larger. It's the only word that covers it, but right now there is so much unliftable fog around that all I can see is vague shapes, no outlines." Jaikie had turned to me. "You're right, today wasn't wasted, the Gaffneys figure somewhere and I'm pretty sure why they killed Charles Drayton sooner rather than later. But who asked them to do it? Julien Raphael on behalf of ASC? And right at the other end of the social spectrum there's Ralph Askew always bloody well there when I turn round, wings flapping like some demented harpy."

As if to prove my point, he had phoned earlier in the day to invite me and Laura to lunch at the end of the week. We were to bring Jaikie as well. He would get his P.A. to arrange it and she'd phoned back half an hour later with the details. Why, I asked of Jaikie, Laura and the middle-distance, would a government minister be so keen to have lunch with a retired Detective Chief Inspector, a country GP and a money shy film star? Jaikie thought he was the main reason and lowered his voice in deference to Laura, explaining that people like Ralph Askew were known in the business as star-fuckers, sad bastards who would do anything to have some of the glitz and glamour rub off on them. That didn't explain his interest in me and Laura, I said. What did we have that he wanted? What did we know that might be useful, valuable, dangerous…?

"Have you seen George Corrigan today?"

"As a matter of fact I have. He was in the chemist next door to the surgery, buying toothpaste."

Corrigan's role in all this was certainly different to that of the Gaffneys, Julien Raphael or Askew but was he part of the unliftable fog or part of the breeze which would clear it?

13

Rodney Taylor came to this country from Jamaica in the early seventies and set up a small business repairing cars in the nearby village of Ford. Not much has changed about him in the intervening years. The business is still roughly the same size, the prices he charges aren't much different and he can still fix anything that used to move but now doesn't, generally doing so with bits and pieces he finds lying around his yard.

There is one thing about him that's altered, however, and that's his attitude towards me. It's warmed and it's done so without us ever discussing the reason for his initial reserve. It doesn't take a genius to work it out. In the sixties and seventies Rodney spent most weekends being stopped and searched by my colleagues on the streets of North London - Holloway, Archway, Islington - for no other reason than the colour of his skin. Truth is, we both know that it was the Met's way of airing its prejudice, proving to demanding task masters that they had 'the situation under control'. The attitude made no sense then and certainly didn't do any good. Ask anyone who was at either of The Notting Hill riots. By the time I joined the police the tide was turning, very slowly, though it hasn't yet made it all the way to the shore.

Strange how in a friendship the taboo subjects are so clearly defined by their absence. I imagine Rodney and I have both wondered what the other's take on the practise of stop and search is, or was then, but we're both too old and too wise to raise the subject over a pint. We'll talk our way through anything else, but we never go back to those nights when he and his family could hardly poke their noses out without committing to a night in the cells of a London nick. He never holds back when it comes to my skills as a mechanic, though.

"Heh, Nathan, how many times I tell you, man?" he said after a brief look under the bonnet of the Land Rover. "You change the air filter on this? Never. I show you how a dozen times, you don't listen."

"You're saying that all it needs is a new air filter?"

"Leave it here, I fit you in. Phone me tomorrow."

Tomorrow, always tomorrow. And as usual it wasn't as simple as a straight air filter. Yes, the engine cutting out was down to that, so to that extent I was vindicated, but he also discovered that I needed 'an adjustment link for the rear suspension'. Whatever that was it had to be ordered, delivered and fitted and that took three days but by the time I drove out of Rodney's yard, the Land Rover which my family and other animals had said was a lost cause was running like a leopard. And all for £73.47.

The three days it took to do the repairs gave us time to organise the trip to London, the main purpose of which was for Laura to visit Julien Raphael at the offices of Argent Sans Cordes. There they would discuss the plans for the new Health Centre, which he'd been sent a week ago, and once any wrinkles had been ironed out, Laura still believed there was every chance that Raphael would hand over a quarter of a million quid.

To our credit she and I managed to steer clear of the fundamental differences in our attitude to ASC, hers based on optimism, mine on the cynicism which came from my years in the service. One of us was going to be proved wrong but until that moment we settled for having a day out in Bloomsbury, decent lunch thrown in courtesy of Ralph Askew, plus the chance to find out what he was really after. Early afternoon, if Laura had her way, we'd move on to The Faberge exhibition at Buckingham Palace.

I'm not sure at what stage Jaikie decided to join us, but I knew why he wanted to come. He was getting twitchy at not being recognised as often as he would've liked and the place to put that right in was London. He arranged a meeting with his agent who, having taken a lush 300 thousand dollars commission from *All Good Men and True*, was only too happy to discuss ways of repeating the exercise. As with most successful actors Jaikie was talking about 'going back to do more theatre'. I reminded him that he hadn't done much in the first place, there being very little on offer when he came out of Central School, and at a rough guess I didn't think his agent would go for a 99.9 per cent pay cut. With the supreme confidence of youth Jaikie assured me that his agent would be thrilled to oversee a change of direction in his career. I then made the mistake of asking what Jodie thought. He said he didn't know because he hadn't asked her.

"I thought we hadn't seen much of her lately," I said, fishing. "Lot of work on?"

My question was misinterpreted as nosiness which, combined with my earlier remarks about going back to the theatre, brought on a spell of actorly introspection, otherwise known as a sulk. By the end of the third day I was forced to point out that he'd hi-jacked the build up to the Julien Raphael visit but, more importantly, none of us should forget that at the heart of this matter lay the murder of a young man whom nobody, not even his own parents, gave a toss about.

On the day we were due to meet Julien Raphael, Jaikie appeared for breakfast having emerged from his sulk without apology or embarrassment and asked what the skedule was. Laura outlined it briefly and he nodded his approval before asking what we should do about George Corrigan. I looked at him for explanation.

"Shouldn't we tell him where we're going?" he said.

"Why?"

"So that he won't bother following. I mean how much looking after does Laura need? You one side, me the other, do we need George bringing up the rear?"

It would turn out to be one of those remarks which lives on beyond its original insignificance which, according to Jaikie, was simply to give the guy a day off. He'd seen him up at *The Crown* the previous evening where Annie MacKinnon had remarked that he seemed to be on his eyelids. Her assessment bothered me, given that she was one of those licensees who kept a sharp eye on her customers, but since there was little I could do about George's state of health I put it to the back of the queue and we set off for London in Laura's Volvo, in spite of my renewed faith in the Land Rover. Jaikie sat beside me in the front while Laura, in the back, alternately nursed and re-read the file of documents covering the proposed Health Centre. She knew them by heart, of course, in her mind she had laid every brick, painted every wall, installed every new piece of equipment so that if Raphael had even the dumbest of questions she'd be ready for him.

Jaikie began smiling at Northolt, the traffic lights at The Polish War Memorial to be precise. We pulled up at them beside a young family in a saloon car and the wife, an attractive if beleaguered thirty something, thought she recognised him. She nudged her husband who turned to check the proposition, at which point Jaikie played weary acceptance of being constantly spotted. He smiled his smile and gave a wave to the three kids in the back. The husband looked at him for a second or two longer then shook his head. I'm no lip reader but the shape his made would have fitted the words, "Nothing like him." The lights went green.

We parked in an underground car park large enough for an entire civilisation to withstand a nuclear war and took the lift up to street level. It had those mirrors in it which make you look wonderful and as I caught sight of us the picture froze to become part of my mental album from that day forward. There we were, in that moment of my irrational fear about the immediate future. One of us was looking straight back at himself without the slightest doubt that he was the best looking thing to go up in that lift since it was built. The second looked elegant, expensively dressed and nervous and didn't pay herself the slightest attention. Her eyes were fixed on the floor numbers over the doors, her mind on the business of the next hour or so. The third looked older than he remembered, though pretty good for all that but, in spite of the darkened mirror smoothing out the edges, maybe Jim Kelloway had been right; a new leather jacket wouldn't go amiss.

Out in the street, I reminded Jaikie that at one o'clock we were all due at Ralph Askew's office in Whitehall. Did he know where it was? No, but the taxi driver probably would, with it being the Department of Energy and Climate Change. He strode off, referring to his iPhone for directions to his agent's office, busily ignoring passers by, which was just as well since most of them were ignoring him back. Laura took a deep breath, the country GP's equivalent of girding the loins. She thanked me for being with her, then added quietly,

"You will try to see this from all angles, won't you?"

"You mean be nice to the bloke? You're forgetting the agreement we made. This visit is all about Patrick Scott…"

She said she knew exactly why we were here and took my arm, gripping it more firmly than usual, then apologised for having done so. It was the last day in October, a degree or two warmer here than in Winchendon, and a good deal sunnier. As we crossed Bloomsbury Square I remember thinking that people weren't in their usual hurry for some reason. Or maybe that's the way it seems looking back with everything in finer detail. At the far gate we crossed the road where even the traffic seemed more willing than usual to let us dodge it.

Raphael's office stood behind iron railings safeguarding a basement which ran the whole length of the building. A few stone steps led up to the ground floor and that was just about as Georgian as the building got. The rest of the frontage had been replaced time and again and in its attempt to fit in with its surroundings had lost all character. The double door entrance was black oak and overhung by a stone canopy. A brass plate at eye-level, nothing more, told us that this was the London office of Argent Sans Cordes.

From the moment I entered the building I was looking for signs that the place didn't ring true, that the organisation had been set up in haste, or was hiding tell-tale signs of its real purpose. Nothing grabbed me. Exotic plants and antique furniture knew their place. They were expensive, item by item, the Ormolu clock, the Paul Klee painting, the bespoke *chaise longue*. Way above them all, price-wise, was the Persian carpet, its design almost certain to lower the visitor's gaze. Was that coincidence or hand to hand psychology at its most effective?

The woman who rose from her leather topped desk to greet us was expensive too, aged thirty and French I thought from the accent, though her politeness suggested otherwise. Laura introduced herself then turned to me.

"This is Mr Nathan Hawk," she said.

The woman smiled, hoping for more than just my name, but it wasn't forthcoming. She was Monsieur Raphael's assistant and if we'd give her two seconds she would tell him that we'd arrived. She checked her on-screen diary and sure enough I wasn't there. She rang through to her boss and my schoolboy French could just about glean that she hadn't really caught my name and what should she do in the circumstances? Her boss must have told her to leave it with him. I've no doubt that he would have kept us waiting longer, more psychology, had he not been slightly unsettled by my presence. He emerged from the nearest room and came towards us as if we were the only two people in the world.

"Doctor Peterson," he said. "At last we meet!"

Laura shook the offered hand and I could see that she was immediately struck by the good looks, the Parisian charm, even the way he turned to me and said, "Monsieur, you are most welcome. A friend of the Doctor is a friend of ours. Your name, I didn't catch…"

"Nathan Hawk," I said, shaking his hand.

He gave a slight nod as if committing the name to memory and led the way back into his office. This too was rich and well ordered, though without a Persian carpet to make me feel penniless. That was achieved by another mirror showing the leather jacket, Jerome Gaffney's bite marks and all, quite in contrast to this latter-day Yves Montand, so perfectly turned out, so absolutely French and about ten years younger than me. As with his lookalike he showed signs of a mis-spent youth but whereas in Montand it added to his mystique, with Raphael it showed itself as arrogant disregard. Furthermore, he dyed his hair. Nobody's hair is that black at forty odd. He ushered us to leather armchairs around a low table on which I could see a copy of the Health Centre plans we'd sent him.

There was a flurry of small talk about our journey, about London, about the resurgent warm weather and then he started to perform, becoming almost speechless with bewilderment.

"Doctor, I cannot see for the life of me why your local Health Trust would not consider this a viable proposition."

Laura glanced at me, smiling. "I'm delighted to hear you say…"

"I've had someone look the plans over. We have a few questions to ask, as you might expect. Another day perhaps."

We'd been in the room five minutes and he was already hedging. Questions? Another day?

"So this meeting is just… broad outlines?" I said.

"Precisely."

"May I ask a question?"

The shrug was as French as they get. "Of course, Monsieur, but allow me to ask one first? The name Nathan Hawk is familiar." He frowned as if bringing to mind some distant headline. "You are a police officer, I think."

"I was, but if you're trying to place me, it's either because of my son, an actor, or The Pollicott Shootings 2001." He raised a finger at the mention of the latter, but allowed me to continue. "Six people killed by a single gunman, a farm worker by the name of Christopher Riley. Perhaps you remember his mother? I called her the seventh victim."

He remembered her only too well and asked if I knew what had become of her. It was the old trick of turning the burden of uncertainty back on the person claiming the original knowledge. I said I'd lost touch with Mrs Riley and returned him to my own question. What line of business was he in before he became Investment Facilitator for A.S.C?

"I was the CEO of a tyre company, based in Marseilles. My daughters run it now. We make tyres for army vehicles, earth movers, combine harvesters." He smiled. "We are not Pirelli, but if Pirelli isn't careful we might soon be."

"And what exactly is Argent Sans Cordes?"

He glanced at Laura. "Didn't Doctor Wilson explain?"

"I'm not sure he knew either," I said.

Raphael's English was perfect, I suspected, but he deliberately lost some of the flow when he needed to give half answers. "We are exactly how it says on the tin. Money with no strings. A group of European businessmen committed to putting back some of what we have taken out."

"And what have you taken out?" Laura asked, more to prevent me from doing all the talking than because she wanted to know.

"Oil, gas, coal, metals, minerals, precious stones. Other things too, more human." He smiled at her. "These things leave holes."

He was playing it with an air of regret, even a touch of guilty conscience, broken when his assistant brought in some of the best coffee I'd tasted in a month. As Laura sipped hers, seated on the edge of the chair, legs leaning to one side, I could sense her doubt that I was 'seeing this from all angles'. When the assistant had left the room, she opened her mouth to speak but I beat her to it.

"Why did Doctor Wilson approach Doctor Peterson and tell her about ASC?"

"You must ask him," said Raphael.

"I see. It was his idea, not yours. Only you spoke as if you knew him."

He wasn't sure if I'd tripped him up on purpose or bumped into him accidentally.

"I know him certainly," he said, with a smile. "He is an English eccentric, a man of values, a great friend of Argent Sans Cordes. For his own reasons, based on a lifetime healing the sick, he is appalled, as we are, that medical money is so hard to come by."

I sat back in the chair as if that answer, bristling with high moral tone, was a satisfactory one. Laura relaxed, as did Raphael, who then tried to steer the conversation towards his real purpose.

"Doctor, as I say, it is amazing that your Health Trust denies you this essential finance. Your work is important, in order to do it you must have staff, equipment and, for God's sake, a suitable building. I have a proposition. I would like to make something of a… test case of your project. I tread carefully here, but you come to us for money - not begging, no, but in need. Is this not shameful?"

Laura wanted to take issue with that, a foreigner on the verge of criticising her beloved NHS; she was allowed to do that, others weren't.

"I agree with you, Monsieur Raphael," I said, quickly. "It goes against the founding precepts of the Health Service. Test case, you say? What did you have in mind?"

He turned to me, sensing reservation in Laura and hoping, believing, that I had influence over her.

"We would film, before and after, but also as we build the new premises. We say it can be done at a reasonable price and look what you get for your money." He gestured down to the plans. "The most up to date, cost effective means of supplying medical care to a community."

"You have people who can bring this into the public arena?" I said.

He smiled. "In my mind I look round the ASC board and I see men who have sold everything to the people of Europe, from cars to cuckoo clocks. We will have no trouble selling this Health Centre."

"I like the sound of it," I said. "You say you've looked at the plans?"

"Briefly. I'm not a qualified architect, of course…"

"You had an architect look for you." He nodded. "I wonder if he had the same misgivings that I did? I'm speaking as a policeman and my concern is security at the rear of the building." I gestured down to the plans. "Pages 18, 19, 20."

"You never mentioned this before," said Laura.

It sounded as if she might want a response to that but something about my demeanour held her back. Raphael smiled as if some old woman was making a fuss and eventually he picked up the plans, flicked over pages 12 and 13, jumped to 16, 17. And then he paused, trying to turn the next three pages.

"They seem to be stuck at the top corner." He swivelled round to his desk and reached for a letter opener. "How has such a thing…?"

"I glued them together," I said.

I heard Laura put cup to saucer, then saw her lean forward and place both on the table. Raphael stopped trying to ease the guilty pages apart, looked at me and then laughed.

"You think it's funny?" I said. "Or is it nerves?"

"You can't have done this," he said. "We have had an architect…"

"There's been no architect any more than you've looked at them yourself."

"Nathan, what the hell do you…?"

I held out my arm to her but she batted it away, rose from the chair and began walking the office. Raphael was still looking at me.

"Why?"

"Because nobody gives away so much money without wanting something in return."

He flared his hands up towards the ceiling. "This is outrageous! You come here in friendly guise, you wait, you wait, and then reveal your little trick. And now you insult me." He turned to Laura who was pretty pissed off with me too. "Doctor, you should choose your friends, your 'advisors', more carefully."

"You've lied twice in twenty minutes," I said. "First about the plans…"

"So what? Diplomacy. I haven't time for studying plans. You want your money or not?"

It was a serious question and he'd fired it straight at Laura who was about to answer.

"Then you lied again," I said. "You pretended not to know me, but I think you knew exactly who I was the moment you clapped eyes."

He gripped his head with the fingertips of both hands. "I had no idea! The name rang a bell. Nathan Hawk. Jesus, I remember the case, The Pollicott Shootings, six people…"

"There was no shooting. I made it up on the spur, to get a measure of you. You followed me, lamb to kebabs, so anxious are you to get into this lady's life, that of her colleagues, her patients, the building she works in, all to see if we've hidden what you're looking for. And you're now willing to pay through the nose for the privilege."

"What is this mysterious thing I look for?" he said in a last ditch attempt at keeping the charade alive.

"It has something to do with a young man called Patrick Scott who disappeared a year ago, murdered I believe."

He walked over to the window, not to get inspiration from the view but to give himself thinking time. When he turned back to us he was no longer the front man of some philanthropic business cartel, all oily charm and diplomacy, he was his real self, the street thug from Marseilles who'd fought his way into money, power and respectability.

"You don't know anything about money, do you, Mr Hawk."

I admitted that I knew very little, never having had more of it than I needed.

"It doesn't mean much these days. You have a saying here. Made round to go round? It does that, faster and faster, moving so quickly that nobody values it. Ideas, they are the lasting currency of our age. You have an idea, it may make you millions, billions, but more than that it can change the future. I argue this: today there is not one idea…" He prodded his head at the side as if he were trying to punch a hole in it. "….not one single idea that cannot be brought to fruition. A hundred years ago, fifty years ago, we had big, fanciful ideas but not the means to realise them. Today we have the means but not the ideas. Have we reached the limit of our imagination, perhaps? I don't know."

I didn't know either, but I had an uncomfortable feeling that he was dropping into broken English again and leading me up some garden path. Laura was listening to him politely, not liking what she heard, which didn't necessarily mean that I'd be in the clear when it came to a showdown about the quarter of a million quid. Nevertheless, something was telling me to grab her by the hand and drag her from the room but as I reached out to her she headed for the door without any help from me. Raphael followed.

"I can make your Health Centre happen, Doctor," he said, trying to regain her confidence. "Do not put it aside because of what's been said today. ASC has money to spend on ideas great and small, be they life changing or simply…" He stroked the plans, as if blessing them, and returned them to her. "…beneficial at a certain time, a certain place. Patrick Scott had a idea, something so revolutionary, so all-changing, that when we heard about it…"

He had slipped Patrick's name into the conversation almost casually, but he must have known that I wouldn't let it pass without comment.

"So, you knew him. Did you also kill him?"

He spoke with a fair imitation of passion, marked by a classic French windmilling of arms. "ASC does not murder people! We provide finance and when something so important is in danger of being whipped away from its creator, it is our duty to step in. With money, yes, but much else besides to help him achieve his goal."

Laura doesn't like waffle at the best of times and certainly not in deliberately awkward English. "What on earth are you talking about?" she asked. "What is this revolutionary idea you keep on about?"

He stopped and smiled, then said quietly, "It was a pleasure meeting you, Doctor."

Laura looked at me, frowning, then back at Raphael. His half baked homily about ASC being the banker of ideas hadn't been waffle at all, it had been carefully aimed at forcing her to reveal that she hadn't the faintest idea what Patrick Scott's creation was. And if she didn't know, the chances were that I didn't either. I had two choices at that point. One was to break a chair over the Frenchman's head, the other was to leave him wondering if I might still turn out to be a pile of trouble. I settled for the latter and with Laura too stunned too object, I pulled her from the room, across the Persian carpet in reception and out onto the street. It was a triumph of restraint on my part, achieved without the aid of The Map.

I'd grabbed her coat on the way out and now held it open for her to slip into but she must have seen it as the bull sees the matador's cape. She didn't charge at me, she yelled, quite out of character.

"What the bloody hell were you doing in there?"

"Exposing him for the fraud he is."

"His morality is his affair. I came to see him because I want money which no one else is willing to give me."

"We agreed that today wasn't about money."

I flung her coat over my shoulder and crossed the road, dodging some bad-tempered traffic. She came after me, hampered by the daft shoes she was wearing, part of the impression she'd wanted to make on Julien Raphael.

"Wait!" she shouted. "This is salvageable."

"You don't want his cash, Laura. I saw you in there, the moment you decided to turn it down."

"We all know what a mind reader you are. Pity you're so often wrong. I need that money. Winchendon Health Centre needs it."

I was at the gate in the iron railings which surrounded the small square, aware in the moment I turned to her of so many details, courtesy a rush of adrenalin which was doubtless trying to forewarn me. A young man in his late twenties was crossing the park with a girl, laughing as they approached until they heard our raised voices. They stopped, fell silent, wondering what to do. Some children were playing on a slide twenty yards away, watched over by their mothers one of whom turned towards me and alerted her companion. The children played on.

"You've become one of those people who sees crime as incidental to another purpose, even expedient," I shouted. "If you get your money, Patrick Scott's death will have been worth it."

"How dare you accuse me of that!"

She made a grab for me but I'd opened the gate and entered. She stumbled, again the fault of the shoes. The gate slammed before she could follow me. My mobile rang. I glanced at it. Jaikie. I didn't answer it, just walked the path to the far side. Laura entered behind me, calling out for me to stop. People, other than the young couple, the mothers and children, were turning to me. Laura was catching up. Her own mobile rang. Jaikie I presumed. She ignored it. I could see the cars on the other side of the far railings. One of them was a metallic silver Volvo saloon. They don't come any more ordinary than that.

"What if everything he said was as innocent as pie?" Laura yelled at me. "He *didn't* have time to read the plans, he *was* being diplomatic. That is still what they do. They give money…"

I stopped and turned to her. "And your friend Doctor Wilson, how does he know about them? An enquiring mind? Or did somebody pay off the mortgage on his place in St Lucia?"

She drew level with me, still shouting. "Why does everyone have to be a criminal?"

"Because too bloody many of them are. Hardened or in the making. And age doesn't have anything to do with it."

"He's a doctor, for God's sake!"

"So was Harold Shipman!"

I turned to carry on walking and that's when I saw George Corrigan, approaching from the far corner. He was dressed in the sheepskin flying jacket, open to reveal a denim shirt. The check must have been in the wash, I remember thinking. I glared at him and Laura was asking me what he was doing here. He came near enough for her to ask him herself.

"Sergeant Corrigan, talk about unpropitious moment. Would you care to explain?

"She means fuck off, George. This is private time, a day out with friends."

"Hold on a second," he tried.

The strangest things put a stamp on momentous events, as if to give them ease of recall. For me that day it was a branch from one of the trees overhanging the footpath in the park, some leaves still on it from the Summer gone, some buds opening for the Spring to come, both anomalies of the volatile weather which marked out that year.

I reached the far gate before Corrigan did and closed it behind me. I turned sharply and made off up the pavement, opposite The British Museum. I could see them, eyes in the back of my head, as he opened the gate and let Laura through first, then hurried past her to catch me up.

More people stopped to observe. Not everyone. One man, mid-forties crossed the road at an angle way ahead of me. Old donkey jacket, hands in the pockets of it, jeans and Doc Martins, greying hair held close beneath a greasy baseball cap. I stopped because I recognised him. And as Corrigan drew level with me, followed by Laura still berating me, so the donkey jacket stopped and took his hands from his pockets. He was holding a semi-automatic pistol and extended both arms. The whole combination locked - hand, elbow, shoulder - as he took aim and fired then turned with such agility that I remember thinking he must be a great deal fitter than his age suggested. He looked back as he ran, saw the mistake he'd made. Somehow he had shot the wrong man. He considered returning to put it right but his ride home was already braking in the stuttering traffic. The donkey jacket climbed in and sped off in the metallic silver Volvo saloon.

And as Corrigan bent at the waist and staggered forward he dropped his own side-arm and clutched his stomach. He was falling. I'm not sure if people around were screaming or not, I would imagine they were, but I could have heard a pin drop. And in that collage of terror only Laura seemed to be moving, shoes abandoned as part of her trademark response to a crisis. As Corrigan fell into the gutter she turned him, pulled open the sheepskin, ripped the denim shirt wide, unfastened the belt to his jeans and leaned as if she were about to perform CPR. She was too low down on his body for that and, as it flashed through my mind to tell her so, she called for the plans to the surgery. I wanted to ask why but didn't, just took them from her handbag. It wasn't the plans so much as their polythene cover she needed and placed it over his bare midriff and applied pressure. The blood foamed away beneath it as he exhaled.

Sirens were already beginning to break up the unnatural quietness, allowing panicky chatter to build and people to approach. They stood back again when the paramedics arrived. When the police came they took control of people and traffic. All I could see throughout was our local GP, expensively dressed and shoeless, kneeling in the gutter, weight and effort all focussed on the man whose life she was trying to save.

14

I don't remember the last time I was in the women's fashion section of a department store but it was probably with Maggie, watching her try on twenty outfits and then settle for the one which had first caught her eye. I'm told it was a privilege to have been a bystander at this ritual. Today my task was a macabre necessity.

As we'd sat in the back of the ambulance, screeching through London streets on our way to University College Hospital with George Corrigan flat on his back and hooked up to an octopus of live-saving equipment, Laura had looked across at me and said, "You were right. I'd forgotten the real reason we called on Julien Raphael."

I told her there was no need to apologise. She wasn't apologising, she said as sharply as you can in front of a dying man.

"Did Raphael come out when the shot was fired?" she asked. "The rest of London seemed to."

"He stayed indoors. Diplomatic."

She looked down at herself. Her blue, knock-'em-dead outfit was turning purple, wet with more blood than it seemed Corrigan might have had in his veins to begin with. Her hands and arms were covered with it as well, her face streaked and spattered.

"You'll have to go to Debenhams for me. I can't walk around like this all day."

"Not your colour," I muttered, feebly.

"I'll give you a list. Sizes. You choose the colour."

I nodded at Corrigan. "Will he be alright?"

"I don't know."

"I want to see Jaikie."

I phoned him immediately and left a message, telling him that our plans had changed. He was to meet me in Debenhams, Oxford Street as soon as possible. Ladieswear.

A few seconds later the ambulance braked, the doors were yanked open and Corrigan was handed over to people who save incoming lives on a daily basis and know the difference between a pain in the neck and a bullet in the guts. We fell back as a young Staff Nurse joined us and ran alongside the trolley taking in information from the Paramedics whom she then dismissed. She told the rest of us - Laura, me, police - to wait and pointed at a row of chairs. And as doors clattered open and closed behind Corrigan I had an uneasy feeling that it was the last I'd see of him...

"He needs a heart surgeon," I said to Laura, as if I knew what I was talking about. She patted my arm as if I didn't. And probably in response to the gawping sprained ankles and sore thumbs all around, she asked a passing orderly if she could have a patients' gown to change into. She took it behind a curtain and emerged five minutes later in the guise of one of the customers, her hands, arms and face washed, blood soaked clothes in a Waitrose carrier bag.

One of the young coppers wanted to know if now would be a good time to ask what had happened. She told him it wouldn't be and took pencil and paper from her handbag. She'd dropped it in the gutter before going to work on Corrigan but even so the spurting blood had reached it. Would she wipe it off and carry on using the bag, I wondered? Or would she chuck it, use the event as an excuse to buy a new one? For me it would've depended on whether he lived or died.

Meantime, here I was in Debenhams about to buy a dress. I'd attracted the attention of a standardly beautiful floor walker who inevitably came over and asked if she could help me. It didn't seem right to tell her that my friend had been covered in the blood of a man who'd been shot in Bloomsbury Square, so I paraphrased it to, "Do you have this in a quieter colour?"

I pointed at a mannequin in a noisily red dress.

"As a matter of fact we do, sir. A subdued but very elegant green."

"I'd like underwear to go with it - bra, pants, tights."

I really must find out why most men of 54 have difficulty talking to women half their age about underwear. Mind you, I'm not sure this girl was fully at ease with the conversation either, unsure perhaps of who the clothes were meant for.

"What size are we talking about, sir?" she said, lightly.

I handed her the piece of paper which Laura had given me and she smiled. The dress, at size twelve, clearly wasn't for me. I'm at least an eighteen.

"If you'd care to wait by the checkout, sir, I'll bring the garments over for you to see."

I thanked her and loitered by the till. Once I'd approved the clothes, in the same self-conscious manner that I taste a bottle of wine in a restaurant, an assistant wrapped them and I paid. And at that point the surrealism of the occasion was compounded as the star of *All Good Men and True* crested the escalator and walked over to me.

"Is he dead?" he asked, anxiously.

The film star, the frock and the frilly underwear, it might have been called. We forbore to explain anything to those around us and hurried from the store, back to UCH.

I thought she looked pretty good in the dress. We all thought so, even Laura, and then she reminded us that it wasn't a fashion parade but the serious business of waiting to hear if a friend was going to pull through. We sat in the surgical waiting area like the front row of a Sunday congregation, eyes front, contemplating miracles. Corrigan was in operating theatre two, having his heart started, stopped and started again, presumably to some purpose. Police were everywhere and I heard on the fringe of their chat that word was abroad of an S.O.U. Sergeant being gunned down in the street. It sounded as if a Chicago style shootout had taken place in good old Bloomsbury Square and that George Corrigan had been the intended target. Neither was true. It had been a single shot and it hadn't been aimed at him.

It was another two hours before a po-fagged cardio surgeon emerged from the operating theatre, looked round and beckoned Laura. She went over and they broke into medi-speak and, not for the first time since Patrick Scott had come into my life, I felt utterly superfluous. A month ago Jaikie had had mock acid thrown at him and I'd frozen. Laura had stepped in. Three hours ago she'd done so again, to stop the blood pumping out of George Corrigan. If I didn't know myself better I'd say I was … concerned that all the presence of mind, all the effective action in this case, was being shown by a fifty year old lady doctor.

The surgeon finished his summary of the work he and his team had done. His body language, full of helpless shrugs and weary sighs, said that Corrigan's chances were now in the lap of the Gods and I considered that to be typical of a man covering his back. I wanted his opinion, a percentage figure, on how likely Corrigan was to make it. I went over and put it to him but he scissored my question away.

"Doctor Peterson'll give you the lay version. Suffice to say that your friend is a very lucky man."

The words were spoken in a tone of near resentment, critical that a man had so recklessly gambled with his own life as to be shot in the guts and get away with it. Before I could respond, Jaikie was beside me, hand on my arm, steering me towards moderation. He gave the surgeon a reduced version of his smile and thanked him. I watched the man stagger away.

"Why do surgeons think they're God Almighty?" I asked, quietly. Another question ignored.

"Nathan, the bullet struck him right here," Laura said, pointing with bunched fingers just above her own navel. "And the reason he's lucky is that it hit the buckle of his belt first, which not only slowed it down but altered its direction. Upwards. It punctured his diaphragm, kept going, missed every vein and artery that would have … bled him out, as the Americans so vulgarly put it. Nevertheless it has penetrated his left lung. Not enough to collapse it. The bullet ended up lodged somewhere between his left atrium and the superior lingula … left lung."

"Where is it now?" Jaikie asked.

"Still inside him."

Again I reacted as if I knew what was best for Corrigan, far better than any good looking surgeon. I guess it comes from years of needing to take control of a situation immediately or forever remain peripheral to it. Evidently, I made a move to follow the surgeon and have it out with him but Laura said, loud enough to stop me,

"More deaths occur from surgeons poking around for objects when they should have left well alone, at least until his other organs repaired."

"What about all the blood he lost?" Jaikie asked.

"Ink spilled on the floor, always seems twice the amount that was in the bottle." She laughed. "Hark at me, talking as if your generation uses fountain pens. The main problem wasn't to stop blood escaping but to prevent air entering. Hence the polythene cover to the plans. I knew they'd come in useful one day."

Hospital canteens belong to that soulless family of eating places, along with railway buffets and motorway service stations, which offer food and drink while ensuring that whoever buys the stuff won't hang around for longer than it takes to swallow it. I shared this thought with Laura and Jaikie, adding that this particular carrot cake, baked in China no doubt, had never seen a root vegetable in its life.

"Dad, you should be rejoicing," said Jaikie. "The guy is still alive."

I looked at him across the top of my plastic cup as I blew on the tea to warm it. He had a point. Complaining was my watered down version of kicking the cat. I'd already tried to wind up the surgeon and failed, the canteen tea and cake showed every sign of being just as unresponsive, which left me with Laura and Jaikie. If they weren't careful they'd take the full brunt of my guilt trip. That's what it was, common or garden guilt. I won't say that I'd led Corrigan into this mess, but could I have done more to forewarn him? If I'd taken Jaikie's advice and told him, first thing in the morning, that we were heading into London, there was no need to follow us … I would probably be dead.

"You do know what happened out there, don't you?" I said.

"Somebody jumped out of the bushes, ran up to George and shot him," said Jaikie.

"No, you bloody fool…" I caught myself and modified my reaction. "No, somebody jumped out of the bushes and ran up to *me*. George put himself between us."

The eyes widened with fear and excitement. "You mean he took a bullet for you?"

"Oh, for Christ's sake…"

If hospital canteens have any merit it's their anonymity. Nobody hears when you raise your voice, at least to a certain level, and nobody really cares if you're a film star. Essentially you're just another number, waiting in line. Jaikie was already apologising for his unguarded lapse into Hollywood and I was breathing deeply. Laura was merely being horrified at the substance of what I'd said.

"You mean someone tried to kill you?"

"Yes, and what's more I recognised him. From the premier of *All Good Men and True*. On that occasion he was better dressed, wearing a bog standard dinner jacket and threw mock acid in my son's face. Jealous nutter or serious player? I say the latter. And he just upped his game by trying to kill me."

It was eight o'clock the same evening when we heard that Sergeant Corrigan was now in the recovery suite and had come round from the anaesthetic, presumably the one he'd been given when they anchored the bullet to an unsuspecting internal organ. The nurse who delivered the news wasn't prepared to say if he was going to live, but at the same time she was adamant that he wasn't going to die. All eventualities covered then, I said, trying to pull her off the fence. At Laura's suggestion we took what the nurse had said as good news and I told her it was time that she and Jaikie headed for home. I wanted to stay on, at least until I could look Corrigan in the eye and thank him for saving my life. As I rehearsed in my head the various ways of putting it, they all seemed insufficient, insulting, insincere, but I could hardly leave it unsaid.

The time line for the next twelve hours was punctuated by negatives, apart from when Jaikie phoned to say they'd arrived home safely. I was in a pub at the time, helping myself to think straight, ice all the way to the brim. Back at UCH the canteen closed at ten and I was moved on by a black bear of a security guard. We met again, an hour later, when he found me asleep in a corner of the X-Ray Department's waiting area. I was being worked around by a squad of cleaners, one of whom must have summoned him. His attitude was hostile. I tried to turn him but he wouldn't shift. He had rules to follow, he said, and one of them was to throw people like me out by midnight. I moved on to Neuroscience and nodded off beneath a poster of a schizophrenic who was telling me that I shouldn't be afraid of her. The next thing I remember was the security guard, hand on my shoulder, saying, "I told you not to come back. Why have you come back?"

I could hardly blame him. I was feeling and no doubt looking pretty rough by then: I certainly needed a shave, the scotch was probably still on my breath and the savaged sleeve of a well-worn leather jacket wasn't helping. I opted for the line of least resistance and on the way to the main entrance the guard allowed his true self a moment's free rein, paused at a cupboard and took out a blanket and handed it to me. He thought I was a down and out. That was a first for me, but to have disabused him would have been unmannerly…

Outside on the street it was cold and as I tried to settle in the doorway of one of London University's many superfluous buildings, it occurred to me that I was probably in the throes of some psychological reckoning. Not too deep down, by allowing myself to be removed from the hospital like some pathetic old drunk, I was trying to apologise for being alive while Corrigan's chances were still fifty fifty. Nearer the surface, I was probably in shock which was why the blanket came in handy, but in spite of it I slept as badly as I'd expected to, propped in a sitting position hard up against some fancy brickwork.

It's easy to forget, in the comfort of a reasonable pension and a decent place to live, just how debilitating rough living can be and my own refresher course on the subject was cut short at five thirty in the morning when a boiler, which must have been the size of an ocean liner's, burst into life in the basement across the street and started chucking out steam and carbon monoxide in equal measures. I stretched myself into human form, folded the blanket, and set off back to UCH.

Hospital security is a strange animal. In some places you can't pass the barrier without a full scale inquisition, others you could jog round naked without anyone batting an eyelid. I thought UCH would fall somewhere in the middle, so I entered via A and E, hoping I'd be recognised from the previous day which would give me credibility. It was a smart move and as I strode into the waiting area, past the early morning cyclist knocked off his bike by a taxi, a scalded face from a breakfast kettle and a laid out drunk from the previous night, I spotted the Staff Nurse who had first received Corrigan. I paused, hoping to ease my way by thanking her for what she'd done yesterday but before I could speak she said,

"How is he?"

"Just going up to see. How do I get to the Recovery Suite?"

She gave me directions, I gave her the blanket. She didn't question it, simply threw it into a passing laundry trolley and called out for the next casualty.

When I reached the Recovery Suite I was halted like a car at a crossroads by a uniformed police officer of twelve. Standing squarely in front of me, hand raised, he planned on making sure that I hadn't come to finish the job which Bog Standard had started.

"Go and ask Sergeant Corrigan if he'll see me," I said immediately.

"Who are you?"

"Hawk. I'm not good this early."

"Will he know you:?"

"Take a good look, describe me to him."

He stared at me and recognising a more fragile state of mind than he was prepared to deal with he said, "Wait there."

He returned two or three minutes later and beckoned me to follow him. As we turned a corner the Sister-in-Charge came out of her office and tagged along. We paused at the window of Corrigan's room and through in the morning gloom I could see him, propped up with pillows, a drip feeding into his left arm. For a man who'd been shot less than twenty-four hours ago he looked pretty good, but then he had the advantage over me of a decent night's sleep. The young copper tapped on the window, Corrigan focussed, then nodded to reassure his protector that I was friend not foe. And at that point the Sister came into her own. She told me I had fifteen minutes. No more.

I wasn't the only visitor Corrigan had. In a low, hammock-like chair sat a woman in her early sixties and it was obvious from the general puffiness of her face, to say nothing of the tissues screwed up and dropped in the bin beside her, that she'd been crying. She'd probably slept no better than I had, but she was fully awake now and occupied. She was sewing the top button back onto Corrigan's check shirt.

"My Mum," he said, quietly. "She brought some clean clothes from home."

I went over to her, stooped and offered her my hand. Her own was cold and I instinctively took it in both of mine with a sympathetic wince. It was too forward a gesture. She withdrew her hand and went back to the button.

"I've got fifteen minutes," I said to her son.

"During which time keep your mouth shut and listen." He beckoned me to the bedside. "Jesus, you look like shit."

"You look better than you deserve to." I pulled out a padded bench from beneath the bed and sat down. "What am I listening to? More abuse?"

He lowered his voice to exclude his mother. "This Patrick Scott business has bothered me ever since ... well, ever since I met you. When it came down to it, I didn't really think you'd be wasting your time if there was nothing to it."

"You told me it was out of my league."

"Yes, well, you must have got close to something or why else would they want to shut you up?"

He winced with pain, tried to relax and took a few shallow breaths. His mother came to the bed and elbowed me aside, asking him what he needed.

"Mum, I'm fine. This is business, things that need sorting out, just Mr Hawk and me."

With an accusatory glance in my direction, she returned to her chair and picked up the needle and thread.

"I talked it over with my boss. He said I should 'pick away at the scab, see if there was any pus underneath'."

I nodded. "I used to have one who spoke like that. Point is, do you trust him?"

"Sort of. Mind you, he didn't give me the resources I needed." He broke off and, with a separate effort, smiled. "I called in one of 'those' favours. A girl who used to work on the Police National Computer. She got onto a friend who's still there and you know what? Patrick Scott *was* reported missing."

"By Belinda Hewitt."

"How come you know that?"

"She told me, I believed her."

He paused to compute the implications of that, the main one being that I'd found Patrick Scott's girlfriend and paid her a visit.

"If it's on the Police Computer, how come Jim Kelloway didn't pick it up?" I said. "Or is this where it gets out of my league?"

"Mine too. There's a database, tucked away behind a pack of firewalls, stuff that doesn't get deleted so much as back-burnered. It's the kind of crap that might jump up and bite police in the arse one day, so we need to know what it was all about in the first place."

"And me bringing Patrick to life falls into that category?"

"He's on the database sure enough but there's precious little intel to go with him."

He was searching my face, wondering how much more to tell me and he needed prompting. "Precious little doesn't mean nothing."

"One name attached. Maybe a suspect, maybe not…"

"If not a suspect, then what?"

He scanned my face again and I saw the moment when he decided to take me all the way into his confidence.

"That's where I was heading before yesterday. I'd fixed up to meet him next week, Monday, but as you can see I may not be able to make it. Why don't you go in my place?"

"What's the name?"

"Edward Rochester. He's some kind of crank philanthropist, money to burn, no sense of how to put out the fire."

"Rochester?" I muttered.

"Like the town in Kent."

"Like the bloke in *Jane Eyre*." Maybe Marion Scott hadn't simply drawn on her core memory for the name. The man really had existed. "Where will I find him?"

He winced, though not with pain this time. "Easy enough to find, not so easy to reach. Sodding great security jungle between him and the outside world."

"I'll manage."

I slid the bench back away from the bed and leaned forward, elbows to knees. I must have looked especially worried.

"What's wrong?" said Corrigan.

"I've never been in this position before, needing to thank someone for saving for my life."

He would have laughed out loud if he'd been sure that it wouldn't damage him. "Don't go thinking I wanted to do it, Hawk. It was Pavlov's dog. The gun came out, I dived in front of it."

"Why were you there in the first place?"

"I was protecting Doctor Peterson and not, repeat not, because you asked me to, but because I was assigned. You went into see Raphael, I did a sweep of the square on foot. Saw the same guy twice, thought I recognised him."

"You did. He threw vinegar at my son."

He nodded. "I went round a third time. He'd gone. That bothered me even more."

I could see the young police officer and the Sister outside in the corridor, checking their stop watches no doubt. I'd been there ten minutes at the most.

"I'll keep you posted," I said, rising from the bench. "I meant more than just thanks, George…"

He gave me a withering look and said, "Woof."

I said a quiet goodbye to his mother and left.

15

By Monday morning Corrigan had improved more than he'd been expected to in such a short space of time and was pushing to be discharged. With damned good reason, he told me in a text message. Having survived a bullet in the guts, he didn't fancy being killed off by an in-house bug. They may well have sounded like second rate university degrees - MRSA, C.Diff, CRKP - but they still did for you. He then tacked on Rochester's address, Number Seven, Hyde Park Close, London, and the time he'd fixed up to meet him, 5.00 pm.

He stayed in hospital. The brass at S.O.U. clearly believed he'd been Bog Standard's target and had upped the police detail guarding him which, in a subsequent text, Corrigan said confirmed his long held belief that he was working for a bunch of morons. It bothered me slightly that he hadn't told his purple spouting boss the truth, that the real target was me. My best guess was that he knew it would bring my investigation to an immediate halt, never to be started up again. Then he found himself in a bit of a moral bind and started to worry about me. Hospital does that to you. He'd been assigned to look after us, not chuck us under oncoming danger. At first his messages were jokey, one stating that he hadn't saved my life only for some bastard to have another crack at it. He signed it Ivan Pavlov. I texted back saying that if somebody wanted to blow my brains out there wasn't much either of us could do to stop them. He made the joke more serious. Listen, who the hell is going to jump in front if the bullets start flying again? What about Jaikie? What about Laura? Who'd keep an eye? That woman saved his life. Is this how he intended to repay her?

I didn't reply. However, I did make a gesture towards self-preservation by getting my old Smith & Wesson out of mothballs. I cleaned it, oiled it, took it up into Winchendon Woods and fired it a few times. Frightened the birds.

I took Jaikie with me to meet Rochester, more to keep my eye on him than anything else. We drove to White City, parked in a multi-storey and took the Central Line to Lancaster Gate and walked. He said he missed the London tube. He probably did but more than that he missed the people who rode it staring at him, wondering if it really was him or just some bargain basement lookalike. The trouble was the more curious amongst them had a tendency to come up close and check and I had a Smith & Wesson holstered under my jacket. I'm not saying that if one of his admirers had reached out an inch too far I would have shot them dead, but I wouldn't have stood by and watched.

We reached Hyde Park Close which could just about be called a new-build, in that it hadn't been there long, though that's where any comparison with affordable housing ends. Even Jaikie was silenced into disbelief as he looked up at the three, jenga-like towers and for once had no Los Angeles comparisons to draw. A plush command post straddled the entrance to the complex with a Latin slogan in carved ironwork forming the arch. It said 'Domus Est Ubi Cor', roughly translated as 'Home is where the heart is.'". For all that it struck a chord it might just as well have said 'Arbeit Macht Frei'. It certainly felt as if we were on the threshold of some Godless world. An expensively suited ex-SAS type came out to greet us like long lost enemies.

"Name?"

"Hawk, father and son."

"Who for?"

"Mr Rochester."

He pointed for us to enter the habitable side of the archway where two younger subordinates rose from a sofa to cut off our escape. The man who'd greeted us so warmly told us to empty our pockets. The Smith & Wesson marginally increased their interest in us and they examined it by turn as if it were an early flintlock.

"You usually carry this?" the older one asked.

"No."

"Why today?"

"Because three days ago somebody tried to kill me."

He looked at me as if at long last I'd spoken in a language he understood, then said to both of us, "Shoes off."

"What is this? Heathrow?" said Jaikie.

They'd heard it before. They examined our shoes then told us to raise our arms.

"You want me to bend over?" said Jaikie, getting hacked off. They'd heard that one before as well.

"Jaikie, shutup," I suggested.

Our hosts quietly seconded the motion and then returned everything to us except my keys, the pepper spray and the revolver. The older one went over to a computer and must have dialled a number, Skype maybe or something internal. He pointed at a screen on the far wall and after a few moments a man's face flickered into view. He'd be 40 years old next month, he told us three or four times during the next hour, but it wasn't simply his age that didn't tally with our joint preconception of a philanthropist. He was a deeply unattractive man, most of the off-putting details there by design, starting with the long, greasy hair, and unkempt beard.

"Yes, Sergeant?" he said abruptly.

"There's a Mr Hawk and his son to see you, sir."

"Never heard."

The screen went black, the Sergeant turned to me and made to return my other possessions.

"Call him up again and say the name Patrick Scott," I said.

I've often thought it unsettling that if you've been trained to obey orders and they're issued in the right tone of voice, it doesn't much matter who gives them but nine times out of ten they'll be followed. I'm not suggesting that had I told this Sergeant to shoot his two comrades, then himself, he'd have obliged. Nevertheless, without the slightest hesitation he went back to the computer and within a matter of seconds Rochester was up on the screen again.

"What is it now?"

It was an educated voice, once upon a time, roughened at the edges by affectation, a rebellion against all that money, perhaps. 836 million pounds and rising, according to *The Sunday Times* rich list, via Jaikie.

"Sorry to trouble you, sir, man says to mention the name Patrick Scott."

After a brief pause Rochester said, "Bring 'em over."

The Sergeant flicked his head at us in a gesture that said fall in behind me, then led us out of the den and across to the three towers. They were set around a lawn of untreadable grass with flat screen waterfalls in serried ranks and fountains spraying shapes unknown in nature. At the first tower, the doors opened of their own volition to reveal another besuited ex-army type. He acknowledged the Sergeant, though not us, and waited for orders.

"Seven," said the Sergeant, then turned to me and Jaikie. "Collect your stuff when you leave."

He watched as the glorified doorman led us across the marble foyer to the lifts, or elevators as Jaikie now called them. Lifts are apparently heels on a shoe or surgery to a fallen face. This outdated meaning of the word was lined with scented mahogany and silver framed mirrors and took us up seven floors to the penthouse suite in three seconds flat. Our stomachs followed at their own pace. As we stepped out of the lift and began to glide across yet more marble a wall up ahead of us opened, concertina style, lest any visitor should find the business of entering through an ordinary sized door problematic. The other side of where the wall had been stood Edward Rochester, dressed in a black T-shirt and jeans holed above the knee line, a complete picture of anti-social, early middle-age, hardly the dark, mysterious object of Jane Eyre's and Marion Scott's simmering desire. He raised a hand for us to stop, which our escort ensured that we did by thrusting out a beefy forearm. Rochester came right up close and looked us up and down.

"Father and son you say?" He nodded, as if he now believed what up until then was doubtful. "I see the likeness."

He flapped a dismissive hand at the glorified doorman who stepped back into the lift, asked it for the ground floor and it fell to earth. Rochester raised a beckoning arm and we followed him into the penthouse, a fantastical mixture of mechanical utility and over-designed furniture masquerading as simplicity. Acres of space stood between one open-plan area and another, lights switched on, curtains closed and fires lit at the touch of a button. Nothing especially advanced in that, you might say, but when a man speaks into the middle-distance and asks a sofa to move to the window area, and two armchairs to position themselves opposite it, and all three objects obey then, if you're Jaikie, your jaw drops. If you're me you hear your father's voice condemning excess.

"Have a seat," said our host. "I don't get many visitors, don't get much chance to show off the latest gadgets. What do you reckon?" He smiled. Yellow teeth, a colour match for the facial hair, both tarnished by nicotine. "Careful how you answer, we've just put a sizeable chunk into a company that makes this crap."

"Why?" I asked.

The smile faded and he looked at me as if I had half a brain. "Can you imagine the difference that responsive furniture would make to the lives of your average disabled man or woman?"

He wanted me to believe that altruism lay at the core of this extravagance, then. From the little I knew about robotics, the armchair I was about to sit in probably cost more than the new Land Rover I was trying not to think about, but at least I actually settled in it. Jaikie circled his a couple of times before perching on the edge.

"I'm told the only real thing about this place is the view," said Rochester, nodding out over Hyde Park across to the river at Chelsea, visible in hundred metre stretches between competing buildings. "The girls don't get so worked up about it as I do, but then they're not British."

The girls he'd referred to were several versions of Tretchikoff's green lady, mounted on a nearby wall.

"You want something to drink?"

"Thanks. Scotch, with ice to the top of the glass."

He turned to Jaikie. "I know you, don't I?"

"I don't think so," said Jaikie, with feeling. "Orange juice, please."

Rochester addressed the middle-distance again. "Yi Ling, scotch with ice to the brim, same for the straight and an orange juice." He tugged at the ragged beard for a moment, then flattened the strands he'd dislodged. "I was expecting Sergeant Corrigan."

"He was shot on Friday," I said.

"That doesn't tell me why you've come in his place. Are you a cop too?"

"I was."

He nodded, still weighing us up, still believing that he knew Jaikie from somewhere.

"You've never come to me for finance? What line of work are you in?"

"Actor."

Rochester snapped his fingers. "You're in that war film, what's it called?"

"*All Good Men and True*," said Jaikie quietly, no smile.

"I saw you on telly, talking to that bunch of women, lunchtime. Christ, they were all over you, two of 'em old enough to be your granny. I knew I knew you, it wasn't just the old cogs slipping, now I'm forty…"

We turned as a girl in her early twenties entered, Singaporean so Jaikie told me later, and discreetly immune to any of his charm. She was carrying a tray with our drinks on it and Rochester asked a low table to come and join us. It settled itself between the sofa and the armchairs and Yi Ling set down our drinks on it.

"Why did you agree to see me, Mr Rochester, but not until I mentioned Patrick Scott's name?"

It was only for a split second, but he thought about his answer to that. "I hoped you might know where he is. Haven't heard from him for over a year. I've invited him to my fortieth, he hasn't replied."

"That's because he's dead."

He nodded. "I did wonder, in spite of his old man insisting otherwise."

"Murdered."

He went onto the back foot, fiddled with the beard again. "And that's what Corrigan wanted to see me about?"

"No, he was going to ask if you'd lent Patrick any money lately."

"Twenty five thousand pounds."

"What for?"

He shrugged. "It's what I do. I give money away, but only to people with good ideas. Patrick had a brilliant one…"

"You're the second person I've met this week who's sung the praises of good ideas."

"What was the brilliant idea?" Jaikie asked.

"He claimed that it would make the desert bloom," Rochester said. "He called it The Magic Carpet."

He looked from one of us to the other and, gambling that I didn't know that he was lying, he went on to describe The Magic Carpet with boyish enthusiasm. It was a carpet like any other, to be produced in rolls and sold by the metre. He rose from the sofa and went over to a Georgian desk, one which apparently still had a mind of its own, so he didn't bother giving it instructions. He took a large pliable sheet of something from the central drawer and brought it over to us. This was it, he said handing it to Jaikie, but unlike the carpet you walk on, it was made of a peat based compost with a bio-degradable, waterproof surface. Into the carpet itself, seeds would be set. In this example it was grass but the possibilities were limitless - grass for livestock, wheat for bread, sunflowers for oil - and all one had to do was to roll it out on barren land, waterproof side up and the moisture which is always present, no matter how dry the land seems, would rise and be trapped, the seeds would germinate and the desert would bloom. He paused, presumably for our appreciation.

"You gave him money for *that*?"

He smiled. "You sound like my father, Mr Hawk. I gave Patrick a cheque for 25K, told him to make a prototype."

"And a week later he disappeared?"

"That'll be the ex policeman in you. You're right, though, I didn't see him again, but the cheque was never cashed either."

"Do you remember the date on it?"

"November the first, last year."

"Odd that you remember such a specific date."

He shrugged at that. "You can't have it both ways. You want information, so I tell you what I know."

"Why do you go back to visit the Scotts, Gerald and Marion?"

"Courtesy, empathy."

"You've lost a child yourself?"

"Never had one to lose."

"Then you mean sympathy, surely. And maybe you'd like an off cut from The Magic Carpet?"

He bridled at that and set down his drink on the table. "If the project goes ahead then the rights to it will belong to Gerald and Marion Scott and I will ensure that they get them."

"What's the whisky, by the way?"

"Glendaloch, bottled in 1968."

"Too good to drink, really."

He chuckled. "Yi Ling, another scotch for my guest."

"No ice this time, Yi Ling. In your sympathy trips to the Scotts did you ever come across two men, uncle and nephew, by the name of Gaffney?"

The yellow smile was getting thinner the more he used it. "Now you want to question me, like I was a witness?"

"Suspect actually."

He paused and searched his memory. "Gaffney? No. Who are they?"

"They killed a man called Charles Drayton."

"It's been a good week for the grim reaper, by the sound of it, but to answer your question I don't have many friends who are murderers."

"Charles Drayton disposed of Patrick's body, turned it into dog food. Would you call that a 'good idea'? The reason I ask is that Drayton was paid handsomely for it … about twenty-five grand, strangely enough."

He took a sip of his own drink, keeping his eye on me. "Maybe this Drayton killed Patrick in the first place?"

"Did his parents ever speak to you of people who were in competition with him, people he owed money to…" He was shaking his head, before the questions were fully asked. "…people who envied him, or just plain disliked him?"

"No."

"You never met his girlfriend, Belinda?"

He laughed. "Christ, I was going to give him money, not take charge of his fucking life."

"There was another girl, Henrietta…"

And that's where he drew the line in his stream of denial. The name had meant something to him but he tried to cover it by taking offence. He put his glass down and stood up.

"I've had enough. Thanks for dropping in. If and when the real police need help with this case, tell 'em to call me. Door open."

And as the wall performed its party trick, so Yi Ling entered with my second drink, no ice, just the scotch. Rochester and Jaikie stood watching as I savoured it, one sip at a time, then handed back the glass. We walked over to the lift which swallowed us with all the stealth of a shark and then dived.

We met Laura for supper at *The Crown* where, at least amongst the regulars, Jaikie's celebrity gloss had lost some of its shine. Familiarity had reassured people who knew him, like his old teacher John Demise, that he was still just an ordinary bloke. Ordinary-ish. My qualification.

There was one new face at the bar, drinking lime and soda. He was Corrigan's replacement - or temporary relief, as both men preferred to call it. His name was Mark Granger, six months in the job, and the stress of it was already beginning to show. He was suffering from every ailment known to his age group and, halfway through the day, had engaged Laura in conversation prior to showing her the moles on his back.

Meeting Edward Rochester had had more of an effect on Jaikie than I'd expected.

"Can't get a toehold on the guy," he said. "All that money, he dresses like a slob, long greasy hair and beard. Stank as well, common or garden B.O."

"Oh dear," said Laura. "Did he have no saving grace whatsoever?"

Jaikie passed that one on to me. "The whisky, best I've ever tasted."

She smiled. "I knew there's be something."

"With all that money, you'd think he'd employ one of these life-style coaches," Jaikie went on. "But do you know what he had dotted around the room, like mildewed pole dancers? That green woman my mother used to loath. I thought there was just one of her but turns out there's dozens…"

"Vladimir Tretohikoff," I clarified for Laura. "Thing is, Jaikie, your Mum was talking about posters, ten quid a time. What Ted Rochester had were the originals."

Hyde Park Close was a crime against humanity, he pronounced, and should be not allowed to go unpunished. It was the ultimate example of a divided society and according to Google this man, this Edward Rochester, had paid forty seven million pounds for that penthouse. The roof was a full blown garden, with a helipad, trees, fountains, pools. Down in the basement, reached by his own private elevator, there was a panic room, in case of terrorist attack. And if he felt peckish, a well-known gourmet chef was on call to knock him up a gold plated sandwich…

The actor in him was returning and, up on his feet now, the performance widened to include people at nearby tables. It wasn't just a matter of supremely wealthy people living in such places, he went on, while within spitting distance there were children living in poverty. That would be simple to get his head round, but Hyde Park Close was another world, designed for an off-shoot of the human race comprising men like Rochester who spoke to furniture, who were guarded by a militia of morons, and never walked at ground level. There were no words to describe the pure evil of their obscene, appalling wealth. John Demise dared to pull him up on that. The words were there, he said, from Jeremy Bentham and Tom Paine through to Marx and Engels. The trouble was every generation rehashed them, then laid them to one side.

Jaikie paused and for a moment he was back in the classroom, showing respect for the teacher. It wasn't just a matter of words, he said. They can be made to mean anything. It was about substance. Was John aware that, in spite of his own excellence as a teacher, his generation was the first in history to teach the one below it less than it knew itself? And the biggest shortfall was in morality. One or two people clapped feebly but before Jaikie could acknowledge them Laura called softly to him. She smiled, patted the seat beside her and he re-took it.

Fifteen minutes later with a bowl of Annie MacKinnon's venison stew to work on, Jaikie said quietly, "Sorry about that. Meant what I said, though, just didn't mean it so loudly."

Ever indulgent, Laura said she'd enjoyed hearing him, that actor's voice, holding everyone in the room rapt. Jaikie nodded, and turned to me.

"So what about Ted Rochester, Dad? I've diminished to Ted, it helps me cope with him."

"He lied to us, for a start. All that stuff about The Magic Carpet was bollocks."

Jaikie gave Laura a cut down version of what Rochester had told us, the actor's voice again holding her rapt.

"It's certainly a clever idea," she said, when he'd finished. "And like all the best ones, extremely simple."

"Which is why it isn't what the Gaffneys, Raphael, Askew, or whoever turned your cottage over, were after."

"How can you be sure?"

"Because you wouldn't need detailed plans for a carpet with seeds in it. You wouldn't have to float a 250K bribe, let alone murder its inventor to get hold of it. Christ, Jaikie and I could stamp out a roll of the stuff in my garden shed next week, just from hearing about it."

"So why did he lie to you?" said Laura.

"First answer is he wants Patrick's 'brilliant idea' all to himself."

"Second?"

"He's that rare thing in our midst, a thoroughly good man. Yes, he's a smelly, scruffbag but he might just believe what he said, that any rights to whatever we're talking about belong to Gerald and Marion Scott. Who's for dessert?"

Laura glanced at her watch. "Ah, I said we'd be home by eight-thirty. Jodie Falconer's coming round."

Jaikie stopped eating, mid-mouthful, and tensed up. "Why?"

"Just to see us, she said on the phone. It's been a while." She looked from Jaikie to me and back again. "Is there a problem?"

"No," said Jaikie.

The waitress brought the bill to me out of habit. Jaikie didn't even notice her, let alone my credit card going down on the little silver tray. He was more concerned about the visit from Jodie.

Laura drove back to Beech Tree in her car, I drove the Land Rover and Jaikie. It's a mile at the most but halfway home he asked if I would pull onto the verge and switch off the engine. The headlights died and, since the bulb in the map locker had blown long ago, we sat in near darkness.

"If this is about Jodie…" I began.

"It isn't," he said quickly. "Well, it is and it isn't. It's about money. And the fact that I haven't got any."

"Would you care to repeat that?"

"You heard the first time."

"You were paid two million dollars for that film."

He sighed melodramatically and flopped back into the seat as if he wouldn't mind being swallowed up by it.

"I invested in an L.A. property company. Lost it."

Never having earned more than a D.C.I.'s pay I was in uncharted waters. I gave the news a few moments to sink in, then said, "Of my four children I always thought you might be the one who, in years to come, would look after the rest of us. You, with your nose for luck and money." I needed confirmation. "Say again, for the record, how much have you lost?"

"Had stolen. Two million. It's only dollars, remember, not pounds…"

I was trying to keep calm and not making too bad a job of it, I thought, but what I really needed was The Map. I felt for it in the inside pocket of my jacket.

"How many times have I said to you: never put all your eggs in one basket?"

He played hurt. "You're making it sound as if I did it on purpose. I was conned."

"To the tune of two million dollars?"

"Will you stop repeating the figure."

"Okay, then, who relieved you of the aforementioned sum?"

"His name is Jason R. Tanner. And I wasn't his only victim. That's where you come in. I told my friends I'd get you to pop over to L.A. and track him down."

"I can just see me with a plaster over the bridge of my nose…"

He pointed at me. "Jack Nicholson, *Chinatown.*"

"Shutup! You fill some flibernite's boots, money you'll never see again, then scrounge off me, Laura, Jamal no doubt?"

"George Corrigan, too," he added quietly. "I owe him seventy."

"Jodie?"

He nodded. "Jodie was the proverbial brick wall. Wouldn't play more than once. Instead she made me promise to tell you. That's why she's at home now, to see if I've done it. It hasn't been easy, Dad…"

I stopped listening to him and recalled the last time we'd fallen out. He was eighteen, still raw from his mother's death and he and I were just about to lock horns when I was struck by a dose of lateral thinking. I told him we weren't going to play this game anymore. We were never going to fall out again, be it over trivial nonsense or fundamental differences. He was surprised at the time, I was surprised, but from that day forward we managed to stick to the agreement and I had no intention of breaking it now. I took The Map from my inside pocket and spread it out on the dashboard, closed my eyes and brought my finger down on a small village in Nepal, the one where Ellie was working in an orphanage. She'd gone there with an American boy called Rick

Bettucio. 'Terrific Rick' we called him because terrific was his favourite word. I'd emailed her the other day, just before leaving for Belinda's antique shop. I'd wittered on about nothing in particular, then ended with, "Funny thing, though. Jaikie never seems to have any money on him these days. Borrows. Answers on a postcard, please. Or email."

I'd received a swift reply. "Dad, why does every parent think that when their kids borrow money from them it's to buy vast amounts of the Devil's Dandruff? Jaikie could buy up the entire coke output of Bolivia, from what I hear. Besides, he'd never do drugs. Mess up the face, darling? I should coke-oh! Anyway, miss you. Home for Xmas. Love Ellie x."

The home for Christmas bit I'd liked, but why had she gone straight for the drugs angle? Did she know something and wasn't telling? Did it say something about her that I wasn't...?

Jaikie's voice broke in. "Dad, that's The Map. You use it against scumbags, not family."

"Just be grateful that it's working. And given that you aren't going to see that money again, what are you planning to do?"

His reply was characteristically artless. He was going to stay on with me for a bit while his agent found him another film. Any residuals which came from *All Good Men and True* would be placed in an account which Jaikie couldn't pilfer.

I lowered my voice as far as it would go. "Day to day, how does that work? Food, coffees, pub lunches?"

With the same lack of guile he said he would eat from the freezer and borrow money from me only when necessary, pay me back as soon as possible. I told him that even though my police pension was worth just two percent per annum of the two million he'd received we'd rub along on it somehow. With a matey dig in my ribs he said we'd be fine and thanked me for being so understanding. I wasn't aware that I had been.

"I want you to do something for me," I said.

"Name it."

I told him I wanted everyone home for Christmas. Ellie was coming anyway, probably with Terrific Rick, but that was okay. Polite enough bloke. I hadn't seen Fee since last summer in L.A. though it felt more like last week. And Con. I was never at ease about Con, though people kept saying he was fine. I needed to have him face to face and make up my own mind.

"Then worry at your leisure?" Jaikie said.

"Do that for me?"

He nodded. "Am I invited?"

I smiled at him, or at least I think I did. "You're cooking dinner."

When we arrived back at Beech Tree, Jodie's car was there. Jaikie got out of the Land Rover, hurried over to the back door and straight into the kitchen. He paused and looked across at her and just as I walked in she reached up and kissed him on the cheek. Paradise was back on earth. I went over to the phone and checked my messages. There was only one. It was from Imogen Slater, timed at ten that evening and she wanted me to phone her back, no matter how late I got in. So I did.

16

The Slaters' London pad was a mews house in Notting Hill, a two up two downer and, in its time as the address suggested, the street had provided luxurious accommodation for horses. Now it offered pokey homes for upwardly mobile human beings or, as with the Slaters, somewhere for those who'd reached the top to crash out before the morning slog back to the country. Number 47 Carnegie Mews was an odd mixture of Victorian charm and modern absurdity. The street itself was cobbled with a drainage channel running down the centre of it, but a sign of more recent times was the size of the garages, in most cases larger than the living space.

We'd parked the Land Rover a fair distance from it, on an example of that endangered species, a parking meter and if it hadn't been for the desperation in Imogen Slater's voice last night, asking that I visit her at the earliest opportunity, it would have had all the promise of a Great Day Out, father and Son. For a start my fear about why he never had any money had been allayed. It wasn't flagrant excess, it was innocence, naivety, carelessness. Some would say stupidity. To the tune of two million dollars. Okay, so it was dollars not pounds, as Jaikie insisted, but according to my iPhone that morning that made it 1,290,407 quid and how in God's name anyone in their right mind could give another human…

I swung my mind back to the immediate concern. Imogen Slater wouldn't tell me over the phone what was troubling her. I took it to mean that it was something she didn't want her husband to know about and indeed her phone manner, whispering, rather than speaking in a normal voice, endorsed that. I was wrong, though, and while she was the one to open the door, Richard was right behind her, descending the open stairs to greet us like the best friends he'd never had. He was delighted to see us, what a pleasure, what an absolute joy and he still couldn't get that performance out of his head, the number of people who had sung its praises…

His wife called a halt causing Richard to ask if he'd been going on a bit. To our shame we denied it. Part of me was wondering if Imogen would suddenly dismiss her husband and then pitch in with what she wanted to talk about, but Richard was staying close. This was to be a joint effort and they were twitchy about it.

"How is that young man, Mr Hawk?" she asked, measuring out coffee into a percolator.

"Sergeant Corrigan? He's improving by the day."

"I'm so glad to hear it. Does he have family, a wife, children?"

"No wife or kids. A mother."

She nodded, turned back to the coffee. "Dammit! Always happens."

"Eight," said Jaikie, reminding her of where she'd got to, spoon-wise.

"I don't quite know how to put this to you, Mr Hawk." She laughed. "Me, the hard bitch gardening editor of *Home Weekly,* eh?"

"From the hip," I said. "You mind if we…?"

I gestured to a clutch of armchairs near the stairs and Richard apologised for not having seated us. When he'd stopped beating himself up about it, he handed the conch back to Imogen who closed her eyes and began searching for words to describe a very simple state of affairs.

"You should know that Ralph Askew and I were an item at Cambridge," she began. "People often feel they have a right to exploit the familiarities of those halcyon days. He rang here yesterday morning and said he'd be round for lunch, one o'clock."

"Invited himself?" I said.

"Ostensibly to pick up some research Dickie had done for him. We were perfectly agreeable, I mean we hadn't seen him, apart from at the film premier, for what…?"

"Twelve years," Jaikie said.

"Yes, so round he came. Strange when you know someone's weaknesses. One is inclined to play on them if one needs to."

I smiled. "What are Ralph's?"

"He could never drink, not with any safety, so I asked Richard to open a bottle of Rovero. It's a favourite of ours and I knew Ralph wouldn't say no."

"Why did you feel the need? Something must have forewarned you."

"I knew he wasn't coming round just to pick up his wretched research. Someone from his office could've done that. No, there'd be a greater purpose and with a drink inside him…"

"He'd talk. So what did he say?"

"It didn't strike us at the time, but after he'd gone, we sort of turned to each other and said 'What was all that about?' He neither asked us about ourselves, the children, the house in Provence, nor did he tell us anything about his own son, ex-wife, his job. On top of which he left the research here."

"What was it?"

"He wanted me to find out about a man called Edward Rochester," said Richard.

I could feel Jaikie about to reveal that we knew Rochester, but a sharp glance kept him quiet.

"You'd think he'd have enough resources at his own disposal, wouldn't you," I said.

"He wanted it done discreetly, and in the old-fashioned way, A4 sheets, stapled at the corner. He didn't want other people in the office knowing about it, I imagine."

"May I see it?"

He rose and went over to a desk at the other side of the room, took out a box file. It contained a jumble of photocopied documents, handwritten pages torn from notebooks, envelopes stuffed with scraps of paper relevant to various projects Slater was working on. The stuff about Edward Rochester was a sheaf of crumpled paper, clipped with a bulldog. The top page was a hand-written list of names, a roll-call of Rochester's good ideas. When I asked how Slater had obtained the info he said he'd started with tax returns, records of charitable donations, and then drawn on a wealth of contacts in the gossip industry.

"Most of these are high-minded and worthy, I'm afraid, and I know Ralph wanted dirt, dirt and more dirt." Slater picked out an item on the list at random. "Recon Ltd. They could not be more tree-hugging if they lived in the woods."

His wife shuffled the bits of paper and found reference to a young company based in Cambridge that wanted to recycle waste food, turn it into a delicious and nutritious substitute and ship it off to the starving millions.

"Recycled burgers and chips, pizzas, kebabs?" Jaikie said, grimacing.

"Presumably."

"Is there something there called The Magic Carpet?" I asked.

He looked down his list. "Yes, it's evidently a means of making the desert bloom. Rushfarthing Enterprises. And they take the idea of extracting water from the driest of land even further. Aquatrap. It's a means of harvesting condensation over vast areas, containing it between two waterproof layers and channelling it. Clever."

"How do they get water to rise up through one layer and stay there, not sink back," Jaikie asked.

"That's the clever bit," said Imogen. "It's porous one way, not the other. Based on the idea of disposable nappies."

So Rochester hadn't exactly lied to us, in that The Magic Carpet was an idea dreamed up by Patrick Scott. It just wasn't the invention everybody was keen to get hold of and certainly wasn't worth murdering for.

"He also asked about you and Doctor Peterson," said Richard.

"What exactly?"

"Started off with how well did we know you. I mean fair enough, he just dropped your name into the conversation and asked a passing question. But he wouldn't accept that we didn't know you very well. When did we meet? Did we know if you were retired officially, or did you perhaps work for some security firm? What did we know about Doctor Peterson? Then, had you ever mentioned a young man by the name of Patrick Scott?"

"So he knows I'm interested. Why would he think I told you all about it?"

Jaikie gave a nervous cough. "When Richard interviewed me I mentioned that you were looking into his disappearance, Dad."

I turned back to the Slaters. "Anything else?"

"Only that, as Dickie says, he wouldn't let it drop. He wanted us to speculate on why Doctor Peterson's house had been broken into. We said we didn't know that it had been but he wasn't satisfied. You must know, you're a bloody journalist, it must be on the grapevine."

Richard held up a hand. "Worth saying here that we were onto the second bottle of Rovero by then."

"In the end I became quite scratchy and, calling on those past familiarities, I said I wanted to talk about something else other than you, Mr Hawk." She smiled, gently "No offence. He could sense that he'd overstepped the mark, called up his driver and twenty minutes later he left."

"We thought you should know," said Richard. "With there being a murder to answer for."

"If not two. May I have a copy of that research?"

Imogen went over to a printer, began scanning the documents and rolling them off.

"Coffee's done," said Jaikie, nodding to it.

Slater over-apologised for not having noticed himself, poured four cups and dug out some biscuits. He was sorry about those as well, but he and Imogen weren't great biscuit eaters.

"Now let me turn the tables on Ralph Askew," I said. "What do you know about *him*?"

"Apart from the fact that he broke my girly heart," she said, lightly.

"How did he get into politics?"

"Father's footsteps. In our final year a local Tory party back home at Selingthwaite, asked if he'd be their next candidate. He was 23 years old and flattered beyond belief. We'd get married, he promised, have a flat in London, a home in the North, I'd go into journalism, he'd be an MP."

"So what went wrong?"

"One evening, in *vino veritas* he told me that an MI5 recruiting office had approached him. It was the days when they still trawled Oxbridge shamelessly for new blood. Wouldn't it interfere with him being an MP, I asked, like a fool. Not at all, he replied."

"They wanted him to be their man at Westminster?"

She nodded. "There was one problem, however. My father was a journalist, quite a firebrand, left wing and anti-establishment and I was hellbent on following in his footsteps. Not the sort of wife Ralph wanted so three days later he finished with me. At the time I was heartbroken, now I think of it as a close shave."

"He's a most unlikely looking spy," said Jaikie, through a mouthful of shortbread.

I appealed to the Slaters. "I keep telling him they bear more resemblance to the man next door than to George Clooney."

"Whatever they look like, I've always thought of them as snappers up of unconsidered trifles," said Richard. "People who listen at keyholes, compute gossip into allegations, turn smears into damning evidence. For all their apparent paltriness they are highly dangerous."

"Yet you refer to Ralph as an old friend," I said.

"Then let me put it on the record now. He isn't. And never was."

It sounds bizarre I know, but we went from the Slaters' house to The Natural History Museum and for several reasons which jostle for position as I recall them. I needed to think over what Imogen and Richard Slater had told me, and to do so without Jaikie offering his opinion at every turn. I also wanted to bask in the memories of Family which it evoked. We lost Con there once when he was eight years old, though only for an hour, and found him transfixed by the fossilised skeleton of a mosasaur, *Platycarpus ictericus* to be precise, an 81 million year old lizard. As a result of the experience none of us has ever forgotten what that creature looked like. An odd-shaped couple of hours, then, and just as we were leaving I received a text from Detective Sergeant Alan Baker at Tilbury. It was brief and to the point. 'No joy with Gaffneys. Releasing them today. AB.'

With the kind of unthinking arrogance which assured me I could do something about that, point something out which Baker had missed, find another reason for holding the Gaffneys, I decided to take a preposterous detour home to Winchendon via Tilbury. Jaikie insisted on driving, in the belief that it was safest for both of us, and only became uneasy as we drove into the visitors' car park at Tilbury nick. He was, after all, still uninsured on the Land Rover which, during the journey, had started playing up again.

God knows what Tilbury nick is made of but the slabs it's rendered with are blue and grey, the bolted on lettering more suited to a cheap diner than a police station. The front line of the local battle against crime was manned by a uniformed PC, early thirties and glasses, locked in a steel cage whereas once he'd have had twenty twenty vision and stood six feet tall the other side of an elm counter, as if at any moment he might reach down and pull you a pint. This bloke recognised Jaikie, though he wasn't sure where from.

"Yeah, what can I do for you?" he asked, whereas once he'd have called us 'sir' and asked how he could help.

"I'd like to speak to DS Baker."

"Who shall I say…?"

"Nathan Hawk."

He ran the name and face through his memory but nothing came back.

"Take a seat," he said, whereas once he'd have asked us if we minded waiting. In spite of an overwhelming desire to challenge him with this decline in standards, I held off.

When Baker eventually appeared he beckoned us through the security arch and tried to be friendly, but quickly realised there wasn't much point in my case and turned his attention to Jaikie. As we walked up to his office - the elevator had broken - he bragged about his 16 year old daughter, Emma. She was pleased as punch to have got his autograph. She was thinking of going into acting herself. She did it at school, belonged to a local amdram group, had applied to go on 'Britain's Got Talent' but hadn't heard back yet…

"You want tea, coffee?" he said when we reached his office.

"I'd prefer an explanation," I said. "No sugar."

He chose not to see it as a challenge, but an exchange of information between two professionals.

"Guvnor, we've had the bastards here for 96 hours. I tried for another extension, magistrate wouldn't play ball…"

"So you let 'em go?"

"Neil Manning's next door doing the paperwork."

Jerome and Trader Gaffney were still in the building, then, the other side of the dividing wall. At best it was stud and plaster.

"I could have filled you in over the phone," he went on. "Saved you the journey."

"I was told you were the hard man on this manor."

He shook his head slowly, warning me. "You know what the problems are. Don't make it personal."

"So what did you find out from the Gaffneys, apart from fuck all? Who are they working for?"

"They wouldn't say, either on or off tape. I've no doubt they killed Charles Drayton but there's no trace of them in that back room where he died. Yes, there are prints in the kitchen, on tea cups, on bank notes. It means they were there but only to buy the MG Sports Car. They gave the wife two grand for it, and yes it was worth ten, but whichever one of them slipped away to kill Charlie wore Marigolds."

"No link to Patrick Scott?"

He shrugged. "The day you were at his parents house, they came to pick up money he owed them, they say. And no I don't believe that either, but Gerald Scott says it's true."

"Then he's lying as well."

"Can you blame the poor bastard? His wife is so scrambled you could eat her off toast."

The phone on his desk buzzed and he lifted the receiver. He didn't even say okay, just kay, then turned to us, big smile.

"Bite to eat in the canteen before you go, guys?"

"No thanks."

"It wasn't an offer." He held the smile, no doubt hoping that I'd smile back. "More of a Health and Safety requirement."

The reason for it became clear five minutes after we'd sat down at a canteen table, Jaikie and Baker with chunks of Dundee cake, me with a straight cup of tea. Through the window I caught sight of Neil Manning leading Trader and his uncle to a car. To Baker's consternation I rose and tapped on the window. Trader turned, surprised to see me at first, then he raised his hand and waved back, just with the tips of his fingers. Manning shoved him on his way. I sat down again.

"Watch your back, Nathan, that's all I can say. Apart from sorry."

There was a log jam on the M25 so, Hobson's choice, we went through the centre of London and hit serious traffic on the Marylebone Road. But at least the spell in Tilbury nick's car park had given the Land Rover a new burst of energy and I was now in a reasonably fit state of mind to drive it. Jaikie was studying Richard Slater's research on Edward Rochester. Occasionally he would break off and invite me to pour scorn on some of the projects Rochester had thrown money into.

"Does anyone really want to spend their holiday in an undersea hotel? Somebody came to him, crackpot idea, he put in ten million dollars."

"Investment or donation?" I asked.

"Either way its money down the drain. Okay, so spray on skin. Good idea. So too most of the medical stuff here, but Christ, why don't governments put money into this?" He tapped an item on the list. "Two hundred grand for a body part farm. That's just sick."

"Unless you're the one who needs the part. Like this bastard behind me who'll be a prime candidate if he doesn't pull back."

Jaikie turned to see a sports car accelerating the ten yard distance between us, coming to within a foot of my bumper, then braking hard. It was a Mazda RX8, Jaikie informed me before going back to the research.

"Teleportation. Beam me up, Scottie. It's on the cards, evidently, and Rochester's in there. A whole bunch of green stuff as well as medical projects, but do we really need vertical farms? Or am I becoming a luddite just like you?"

The driver behind me did it again. He allowed a gap to develop then roared his way to closing it. People on the pavement turned, unimpressed.

"Rough guesstimate, he's given away a hundred million dollars in the last five years," Jaikie went on. "It's some kind of guilt thing, surely. Cell regeneration, anti-ageing, fair enough, but here it is … the idea that we could live forever. Pure Hollywood."

I asked if there was anything on the list about regenerating old Land Rovers since mine had just begun to object to the stop start nature of our progress. Jaikie said there was nothing specific to Land Rovers but Rochester had given a fair old chunk to some guys who'd designed a water car.

"And look at this!" He laughed. "He's backed a company that's taken fireflies to bits, the insects, to get the secret of their luminescence. In ten years time the streets'll be lit in the same way as a firefly's arse."

We were approaching Madame Tussaud's waxworks where Jaikie's attention wandered from the list and over to the museum and the queue outside it, then inevitably to the exhibits inside. In time he muttered, "One day, eh, Dad?"

"Me or you?"

He laughed. The traffic stopped at the junction. The Land Rover stalled. I turned the key. Nothing happened. I gave it a moment and tried again. Nothing. Again. Even less.

"Don't do this to me," I whispered.

I gave it a long, aggressive turn and the starter motor began to groan. The traffic ahead moved off on a green light. We didn't. The Mazda moron leaned on his horn. In the rear view mirror I could see him waving me on. The mist began to gather, same colour as his car.

"Dad, The Map."

"Fuck The Map."

I got out of the Land Rover, threw the door shut behind me. Jaikie followed, saying something I couldn't hear. The man I was about to break in half wound his window down and I got a double reflection of myself in his sun-glasses, caught a whiff of his shoddy perfume.

"Look what we've got here," I said to anyone listening, and there were quite a few by then. "A carbon guzzling tosser in such a hurry to go nowhere, except into me."

He tried to open the door to get out, I slammed it back on him. I made a grab for the sunglasses and they fell off as he turned his head to avoid my hand. Jaikie took me by the arm but all that did was give the thirty-something a chance to get out of the car. Others were now hooting or trying to work their way round us. The queue outside Madame Tussaud was enthralled. A free show. My adversary was big and he wasn't afraid, but nor was he the dirty fighter those years on the streets had made me. Jaikie got between us, one arm stretched out to each man. I could see his lips moving, no doubt talking sense. I saw the moment when the thirty-something recognised him and calmed down by one degree. I still wanted to punch his lights out, his and the Mazda's, and Alan Baker's, and Neil Manning's, and Trader Gaffney's, and his uncle Jerome's and anyone else I held responsible for the year long silence about Patrick Scott. And all of a sudden I didn't. The change was so dramatic that it bothered Jaikie.

"Dad, what is it?"

"I've got it."

"What?"

"I know what they're all so exercised about. Askew, Raphael, Rochester." I turned and headed for the Land Rover. "Let's go."

"Dad, Land Rover's dead."

I remember thinking that at least it had waited until I'd worked out the reason for Patrick Scott's disappearance and his probable murder. There it sat in all its glory, still dignified, its final act of nobility being to bring a section of London traffic to a halt.

"Get your stuff from it," I said.

I turned to the thirty-something and believe it or not I thanked him.

I was monosyllabic on the way home, according to Jaikie, and it wasn't simply because I hadn't travelled on a train in over six months, or that I was mourning the loss of my four wheeled friend. The journey from Marylebone Station took under an hour, but top and tail that with getting a vehicle recovery firm to cart the Land Rover away, then at the other end have Laura pick us up from Haddenham Station, it turned into a three hour marathon.

Once inside the kitchen at Beech Tree I asked Jaikie to call Jodie and have her join us. Fresh pair of eyes, sharp mind, and a healthy distance from the jumble of facts surrounding the case. She drove over in her father's pickup.

"What I really need is a big, office whiteboard," I said. "Dresser, move."

Jaikie laughed and explained to Jodie, "Ted Rochester had robotic furniture, responded to his voice."

"Jaikie, grab that end, move it into the corner."

He paused for a moment, then realised I was serious and did as I'd asked. Laura stepped in to save the odd item from falling, Jodie watched in restrained disbelief. The wallspace we created was white, whiter than the rest of the room and fringed by cobwebs which provided a useful frame. I took the black marker pen from the dresser drawer.

"What are we actually doing?" asked Jodie.

"I want you to join up dots for me. It's a self-doubt thing. Had it all my life. I know I'm right but could be wrong."

There were two kinds of suspects in this case, I explained. The ones we went looking for - Kevin Stapleton, the girlfriend, Belinda, the Gaffneys, Rochester. And the ones who came to us - Raphael, Wilson, Askew. I decided to lay it out in columns and in the first wrote Raphael stroke ASC 250k. Lies. Didn't read plans. But who were these European companies so anxious to put back into the community?

Jaikie came up with them from memory and I wrote them down. Tata Steel. MacDonald's, of course. Toyota. Danone. Coca-Cola, surprise surprise. Trans World Haulage. Walmart. Shell BP. Glaxo Smith Kline. Bloomberg. Nokia. BMW. Roche.

"That's the main board," he said. "There are smaller fish. You want me to open their page?"

I shook my head.

"Where does Doctor Wilson fit in?" Laura asked.

"He's Raphael's man, certainly, but he hasn't killed Patrick Scott. He might know why somebody else has, though."

I put his name in the Raphael column and headed column two Edward Rochester. There wasn't room on the Great Wall of China, never mind my kitchen wall, for all that he was into but Jaikie read from the list which Slater had given us and I added them.

"Undersea Hotels Inc. Spray on skin. Body Part Farm. A Swedish company, Partikel Blanda, their game is teleportation. Cell regeneration, Time Light Inc. Kirkland Water Power, a car you fill up from the tap. My favourite, Luminette Co. a company who will light our cities in the same way a firefly glows in the dark. Vertical farms. Food pills.

"The day we met him he gave us all that bullshit about The Magic Carpet because he was hiding something much bigger," I reminded them. "Then he got snotty at the mention of Henrietta. Why does everyone curl into a ball at the mention of this woman's name?"

I drew a line for column three. Ralph Askew. Junior Government Minister.

"Our new friends the Slaters reckon he's dangerous and I'm inclined to agree. MI5 connections, if not full blown membership, we learned today. Under Secretary at the Department of Energy and Climate Change. That at least gives him access to NHS records. And may be the Police National Computer?"

"Askew and Raphael have something else in common," said Jaikie. "Ever since George Corrigan was shot, nobody's heard from them."

It was a good point. Raphael didn't even poke his nose out in Bloomsbury Square after the shooting. Perhaps he and Askew were trying to keep a lid on something, lower its profile.

Column four. Patrick's Friends and Family. Into it went Kevin Stapleton, girlfriend Belinda and Gerald and Marion Scott. I tacked on The Gaffneys, for want of knowing who they were working for.

"Why not put them in a column five?" asked Laura, with her need for absolute precision. 'Miscellaneous."

I was just about to do as she'd suggested when Jodie pointed both forefingers at the lists and said, "Does this have something do do with the motor industry?"

I smiled at her. "It sure does. It hit me outside Madame Tussaud's and you've seen it too. I knew you'd be good for this family."

"Explain," said Laura.

"It's all there, on that wall. Toyota, Shell BP, BMW, Raphael's tyre company, Rochester's water powered car, our friend Askew at the Department of Energy and Climate Change. Stick my neck out? I think Patrick Scott invented some kind of automotive engine, far more viable than anything that runs on tap water, and it frightened the beJesus out of these guys. And they're still anxious about it, enough to get Charles Drayton and me out of the way."

"So that's the car the Gaffneys were looking for?" said Jaikie.

I nodded. "Gerald Scott is the canniest man I've met in a long time. He not only knows what Patrick was working on, I think he knows where it is."

I hired a French biscuit tin to drive over to Rushfarthing House the following day and I would have put Jaikie on the insurance if it hadn't been prohibitive. Thirty years old, you pay through the nose anyway, but if you're a thirty year old actor it isn't only your nose. God only knows why I'd suddenly become conscientious about his insurance.

Marion Scott came out to the iron gates, in answer to our ring at the bell. She was carrying the console in one hand, secateurs in the other, and was dressed as we'd seen her a couple of weeks previously, sheepskin body-warmer, tough old shoes and gardening gloves, as if they were a second skin. She came right up to the gates, fully expecting to see her husband the other side of them but when she saw me she froze in fear.

"Marion, how lovely to see you again. How are you and Gerald?"

She put everything I'd just said into one bag and shook it and out came the responses she'd intended, but the words landed in the wrong order like some diabolical crossword clue.

"Where is Gerald? Fine. I don't remember you. Thank you. Who are you?"

"It's Edward Rochester, Marion."

Her face cleared and slowly she smiled. "Oh, do come in Mr Rochester."

She looked down at the console in her hand and her face clouded again. She couldn't press the buttons while holding the secateurs.

"Allow me," I said, reaching through the bars.

I opened the gates and she led us into the house, trotting out the usual niceties afforded a visitor. How had the journey been, had we come far, had we had lunch…? She turned to us with an intensity which the subject matter didn't warrant: she had made sandwiches for her husband, but there were plenty to go round. Ham with pickle.

"And who is this young man?" she asked of Jaikie.

"My son, Jacob."

He gave her his smile and she returned it. A car the other side of the gates hooted.

"There he is, there's…"

His Christian name which she must have used a hundred thousand times over the last forty years, wasn't there at the forefront of her mind.

"Gerald?" I said.

"Yes, Gerald."

"You stay and talk to Jaikie. I'll go and let him in."

Gerald Scott was at the wheel of an old Skoda, the window wound right down ready for him to shout instructions to his wife. He saw me approaching from the house and, as far as I could tell, his expression barely changed.

"Mr Hawk," he said as he drove past me. "What news?"

"Lunch is ready. Ham and pickle."

He smiled, wearily. "Oh, good."

Getting through those sandwiches was quite an ordeal for most of us, the exception being Jaikie. That was down to the pickle, homemade by Marion who couldn't remember having done so and, consequently, what it consisted of. The tea we drank was unstirrable but I persuaded Gerald that he and I should take it through to the living room and talk business. He was anxious at the prospect of leaving his wife unguarded in the company of a professional charmer, but by the time he'd fashioned an objection, I'd already left the room.

The living room still embodied that sense of abandonment which I'd noticed on my last visit, the result of a woman having lost her son and now losing her grip, the father caught in a pincer of his own anguish and duty to his wife.

"How is she?" I asked, as we settled.

"Dementia is a strange affliction in terms of progress - sudden downward slides to a plateau that will stretch out for months. Why have you come?"

"To tell you that I know what Patrick was working on when he disappeared."

I was hoping that his face would betray relief or at least an understanding of what I meant, but Gerald remained as unreadable as ever, and waited.

"I know the Gaffneys were trying to find it, that Edward Rochester kept returning to talk about it." He looked away in disinterest. "You told me Patrick wasn't very clever but the opposite's true, of course, and I think he was killed as a result of it. I thought it was just some tinny old MG they were after, but it was much, much more than that. It would help if I had details."

He took a deep breath, no doubt wondering how much of the concept would go over my head, and how little I would understand. He began by asking if I knew what photovoltaic meant. I confessed it wasn't a word I used every day, but presumably it had something to do with light, being the 'photo' part of the word, and electricity, the 'voltaic' half. He nodded, approvingly. I was no doubt familiar with solar panels, he went on, monstrous looking sheets on the roofs of houses, and the fact that they were a collection of silicon cells, semi-conductors. My face must have betrayed a certain lack of familiarity with the subject. He tried again.

"Sunlight hits the cell, a proportion of it is absorbed within the semi-conductor, electrons are loosened and they flow as electricity. Even if you don't understand it can you hold it in your mind as a workable theory? Now place it to one side."

Easily done. He sat forward in his chair, hands dividing up the lesson he was giving me, saying that it was the use of nanotechnology which made Patrick's motor a force to be reckoned with. Did I know what nanotechnology was? Again he was impressed when I suggested that it was the reduction of ordinary technology to microscopic levels. Apply it to silicon, he said, and imagine the number of surfaces which light could strike. That dreadful mug of tea in your hand, which should be emptied forthwith into the *ficus benjamina* beside me, would hold a mile of surface ready to absorb light and transform it into electric current. I poured the tea away and waited for him to continue.

"You don't seem as bowled over as you should be, Mr Hawk."

"I'm sorry, I thought there was more."

"Isn't that enough? Up until the present time a mere ten percent was the most a semi-conductor could absorb; with nanotechnology we'd be looking at forty, fifty percent. Far be it from me to suggest that perpetual energy is on the cards, it's another concept altogether, but if its fifty percent today, why not sixty, seventy in five years time? Unabsorbed light reflected, absorbed, reflected, absorbed, reflected…"

"So, what did he actually produce, Gerald? What are the nuts and bolts of all this work that might have led someone to kill him?"

He wasn't keen to be drawn away from the brilliance of Patrick's invention and back to the reality of his disappearance but I forced him.

"He built a prototype. Here, in the back room."

"Where is it now?"

He shook his head, again a convincing display of weariness at being asked the same question time and time again. "I've simply no idea what happened to her. Why is it that motor cars are always female?"

"Because they're an object of desire, I imagine. Was this one called Henrietta?"

He nodded, then asked if I knew what had happened to his son, if I was certain that he'd been killed. I said, rather feebly, that in my opinion the car was motive enough for people to have wanted Patrick out of the way. And for all the usual reasons: envy, greed, expedience or perhaps to justify a hare-brained scheme of their own. The Kirkland Water Car, for example, which Rochester put cash into might not have survived the competition…

"But Rochester gave him money," said Gerald. "I still have the cheque somewhere."

A sudden burst of laughter from the kitchen reminded him that Marion was alone with Jaikie and by the sound of it they were getting along all too well. He rose to go and join them. I remained seated.

"When D.S Baker at Tilbury said he'd charge Trader Gaffney and the uncle, why didn't you co-operate?"

"I told him as much as I knew…"

"No. The day I was here they were asking for the car and a computer disc, one the finished article, the other detailed plans of how to construct it. You didn't want them charged because you didn't want the police tramping over the house and gardens again in case they found what everyone's been looking for."

He'd reached the door by now but turned back and, for the first time in our acquaintanceship, raised his voice which I took to be a sign that I must have drilled into a nerve.

"They've all been here before," he said, shrilly. "They've examined every inch of the place. Why let them do it again? Marion could barely cope the last time."

It sounded as if there'd been more than just a few coppers strolling the grounds, looking for clues.

"When was this?"

"February before last. Cold winter, the ground was like rock but it was routine stuff, they said. When someone goes missing, sooner or later the police search his back garden."

"They weren't looking for your son's body, Gerald, and they probably weren't police."

He shrugged. "Whoever they were, whatever they came for they went away empty-handed."

Believing that to be the last word on the matter, he hurried away to the kitchen.

We stopped off on the way home, not at the place where we'd had the *moules marinière* but at a lay-by cafe, a caravan from which a guy with no smile, no idle chat, just please and thank-you, dispensed surprisingly good coffee and decent sponge cake. Presumably his name was Frederick, since the word 'Freddie's' was stencilled along both flanks of the trailer. We settled ourselves on fold-up chairs beside a couple of French lorry drivers who were taking a break before heading down to the channel tunnel, I guess.

"Your game's a lot like mine, Dad," said Jaikie, quietly. "It's as much about brass neck as having any recognisable skill, a matter of getting people on side, persuading them you're really interested in what they're saying, then extracting the stuff you need. Sounds more like dentistry than acting or police work, doesn't it. One sided conversation and then yank it out of them."

"What did she tell you?"

"After giving me the life story of that pickle, or what she could remember of it, she suddenly dropped her voice to a whisper and said, 'There are things I've been told not to tell you.' Cruel, really, because I then asked her what they were and she told me as if still keeping a secret."

Evidently, Marion went downstairs early one morning, looked out of the kitchen window and there on the lawn were a dozen men in white coats. In her state of mind, she must have been terrified, but she called for Gerald who read their visitors the riot act and sent them packing. Thing is they weren't exactly white coats, Jaikie said. From Marion's description they were white overalls, and they weren't psychiatric nurses but technicians, and it wasn't rubber truncheons they were carrying but metal detectors. They were Men from the Ministry, she'd said. She didn't know which one.

"Department of Energy and Climate Change?" I suggested.

Jaikie nodded. "She said it happened 'just the other day' which doesn't help, given that everything she remembers occurred that recently."

I shook my head. "I think she might be right this time. It's happened since the last time we were here. Gerald's told her to keep schtum about it, hence the whispering. Well done, for extracting it. How goes the other little job I gave you?"

He said he'd been in touch with Ellie, Fee and Con on Facebook. The girls were coming home for Christmas. Con hadn't got back to him yet but then he'd always been unreliable in that way. He'd regret it this time because Jaikie had set Fee on him. No hiding place. She reckoned it was all the fault of the new girlfriend.

"Looking at her, I can see the distraction," he said.

"You've met her?"

"No, she's on Facebook as well."

I stood up and made to go over and pay Freddie.

"I'll do this, Dad."

I looked at him, trying not to disbelieve. He smiled.

"My agent, David Stanley, sent me a cash card the other day. He's set up an account for me. Annie McKinnon gave me extra money on it last night, up at the pub."

It was residuals from *All Good Men and True*, he explained, and although I wasn't dead keen on a man I'd never met having control over his money, if it worked then who was I to quibble?

"Has he said anything about your plans for a... new direction? Theatre, plays?"

"He's very interested, but thinks now isn't quite the right time. He's lined up a couple of interviews for film parts."

In other words I'd been right and David Stanley wasn't prepared to kiss goodbye to future earnings. Jaikie took some money out of his breast pocket, peeled off a twenty pound note and replaced the rest. He patted it.

"I've already paid Jodie but there's fifty there for Laura, twenty-five for Jamal and seventy for George Corrigan."

My name wasn't on the list, but then I hadn't really expected it to be.

17

That evening I logged on to Ralph Askew's constituency web page and found that it characterised him heroically, as ten years younger than he was, the perfect family man, clever yet of the people, charismatic but approachable, successful yet modest. The date of his next surgery was pencilled in for three days time and should any of his constituents, friends or acquaintances wish to meet him they should email, text, even tweet or simply drop in him for a cup of tea and a chat. Jaikie had an interview with a film producer that same morning and while the film star in him was all for re-skeduling the appointment, I persuaded the part that was 3 million dollars short to stick to the original plan and I set off in the French biscuit tin, alone.

Selingthwaite Community Centre was one of those inexplicably octagonal buildings which made every room in it, even the toilets, an unnatural shape, uneasy on the eye and downright impractical. I arrived at about half eight, having left Winchendon at the crack of dawn, and found Askew already seated at a tubular steel table skimming through a clutch of morning papers. All around him was evidence of a recent jumble sale, a couple of empty clothes rails, wire hangers still bearing the odd T-shirt which no one had wanted, the usual flutter of raffle tickets on the floor. Askew rolled the local *Evening Telegraph* tight, as if he would beat himself over the head with it, punishment for having been caught off guard.

"Mr Hawk, how lovely to see you." He was a great one for raising the hands, palms outward. He'd either been a clown in a former life or had read somewhere that it meant you were telling the truth. "I know, I know, it must seem as if I've been avoiding you but so, so, so busy…"

"We never did have that lunch, did we. You sort of ducked out of sight after Sergeant Corrigan was shot. I expect you visited?"

He tried being languid. "No, no, I didn't. How is he?"

"Improving. Where are all the people?"

"Be fair, we don't start until 9.15." He rose and called through a hatch in the wall to a middle-aged woman who was firing up a tea urn. "It is 9.15 today, Mrs Eames, isn't it?"

Mrs Eames assured him that it was and asked if we wanted tea. He said no, I said yes, then set off round the odd shaped room, feigning an interest in pictures on the walls. I didn't see any reason to continue being polite.

"I'm surprised your party even got a look in here," I said as I reached a beaming poster of him.

"Slim majority, true, and were it not for the plethora of other parties divvying up the floating vote we'd have thought twice about fielding a candidate."

"One man's minority party is another's seventy grand a year plus expenses. Do you know, my father would be appalled to hear the way I'm talking to you. You're someone's Member of Parliament, for God's sake. Their Harold MacMillan, Aneurin Bevan, Jim Callaghan. What happened to his belief that you're all men of honour?"

He shook his head. "So many reasons…"

"Too many for you to pick just one? Try this instead. Did you authorise a team of technicians to search the grounds of Rushfarthing House, to look for the solar powered car which Patrick Scott had built?"

He'd been expecting me to deliver some kind of shock but he wasn't prepared for so direct a current and it robbed him of yet another straight answer.

"When was this?"

"Two weeks ago at the most. So, in the absence of the word 'no' I'll assume that you sent a bunch of white coats to find this car. They didn't. Here's another. Did you have Patrick Scott's NHS records wiped when Doctor Peterson began asking after his health - or lack of it?"

He tried to maintain his poster image, honest, sincere, calm in a crisis with just a hint of future party leadership about him. He smiled and then spoke with a gentle scalding hiss.

"It must be so wonderful being you. No dirty work to do anymore, just high-blown principles to shove down other people's throats. Not simply retired but retired copper. That's one step down from sainthood, surely."

He turned away and focussed on a painting of a local warehouse, Victorian and derelict, blackened stone and broken windows, just the sort of thing you'd want in your living room. His instinct was to drop the glib, personable front and blast me but he knew it wouldn't make me go away. So he tried sweet reason.

"Put yourself in my position for two minutes. You, Hawk, stand alone with your principles, I'm part of a global alliance which has to provide energy for 7 billion people."

"I feel a well-rehearsed excuse coming on."

"And then consider that solar powered car. The technology will come. I can't tell you when: a year, two, ten, but it will come."

"I thought it was here already."

He laughed. "Oh, enough to boil a kettle or heat your baby's bathwater, but I'm not talking about that."

"You mean the nanotechnology which Patrick Scott claimed he was using. Did you ever see the car he made? Or any plans for it?"

"That isn't the point. I've just told you the technology will come, sooner rather than later, and when it does it will change the entire geo-political structure of the world."

He was now giving me the chance to share his horror, to be his equal, but I declined. He shrugged and continued.

"It will mean the implosion of all oil producing nations within five years. That doesn't seem to trouble you much."

"I'll consider it when I've caught the man I'm after, but don't lose your train of thought."

He gave me a look which, in its sheer iciness, suggested that Richard Slater had been correct when he'd labelled Askew as dangerous. As I considered his options I remembered that someone had already tried to silence me. I'd christened him Bog Standard, on account of his M & S dinner jacket, and he'd begun by throwing fake acid at Jaikie and progressed to firing a real gun at George Corrigan. I wondered if he might be a friend of a friend of a friend of Ralph Askew.

"The problem isn't that the USA, or Russia, or The Middle East will all fold in half," Askew continued. "The problem is that after the initial gold rush nobody will own the technology. After all, the fuel comes out of the sky twenty-four hours a day, buckshee and untaxable. So, if no one owns it, nobody can control it, or rather they can't control the people who use it. And that, Mr Hawk, is perfect anarchy. Think of that next time you start your car."

"So, along with all those greedy bastards in ASC you tried to buy it, in order to kill it off?"

"Solar power won't be killed off, merely delayed for a few more years. Julien Raphael knows that, but I imagine that when your Doctor friend started quizzing the NHS computer about Patrick Scott, his radar bleeped." He held up both hands to prevent oncoming questions. "Don't ask me how he found out. Leak, leak, leak."

"Where does Edward Rochester fit in to this, or doesn't anyone know?"

"Tedious man, super rich, stuffed full of principles and yearning for The Greater Good. How on earth does one deal with people like that?"

He smiled, hoping for harmony at least on that subject, then glanced at his watch.

"Are the punters about to storm through the door?" I asked.

"Sadly, no, they don't really play anymore. When my father was an MP they came in droves, twice a month, the whole cross section in a day long surgery. I used to go and watch him sometimes. Quite brilliant. London constituency, teeming with life." He shook his head and returned to the present. "Anything else I can do for you?"

"At what point do any of you - ASC, Rochester, you - stop buying up the ideas and start murdering the people who had them?"

He finally gave up trying to get me on his side and stared at me in genuine disdain. "In other words, did I kill Patrick Scott? Her Majesty's Government does not go round killing off those whom we find inconvenient."

"Please…"

"I know it isn't a popular belief but it happens to be true." The hands were up, palms towards me, fingers splayed. "Besides, he wasn't murdered by someone trying to get their hands on his invention, to use or stifle it. It was being *offered* on the open market. And I was the one who, on behalf of HMG, dealt with these would-be extortionists." He smiled. "Ah, silence at last. That'll be because you've been hunting the wrong fox."

"Who were they?"

The smile became a snigger, brought on by my discomfort. "I thought it might be Patrick Scott himself, or someone on his behalf. His name was mentioned often enough in the conversations I had. Brilliant young engineer, invented this, that and the other. I told the chap, as the price kept going up, that it wasn't a great work of art he was flogging, a Van Gogh, a Picasso, a Cezanne. It was a car so ease up on the rhetoric. He laughed and said it was worth all of their work put together and more. And it wasn't just me they were trying to squeeze. Ask Julien Raphael. I'll bet he was approached."

"When was this?"

"November 3rd to November 10th a year ago. Eight days of phonecalls, from all over the country, including London. Then they just - stopped."

"Maybe someone paid him what he asked."

He shrugged and glanced at his watch again but there was still no sign of constituents at he door. Mrs Eames had placed a china cup of tea, on a real saucer, at the hatch and now asked f I took sugar. I said I didn't and thanked her.

"I do hope you get to the bottom of it, Mr Hawk. What are the plans, if and when you do?"

I told him that his friend Richard Slater would probably write the story up for me, no matter where it fell to earth. Askew said that was a generous choice on my part. Richard was never the most sparkling of journalists but he was thorough, dedicated and honest and his wife ruled him with a rod of iron. He watched me sip my tea.

"I trust I haven't given the impression of being disinterested in this engine," he said.

"Don't worry, Ralph, I know you'd sell your own mother for it. Why else would you have sent people to look for it?"

He nodded. "If you do find it, or plans relating to it, we would be extremely interested. After all, someone has to get there first."

I allowed an almost indecent pause to elapse before saying,

"Didn't I say, Ralph? I've already found it."

I hadn't bought Askew's line that HMG were as innocent as lambs when it came to people who got in their way. Having looked him straight in the eyes again, I thoroughly endorsed Richard Slater's theory that he was dangerous and telling him that I'd already found Patrick Scott's solar powered car was a means of making sure that he would protect my back as opposed to having someone shoot me in it. The same would apply to Laura and Jaikie and over the next few days the S.O.U. detail guarding them both was increased. Mark Granger, the hypochondriacal newby, was given company in the shape of two useful looking blokes, painfully short haircuts and even shorter conversations but apparently in perfect health.

It was late when I got back to Beech Tree, but Laura and Jaikie had waited up for me, the latter to tell me that his meeting that morning had been fruitful. A film part was on offer. He'd think it over. I looked hard at him until he changed that. He'd already thought about it and decided to take it. Meantime, they could both sense that Askew had thrown a couple of spanners in the works, the biggest one being that maybe Patrick Scott wasn't dead after all. Certainly it had been Belinda Hewitt's view, that he'd just walked out on her. Kevin Stapleton had thought so too; his first reaction on the phone had been, 'Don't tell me he's turned up again.' Marion Scott thought her son was still alive but that was rather different...

The other spanner was the fact that the solar powered car had been offered on the open market, dutch auction style, and Ralph Askew thought the man at the other end of the phone, might have been Patrick himself, attempting to cash in. I didn't believe that for one very good reason. The demands for ludicrous sums of money, the argle-bargle which Askew, Raphael, Rochester and no doubt others had been engaged in, came to an abrupt halt. Why would Patrick suddenly do that? A change of heart? Unlikely. A sale to an interested party? Surely we'd have heard something by now, the odd rumour of its development. No, negotiations came to a dead stop on the day Ralph Askew said because somebody silenced Patrick.

"Does that mean he was in on the extortion?" Laura asked. "I don't want him to be."

"Your wish is granted, I think. His girlfriend said she couldn't reach him after she went up north on a buying trip with her assistant at the shop. So where was he between the first and the tenth of November? I think he was being held against his will."

"Where? Who by?" Jaikie said. "It would have taken someone close to him, who knew how the car worked and could explain what was on offer. He didn't have friends, we're told, he didn't have enemies, except maybe Kevin Stapleton. I mean we thought Henrietta would turn out to be flesh and blood, not steel and silicone..."

"He had a father," Jaikie said.

"I don't like that either," Laura muttered.

"He did have one friend, of course, maybe not as friendly as we first thought." I turned to Jaikie. "Will you drive me into London?"

"Now?" he said, glancing at Laura to see if she had an objection.

"Two hours time. Get some sleep."

Jaikie didn't ask what we were up to until we were halfway to London. I asked him to have a guess. Why did he think I'd asked him to wear dark clothes and a pair of old trainers he wouldn't miss? He agreed that it sounded as if we were going housebreaking.

"Golborne Road, off Portobello. Belinda Hewitt's antique shop." He kept his eyes on the road ahead so I couldn't tell if he was excited, alarmed or simply taking it in his stride. "Break another law for me. Use your iPhone. Bring up a map."

He did as I'd asked and handed it to me. At one end, Golborne Road crossed over railway lines and the shop was three or four down from there. A ground view showed the building backing onto a mews and, on both sides, it wasn't overpriced living accommodation for once, it was lock-ups, garages, storage. That would be our point of entry.

As we turned into Campbell Mews Jaikie's nerves got the better of him and he waxed theatrical in order to cope. This was like stepping out from the wings onto a stage, he whispered. As the curtain rose an unknown world would unfold and no matter how well-rehearsed the players, it was the uncertainty of the next few hours that gave his life purpose. I told him to stop talking, especially like that, handed him some gloves, donned a pair myself and took the bolt cutters from the tool bag on the back seat.

At the rear of Belinda's shop I checked the metal garage doors, up and down the jambs, along the top joist. There was nothing, no alarm, no light, not even a tin plate saying burglar beware, just a padlock and chain. The cutters went through it in one, but I fumbled my catch and the padlock fell against the metal door and rang out like stage thunder. We waited. Nobody came to any of the twenty windows within view. Jaikie posted the bolt cutters through the open rear window of the Land Rover as I pulled back one of the heavy doors to Belinda's and stepped in. Jaikie followed and closed it behind him.

I shone a torch on a beaten up VW van which took up most of the garage, forcing us to walk sideways past it towards a door at the end. Through this was a small passageway with rooms off it, the first a utility room, stone floor, butler's sink and a cupboard containing working coffee, tea bags and a packet of Bourbons. There was an electric kettle, milk in the fridge, and mugs on the drainer. Across the passage the toilet was in regular use, soap and towel at the hand basin, air-freshener and hand cream. A lined pedal bin was empty. At the end of the passage, stairs rose to the first floor with an ornate notice on the wall saying, 'More Items Upstairs'.

The middle floor consisted of three rooms, each filled with the more portable stuff of an antiques business: mirrors, pictures, prints, chairs, benches, clocks. Above it was an attic reached via winding stairs. Another notice on the wall said 'Private. Staff Only'. It was a studio flat comprising a cut down kitchen along one wall, a shower room and toilet backing onto it. Jaikie said he needed a pee. I stayed and examined the main room, starting with the bed, currently unused, but half made up. I hadn't expected to see an image of Patrick Scott rise from the mattress, like the Turin shroud, but I had reckoned on finding something of use. I must have voiced the thought.

"You think he was kept here?" Jaikie said from the shower room.

"Not in this particular room, too easy to break out of. Maybe I've got it wrong."

"And maybe you haven't. Take a look at these."

I went over to the doorway and Jaikie nodded to the far wall.

"Recognise them?"

He was referring to three framed posters, advertising forthcoming events of the MG Enthusiasts' Club. They were similar, if not identical, to the ones we'd seen in Charles Drayton's dying room.

"These places have a cellar, you reckon?" I said, more statement than question.

We made our way downstairs and into the main shop. Jaikie took one half of the floor, I took the other. Very little had changed since my last visit and the place was still dominated by the Easter Island type statues. A couple had been sold and as I strolled between those which remained, eyes glued to the floor, I suddenly heard the creak and felt the floorboards rock. Jaikie came over, we moved the Easter Islanders, and got down on hands and knees. It was a trap door sure enough, six foot square, iron hinges at one side, bolts on the opposite corners, securing it to the floor. We opened the door back on itself and led the way down the stone steps. I paused halfway, turned to the joist at shoulder level and switched on the light.

The entire cellar had no more than seven feet of headroom, broken by beams a foot thick which hadn't moved a paper's width in three hundred years. The floor was half earth, half mortar. Belinda kept her stock here and the place was crammed full, but all in an orderly fashion. The metal items were on one side, an ongoing supply of Edwardian fenders, coal scuttles, fire irons. Wooden items were kept on the drier side. It was not only dry but cold. Like a mortuary. I don't know what drew me to the far wall, probably the elevated space there with nothing on it.

Against the wall a cast iron down-pipe stood solid. I shone the torch up and down it and, as usual, the delight at having answered a question which no one else had bothered to ask, was tempered by guilt. There was no reason to be pleased about anything here. At waist height the rusty down-pipe was scratched and gouged and whoever had made those marks had done so out of panic and desperation. On the floor, on crude stone flags, there were dark patches.

"This is where they kept him. Chained to this pipe. Those marks on the stone are blood from his wrists."

"Jesus…"

"Let's go."

Since the refurbishment of Paddington Basin, night time no longer falls on it and yet somehow the 24 hour daylight doesn't make it seem a safer place. Perhaps, on that occasion, our reason for being there had something to do with it, but when I think back to that mix of light which hovered above the station I can't pick out a friendly colour. Halogen orange over the platforms, white light on the footbridge, blue beside the towpath and for all that we could see perfectly, the images seemed forbidding and other worldly, especially the boats. *Scorpius* was moored in the same place as before, at the end of the cobbled promenade behind the new Marks & Spencer offices and when we reached it I still hadn't made up my mind how to play this. What Jaikie wanted, I believe, was for us to storm aboard in our party of two, commandeer the boat and clap Belinda Hewitt in irons. Whether she was actually there or not, whether she was alone or had company, seemed incidental to our purpose.

"Come on," I whispered, and set off again

"Where are we going?"

"Her father's boat is just round the corner," I said.

"You need his help?"

Sweet Lady Jane was moored on a spur of the canal, in a flotilla of five, and so isolating is the effect of still water, we might have been approaching it along any towpath in the world. The boat had a deadness about it, no one appeared to be on board this floating apology for a garden shed with its timber clad cabin, the roof of heavy tarred felt. I didn't want to bang on it and wake the neighbourhood, but just as it began to seem like the only option, Jaikie stepped on the gunwale, halfway along it, and stepped off again. The boat rocked, the water lapped against the starboard side. He did it again. A third time until the boat was straining against its mooring. At the far end of *Sweet Lady Jane*, the bedroom end, a curtain over one of the windows drew back and Mike Hewitt peered out. I moved into view.

"Mike, it's Nathan Hawk. Apologies for the ungodly hour, but I really do need to speak to you."

Half a minute later, having thrown on some clothes, he appeared at the door still buckling the belt to his jeans and welcomed us aboard. The cabin was dimly lit and the section we'd entered was his office, simple and sufficient for his needs, and like most people who are dropped in on unexpectedly, he began to tidy the place needlessly.

"You know Jaikie?"

"Your son, the actor."

"Yes." He nodded, trying to get a measure of why we were there. "We've come about Belinda."

"What's happened to her?"

"Nothing, nothing. I need your help."

He nodded slowly, still half asleep, still at a loss.

"There's no other way of putting this, Mike, other than bluntly. I think she murdered Patrick Scott."

It took him a few seconds to absorb the horror, then he shook his head. "No, no, she was crazy about the guy."

He slumped into an upright chair, his hands went to his face and swept it, as if clearing a cobweb he'd just walked into.

"Why?" he asked. "Why has she…? What evidence is there to suggest it? Like I say she was crazy about him."

"That's often the key to it. Not in this case, though. It's all to do with the car engine Patrick designed. Did you know about it?"

He was even more puzzled now. "Well, yes, I found it fascinating but as for it being practical…"

"Plenty of people thought it was. I think Patrick went north with Belinda on November first last year. She says he didn't, it was just her and Chrissie the Reader from the shop. A buying trip. Can you help me there?"

"Chrissie went with her to drive."

"I think he went too and while they were away Belinda persuaded him to cash in on the solar powered engine, try selling it to interested parties, Ralph Askew at the Department of Energy and Climate Change, Julien Raphael at ASC, Edward Rochester, a host of others I expect. He phoned them from all over the country."

He stood up again, more challenging now, and ready to argue in Belinda's defence. "Why would she kill him, then, if they were in it together?"

I shrugged. "The old story. They fell out. Maybe he had a change of heart. You know her better than I do. Would that have angered her?"

As he frowned, the dim light in the cabin made his brow cast a shadow over the rest of his face. "She was always a fiery character but not enough to murder."

"That's what I'd like to suggest to her, then. Courts are more lenient with crimes of passion, more forgiving."

He took a few steps towards me. "Hang on, you've already got her in front of a judge and jury. You're suggesting that she went north with Chrissie and Patrick, and somewhere on that trip she killed him?"

"No, she killed him when they got back. I think for the last few days of his life she held him against his will."

"Where for Christ's sake?"

"In the cellar at the shop. I've been there tonight, seen where she kept him chained up to a downpipe. The shop was still closed, first two weeks of November, he could've screamed his head off to no avail. There are blood stains on the floor. Someone's tried to get them out but you never can completely."

He shook his head, just the once, left to right and turned away. "This is not my daughter you're talking about. And where is the body?"

"Widely distributed, you might say. A man called Charles Drayton disposed of it for her, in tins of dog food."

On learning that a loved one has acted against all expectation the first response of a close relative is disbelief, the second denial. Those two shifts are straightforward enough but then comes a hint of the relative testing the truth of the matter. They don't accept it right away, sometimes they never do, but they entertain the possibility of it by questioning the accuser. Mike Hewitt didn't do that. He started behaving exactly as I'd thought he would: he started blaming himself.

"This cannot be the daughter I raised," he said. "It isn't. I refuse to believe it."

"That's why I'd like you to come with me, round to *Scorpius*, sort this out. If she's killed him she'll have to account for it. Far better that she tells you and me, as opposed to the copper in charge of the case. His name is Kelloway, an unpleasant man at the best of times." I avoided Jaikie's gaze and he mine. "He'll get the truth out of her one way or another. But whatever she is, whatever she's done, she's still your daughter."

He dug out an old jumper, put on a quilted anorak and the three of us walked round to *Scorpius*. For most of the half mile or so I thought I'd misread Hewitt and began to wonder how far he'd be prepared to go. All the way, I thought, maybe into the main cabin of Belinda's narrowboat and then run alongside my charade that she'd been the one to murder Patrick Scott. Within sight of *Scorpius*, three hundred yards away, he stopped and turned to me.

"I can't do this," he said.

"Can't do what?"

He took a deep breath and sat down on a bollard, one of half a dozen blocking vehicular access up from North Wharf Road. He smiled at himself as he confided his characteristic weakness.

"I can't let you and this... Kelloway terrify the life out of my little girl." He gestured round. "Four in the morning, this godforsaken place, can I watch her be accused of murder? I just can't. I know there isn't one, evil thought in her head, let alone the ability to murder..."

"You've lost me," I said.

He smiled. "I don't think so, Mr Hawk. I think you've played it perfectly." He paused and I was more than happy to wait. "I didn't mean to kill him, but I did. I was pig sick of being poor, having to ask Belinda to sub me every time I wanted to go abroad, buy a painting, new pair of shoes. She didn't mind. I did. So with her and Chrissie out of the shop for ten days I invited him over to *Sweet Lady Jane* and… tested the water. Big companies, governments, competitors would pay through the nose for the idea, I told him. We could make a fortune. He wouldn't listen. The car was for Everyone."

He shook his head, having difficulty with the concept of doing something for no personal gain but for the pleasure of improving life for all.

"Then what?" I asked.

"We parted amicably enough. Next morning I got in touch with a couple of acquaintances…"

"The Gaffneys?"

"Yes. Basically I got them to… kidnap him and take him to the flat over the shop. Keep an eye. When he became difficult, they chained him up in the cellar while I went round the country on a phoning trip. I must have tried tapping twenty people, but the one who showed the most interest was some government lackey from the Department of…"

"Ralph Askew."

He glanced away with a wry twist of his lips. "Do stop me if I'm telling you things you already know."

"You can stop if you like. I just needed to hear you say you'd killed him. And you did, a minute ago." I took out my iPhone and showed it to him. "Crisp and clear. Jaikie's taped it as well. He saw it in a film or ten. If it's any consolation to you I knew you wouldn't let your daughter carry the can. How did you kill him?"

He began to speak with a certain amount of ease now, the kind of relief that comes from a confession. "With a flat iron. One of those heavy old cast iron things our grandmothers used."

He'd gone down to the shop cellar, tenth of November, to try and persuade Patrick for the umpteenth time. To use reason on him. He unchained him and instead of walking calmly up to the flat for a chinwag, Patrick flew at him. Hewitt grabbed at the nearest thing, swung it and it caught Patrick on the temple and he fell.

"What brought you to my cabin door?"

"The little things, as usual. Patrick Scott could be cruel, unforgiving and egomaniacal, according to Belinda. I wouldn't persuade a daughter of mine to stay with such a man, no matter how interesting he turned out to be forty years on. You made her feel stupid for not wanting to. You saw him as a potential money-spinner with an idea that would change our lives."

He smiled. "If it worked."

"The beauty of this was it didn't need to work, just threaten to. The slightest chance that it might and people'd pay good money for it, to bury it or develop it, and you tried to sell it like an art dealer; as if it were 'a Van Gogh, a Picasso, a Cezanne.' Ralph Askew's description of your cheap-jack hustle."

Hewitt nodded. "My old problem, going in way above my head."

"And keeping bad company. Charles Drayton."

"Yes, poor old Charlie. I met him at…"

"…at an MG Enthusiasts' Club event? Useful man, Charlie. He came complete with two heavies - Trader Gaffney and his uncle, so devoid of any morality you got them to kill Charlie as well."

"I paid Charlie twenty-five grand to dispose of the body. Every penny I had. And there he was, the perfect catholic, in fear for his mortal soul, ready to confess his guts out."

I could see that Jaikie was shaken by Hewitt's calm recollection of the bare facts, so as much to distract him as anything I asked him to go and phone Jim Kelloway, get him down here as soon as possible. I tossed him my phone.

"Dad, it's four in the morning."

"It'll be Evelyn you speak to, so use some of that magic charm. And copy everything our friend here said onto the laptop, back seat of the car. Email it to Jim."

He glanced at Hewitt. "Will you be alright, Dad?"

I raised my eyebrows and he set off towards North Wharf Road. I turned back to Hewitt.

"You know, Mike, you gave me the worst three minutes I've had for a long time when that Bog Standard dinner jacket you hired threw mock acid at my son on your instructions."

"When did I do that?"

"Two weeks before you had him try to kill me, in Bloomsbury Square."

He nodded with a world-weary kind of amusement

"I get it. Once a copper, eh? Pin everything you've got onto the nearest sucker."

"Stand up."

He knew the reason I wanted him to and said, "Are you sure you can handle this?"

"Oh, yes."

He got to his feet slowly and took a half classic stance of lead and guard, ready to fight me off as I went close. He expected me to do something similar, I imagine, and straightened up in surprise when I took a spray from my pocket and put a single shot of it between his eyes. He then did what the Gaffneys had done. He rubbed the stuff in and five seconds later was buckling at the waist as he choked on his own spit. I stepped in closer, raised a knee and cracked him in the face. He came upright and reeled back along the cobbles, glancing off the bollards. I went in to kick him, caught him once. He held up his hands, unable to see me, barely able to breath.

"Do what you like," he spluttered. "I'll give you everything on the Gaffneys, but I never, never had anyone attack your son. Or you…"

For some reason I stopped and listened. "Did you turn over Laura Peterson's house?"

"Who the fuck do you think I am? MI95 or somebody? Jesus, what is this stuff?"

I went to kick him again, only to hear Jaikie's voice forbidding it. "Dad, leave him."

I turned to him. "What did Jim say?"

"I haven't phoned him yet. Knew I couldn't trust you. Did you bring any gaffer tape?"

18

Four weeks later a great deal had changed, some of it beyond recognition. Christmas tends to do that of its own accord, without the aid of a murder inquiry coming to an end, and I'd handed over the organisation of the festivities to Laura. She'd agreed to take charge on one or two conditions, the main one being that we returned to pronouncing the word schedule in the way God had intended. Also, fawcetts were to become taps again, elevators lifts, cream milk and guys chaps. It seemed a small price to pay. At the centre of the celebrations would be a Martin Falconer turkey which he gave me as payment for having 'looked into' the titanium plate. I couldn't believe the neck of it, especially as he and Jodie were joining us for dinner. Fee was due home on the 20th of December, Ellie and Terrific Rick the day after. We still hadn't heard from Con but expected to any day now. He'd always been a last minute kind of guy… chap.

Mike Hewitt had pleaded guilty to the kidnap and murder of Patrick Scott and saved us all, especially his daughter, much grief. I visited her just once at Paddington Basin. She was angry with me, naturally. I didn't stay long but in our brief conversation she told me she was selling the business and heading off to Canada. The Gaffneys were scooped up and in custody, down in Tilbury, charged with kidnap, murder and conspiracy, pleading innocence and a bad start in life, but if played off against Hewitt they wouldn't stand a chance. Richard Slater's piece was ready for publication in the New Year but he was having difficulty getting the sensitive bits, the stuff which pointed a finger at the Under Secretary at the Department of Energy and Climate Change, past editors and a convocation of grey suits. Ralph Askew sent me a Christmas card. It arrived early, which I hate, and had a photo of him and his family on the front, which I hate even more. His face looked as slappable as ever and I firmly believed by then that Bog Standard was his man - a friend of a friend of a friend - never mind the crap he'd given me about Her Majesty's Government not killing those whom they found inconvenient. He asked politely if there was anything further on the solar car. He'd obviously assumed that I was boasting when I said that I knew where it was…

The day before Christmas Eve I drove over to Rushfarthing House in the new old Land Rover I'd been forced to buy. There'd been some attempt at celebrating Christmas, centred around the possibility that Patrick would arrive home any day now. Life was confined mainly to the kitchen these days, no doubt because the weather had turned colder. An over-decorated tree was shedding pine needles like mad, because of the heat, lights were strung around the wall and holly had been pinned in every available space. Tesco's had provided the Christmas fare and Gerald offered me a glass of it, ice all the way to the brim.

"Good to see you again, Mr Hawk," he said, several times, giving the impression that he really meant it but I guess any friendly face would have drawn a similar reaction. The man was lonely and it was no wonder. Marion entered from the garden, dressed in her uniform of body-warmer and gardening gloves, brandishing secateurs and carrying yet more sprigs of holly.

"Nathan Hawk," said Gerald, introducing her as if she knew me but the name was eluding her. "Hawk, dear. Subfamily *Accipitrinae*?"

She smiled as if she'd merely had a senior moment. "Mr Hawk, of course. Perhaps I can make you chaps lunch?"

"In a while perhaps, yes. It's only half eleven, but thank you."

"Very well," she said as he took the holly from her. "Call me when you're hungry."

"Fear not about lunch," said Gerald, after she'd gone back to the garden. "There's a wonderful game pâté in the fridge, some granary rolls to go with it. Bit of a mess in here, I know, but shove aside anything that's in your way."

"How is she?" I asked, settling at the cleaner end of the table.

"No better, no worse." He took a sip of the straight scotch he was drinking. "So, you caught your man. It was most gracious of you to keep Pat's death from Marion. She still thinks he'll come home one day, but the interesting thing is she has no sense of despair now, so even if we told her he was dead, she wouldn't see it as a tragedy."

He reached for the scotch and splashed another double measure into my glass, then went to the freezer for more ice. I thanked him and set the drink to one side.

"There is the small matter of the solar-powered car," I said.

"Yes, yes," he replied, almost dreamily. "I don't suppose it matters much to anyone now."

I smiled. "You know that isn't true."

He tried to minimalise the subject. "Well, if certain people could get their hands on it…"

"Gerald, the car is yours, morally and legally, inherited from your son and you and I are still the only two people in the world who know where it is."

He chuckled. "Well, I haven't see it for over a year so how on earth…?"

"That's true."

"And a whole host of government technicians swarmed over the grounds with metal detectors, scoured the house, the loft, the outbuildings for a disc. Every inch was covered."

"Not every inch."

I rose and gestured to the back door. He took an old jacket from over a chair and followed me out onto the patio, bringing our drinks with him. He stopped by a bench and set them down, then watched as I walked to a cluster of sheds and opened the door to the smallest one. In front of me was a round, yellow filter the size of a naval sea-mine. A dial on it offered half a dozen choices and I set the handle to 'empty to waste' and switched on the power. A rush of water hissed through a rubber hose then away into a ditch which ran beside a hedge down to the woodland. Green water. The swimming pool was emptying. He came over to me with a smile and handed me my drink.

"You're a clever chap, Nathan Hawk. How did you know?"

"It was the only place the men from the ministry didn't look. You knew they wouldn't, of course. A car under water?" I shook my head. "I guess you've wrapped it in something watertight…"

"I've vacuum packed it, no less, in heavy duty polythene. A double skin."

I nodded. "When I realised that it must be in the pool I went to the web-site of the people who make the winter safety cover. They boast that it can hold the weight of a Range Rover, there's a photo of one doing just that. So what, you towed it out through the French windows?"

"Drove it, shrink wrapped it, sealed it and lowered it down inch at a time by shortening the winter cover straps very gingerly. Down it went, I topped up the pool and bought a new winter cover."

"When you say you drove it…?"

"Using its own power." He nodded at the pool. "I suppose you'd like to see it?"

"For my own peace of mind. How long does it take to empty the pool?"

It would take six hours to empty it completely, so I said I'd meet him halfway, three hoursworth. He helped me to fold back the cover and expose the algae laden water. *Trachelomonas grandis*, he informed me. Single cell. And within an hour or so the water had lowered enough for us to see the top of a small, Subaru-like car, the shrink-wrap polythene still intact. An hour after that I could make out a rectangular box on the roof, covering the whole area, and made up of microscopic semi-conductors, their miles of surface absorbing, reflecting, absorbing, reflecting…

"The disc which everyone got in such a flap about is inside the car, I take it?"

"Yes. Treble shrink-wrapped, sitting on the passenger seat."

"I've seen enough," I said, at about half past two.

"So now what?"

"That's up to you, but I've no doubt you'll do the right thing. You're that kind of bloke. Meantime, while you decide, fill the pool up again." I glanced over to where Marion was attacking a holly bush and giving it no quarter. "And we didn't have lunch. Game pâté you said?"

At the beginning of the following March I received a letter from Gerald Scott telling me that his wife had died, not as a result of her dementia but a heart attack, which just went to show. He didn't specify *what* it showed but he was clearly relieved for Marion, though his sadness was all too apparent. However, if any man could cope with the double tragedy of losing his son to murder, his wife to the disintegration of her mind and then her sudden death, it was Gerald Scott. He added that she'd been a danger to herself in recent months, so much so that he feared she might fall into the swimming pool and drown. He'd had it filled in and paved over. He hoped me and my family were well.

The next book in the Nathan Hawk Mystery Series is 'Evil Turn'.

Printed in Great Britain
by Amazon

79365830R00122